The Pumpkin Spice Spell

The Pumpkin Spice Spell

Wisteria Cove
Book 1

Erin Branscom

Dedication

To Charlotte,

I love you so much, my sweet, little witch. Keep being the best girl I know that you are and chasing every single one of your dreams. You can do anything that you can dream up. I love you very much, Mom

Content Warning

This book includes "on-page" adult content and language unsuitable for minors.

Chapter 1
Willa

The bells over the heavy wooden door to my bookstore and coffee shop jingle as I finish pouring a maple leaf design onto a pumpkin spice latte in a cauldron-shaped mug. I've lost count of how many pumpkin spice lattes I've made all day, already sealing the sweet, warm scent of cinnamon and clove into every corner of the shop. Fall has moved into Wisteria Cove, and honestly, I couldn't be happier. Sure, this means we're swamped, and all our shops are jam-packed from open to close, but it's my favorite time of year.

And what's better than a cozy bookstore and coffee shop in the fall? Absolutely nothing, that's what.

Inside Wisteria Books & Brews, I've collected mismatched armchairs and carved out little comfy reading nooks, each softened with blankets, pillows, and cushions that invite everyone in to explore the new and old books. Tall shelves with a ladder hold my carefully curated collections, while other shelves hold paperbacks mixed with hardcovers, new finds, and dog-eared favorites. Warmly lit lamps illuminate every corner, and no overhead lights glare in here. This is the ultimate escape for anyone needing a place to call home and curl up with a warm mug and a good book. My shop is eclectic, warm, welcoming, and alive.

This morning, a small coven of incredible women gathered here, as they often do, to celebrate each other's wins, sip coffee, and pull tarot cards between bursts of laughter and knowing nods. They're a tight-knit, deep-soul group who loves fiercely, supports endlessly, and leaves the air humming with good energy. I can't help but smile every time they're in the shop.

Nothing makes me happier than pouring someone their favorite coffee or tea and watching them choose from murder mysteries, fairy tales, gardening guides, or our local Wisteria Cove seaside lore. And I may or may not be reading their futures while they are here in the shop. But I don't tell them that. That's for sure.

My mother, Lilith Maren, and my two sisters and I are all notoriously known as the Maren Witches of Wisteria Cove. People love to make up stories about us flying on brooms and wearing witch costumes. But that's not true. But that's also *not not true,* either. While we don't fly on brooms or wear costumes, we all have unique gifts that we use in our day-to-day lives.

But life has been hard enough for all three of us. We don't need to make it harder by over sharing the things that make us weird. Well, *weirder* to the outside world, but just normal to us. History has called witches weird as a negative connotation in the past. But if being intuitive, helping others, and loving apothecary makes us witches, then I guess that's what we are.

It wasn't always easy growing up as the daughter of Lilith Maren, the town sea witch, as the tourists like to call her. She's infamous around here. Nobody takes our gifts seriously until they need us for something, whether they need a spell from my mother, or something apothecary from my sister, Rowan. I have gifts of discernment and intuition, and Ivy has gifts of care and art. She paints and designs tarot cards and loves to write.

Every year, we host the annual Harvest Moon festival, which attracts even more tourists. Can I move things and fly on a broom? *No.* Can I manifest things into happening? Yeah, I've been known to do that and see things that are going to happen before other people do. But mostly, I just run my coffee shop and bookstore. I find beauty in the magic of everyday things. Like a steaming mug of tea, a conversation with a friend, and curling up with a great book. There's magic in the small, everyday things, and I wish more people knew that.

In the back of my kitchen, my soup station bubbles away. Today's special is butternut squash with sage and cream, served in to-go containers with a fresh sprig of thyme. And in the glass case, we have fresh sandwiches that people can grab and go. This week I was feeling roast turkey, savory brie, and cranberry relish. Their aroma from the neatly stacked sandwiches draws customers in off the street. By the end of the day, the customers will have bought everything. We sell out of everything constantly, and it's been a good problem to have.

Across the shop, my sister Rowan emerges from the back, handing me a wooden box of precisely labeled apothecary jars. All clean line labels with: Ground, Clarity, and Calm. Rowan grew and cultivated all of them carefully from her garden and greenhouse.

"Another tea delivery?" I smile, relief washing over me. We've blown through nearly every blend this week, and my shelves are desperate for a restock. Rowan's tea is phenomenal, grown in her sun-drenched greenhouse and the little garden behind her cozy little cottage.

When she's not teaching yoga classes down at the community center, she's been pouring her heart into opening a yoga and apothecary shop in the vacant building right next door to Wisteria Books & Brews. I can already picture it, the warm scent of herbs against the red brick walls drifting through the door that will connect both of our shops, the hum of music from my shop mingling with her laughter.

Rowan's already the go-to in town for everything from loose-leaf teas to lavender tinctures and magnesium sprays. If you can dream it, she can create it. Potions and remedies that seem to carry a little bit of Wisteria Cove's magic in every drop.

"Not everyone can suffer through your pumpkin spice lattes," she says dryly, her dark wavy hair that matches mine pulled back in a simple knot, her velvety brown eyes shining, silver rings clicking as she sets the jars in place. "But I'll give you props...you sell out of everything, so there's that. People love their pumpkin spice, but I'm not one of them. I'm more of a tea kind of girl."

I theatrically roll my eyes. "And there's nothing wrong with that. I love your teas, too."

My younger sister Ivy bursts in through the front door, her reddish-brown hair wild under an askew knit cap, grinning at us. She's walking dogs today, one of her many part-time jobs. The barking of the dogs has begun outside as they bark and look in the window, their leashes tied to the old iron lamppost out front. And there seem to be three extra loose dogs congregating with the ones tied up.

"Should I even ask, or do I just accept that you're the town's official puppy dealer now?" I grin.

"You guys, it's an emergency." Ivy's infectious grin is bright. Leave it to Ivy to smile through an emergency.

"Mrs. Tourney's golden retrievers escaped and fell into step behind me, so now I look like I'm running Wisteria Cove's unofficial Golden Girls Club."

I chuckle and reach for the phone to call Mrs. Tourney. This kind of thing happens often. Ivy's basically the unofficial dog whisperer of Wisteria Cove—well, all animals, really. I swear there's not a single pet within thirty miles that doesn't know or adore her. She's everyone's go-to for dog walking, pet sitting, you name it, though that's just one of her many gigs.

Ivy's what I like to call a serial job holder. She's worked just about everywhere in this town at least once, and somehow, she's charmed everyone while doing it. If Wisteria Cove has a job, Ivy's probably done it, quit it, and sometimes come back for another round. She always leaves on good terms, though. I'll give her that.

As I hang up the phone with Mrs. Tourney, who tells me she's on her way, Rowan sighs. "Remind me why you prefer dog walking out in the cold and don't want to teach yoga classes this week?"

"Because these dogs are adorable," Ivy shoots back with a grin. "Maybe if you considered goat yoga like I suggested, I'd fill in more."

I make Ivy's favorite drink for her, a Moonrise mocha, pop a lid on it and slide it over to her. She smiles gratefully and takes it, immediately taking a sip. "Mmmm, thank you," she says, closing her eyes.

We all turn and look as all the dogs she's walking peer in the window at Ivy, tails wagging, waiting expectantly.

"Look at them. It's like in Nordic countries where parents leave the babies in strollers outside in the fresh air to sleep," she says proudly of her charges as she sips her coffee.

"Yeah, except they aren't sleeping. They want their pup cups that you've taught them they get every time you come here," Rowan says with a smirk.

I pull out my small paper cups and fill them with whipped cream. Rowan, Ivy, and I carry them out and hand them out since they waited patiently like the good doggies that they are. I pet them and scratch their ears, grateful for the break from the busy day. One of them jumps up to sniff Ivy's coffee, and the outdoor table trembles, the glass lanterns shaking. It's the perfect friendly chaos that I crave in the shop. Magic in everyday moments.

Later, I go back to my cozy, cluttered peace. I glance around, grateful for the magic in the mid-morning mundane. The shop is empty of customers right now, but I'm sure we'll get another rush.

I love this street and always have. From the window of the shop, I can see the way Wisteria Cove folds in on itself, part fishing village, part small-town postcard. Shops like mine, tucked snug between weathered clapboard houses painted in shades of white, gray, and seafoam, line the cobbled street like they've been here forever. The air carries salt and woodsmoke, crisp with the warm autumn air.

Further down, the barber's striped pole spins lazily, bright against the red brick. A gull swoops overhead, its cry louder than the occasional car rumbling by, reminding me that here, the sea always has more presence than traffic. It's the rhythm of this place with the harbor bells, the rustle of dry leaves scraping along the stone, the quiet hum of neighbors calling out hellos.

It's not perfect in a shiny Hallmark way. It's better. Quirky, weathered, stubbornly itself. The shingles are faded from salt wind, the paint peels here and there, and the whole town smells faintly of fish no matter how many pies the bakery turns out. But it's *ours*. And I wouldn't trade it for anywhere else.

My gaze drifts down the street to the Holloway place. The windows stare back at me like eyes that have seen too much. It's different now with overgrown hedges, a porch in need of repair. When I was a girl, I used to run across that yard and lose whole afternoons in their backyard. Just seeing it now sends a wave of nostalgia washing over me, bittersweet as the bite of sea air. The house feels like a ghost of another time, one that's tethered itself to me whether I like it or not.

The Holloway house has sat empty for so long that it almost

feels like part of the scenery now, with weathered shingles, faded paint, and a crooked mailbox with "Holloway" still scrawled across it in peeling black letters.

For a long time after Tate Holloway left, I would glance out, expecting to see a light in a window. Watching for a shape moving past the curtains. Or him stepping out onto that porch like no time had passed at all. But that hope faded years ago when he left and disappeared without a word. People around town said that he took a job offshore somewhere doing deep-sea fishing. And eventually, I stopped watching and waiting for him. But part of me wonders—if the old Holloway house could speak, what stories would it tell? Stories of sadness, grief, and a family robbed of time and memories.

I've poured myself into this place instead, focusing on the dried orange slices hanging from the windows, the books stacked just so, and every cinnamon-sugar swirl on the foam of a latte. I try to romanticize everything in my life and make every day count. That's the only romance I have these days. Wisteria Cove isn't exactly full of eligible bachelors, and even if it were, I'm not sure how many would want to date a sad and lonely witch. I live above my shop in a tiny studio apartment, and this is as exciting as it gets, boys and girls.

The bookstore witch is boring.

I built this life...this sanctuary...this shop filled with the hum of conversation and the scent of coffee, books, and pumpkin spice.

And most of the time, it's enough. But lately it just feels lonely. There has to be more than this, I just don't know what.

About five years ago, a severe storm destroyed my father's fishing boat. There were no survivors, and the boat was never found. My family and this town have never been the same. There were seven people, including our neighbor, Phil Holloway, Tate's father on the Salty Siren that night. That was one of the worst storms in New England history. And that night changed the course of both of our families' lives forever.

The Holloways and Marens were like family to each other once upon a time. We shared family dinners and holidays—even our mothers were friends. My sisters and I and Tate grew up together. Everything changed after that night, though. I have always suspected that the Holloways blamed my father for the boat sinking. He was the captain, and people still talk about it occasionally, whispering that they held him responsible. But nobody will ever know what really happened, because they're gone.

Watching my mother, Lilith, wait out on the widow's peak for him to come home for weeks after the storm was awful. She refused to believe he was gone. She said she could still feel him out there. Part of her died that night with him. The mother that we had after that night wasn't the same mother that we had before the storm, with him gone. He left a crater-sized hole in all our lives. Losing a parent is the worst, and not a club anyone wants a membership to.

April, Tate's mother, moved to Florida right after they declared Phil legally dead. She left the house for Tate, and he stayed for a few years, fishing locally. But then, without warning, he was just gone. Things were never the same between us after the accident. We still talked, but our friendship and closeness took a hit.

I move behind the counter, wiping my hands and brewing a fresh batch of coffee for customers while keeping an eye on the simmering soup. Donna Bennett, the town's self-appointed fairy godmother and my mother's best friend, appears at the counter. Donna is also a famous author who has penned over a hundred romance novels in the past several decades. Most of the locals know her, and it's not a big deal, but she keeps a low profile for the rest of the world.

"Hi, Willa, I need five pumpkin spice scones to go for Remy and Junie," she declares cheerfully, plopping her purse down on the counter.

"Hey, Donna, how are you doing?" I smile as I wash my hands and dry them.

"I'm good, sweetie. Just left a meeting about the upcoming Harvest Moon Festival. It's going to be amazing this year," she says. "Also, why didn't you tell me that Tate's coming back?"

I drop a scone on the floor that I was scooping into the bag.

What did she just say?

My chest tightens, and my hands shake.

"I didn't know about Tate," I say.

"Oh, I figured you knew since you two were always so close," she says, raising her eyebrows.

"Nope," I hand her the bag of scones and head to the register to ring up her order.

"Well, keep me updated. It'll be nice to have him home," she says as she hands me her card to pay.

I nod, even though my outside reaction is not even close to my inside reaction. I am freaking out and trying to keep my hands from shaking right now.

"Gossip is as hot a commodity here as the coffee, but I'm trying to reign in my chaotic emotions, so I give Rowan a nudge, who's sitting at the coffee bar, reading a book.

"Donna, tell me about your tarot session with Lilith," Rowan asks sweetly, getting her to change the subject.

"Thank you," I mouth to her behind Donna.

Donna brightens and, luckily, moves on to that, telling everyone what happened. Before I know it, Lilith Maren, my mother, sweeps in with all the dramatic flair she can possibly muster. She's a petite woman, barely five-three, though she carries herself like she's towering over everyone in the room. A velvet shawl drapes around her shoulders like she's stepping onto a stage, and dried wisteria vines loop over one arm as if she's bringing an offering. Her wrists are stacked with silver bangles that clink and jangle with every gesture, punctuating her words like exclamation marks.

Her hair, long and wild, falls in loose waves the color of burnished copper streaked with silver. She insists it's "witch's hair," untamed and full of secrets, and she refuses to let anyone tame it with scissors. Her eyes are storm-gray with flecks of green and have that mischievous spark that makes people wonder if she knows more than she lets on. Spoiler: she always does.

She's not thin but not full-figured, either; she has that ageless, solid, earthy presence of a woman who's lived fully and refuses to apologize for it. There's something both comforting and chaotic about her, like she could whip up soup to cure your cold while also casually working on a spell for your love life in the same afternoon.

Today she's wearing a layered plum and midnight blue skirt, the hem brushing her boots, and a blouse patterned with tiny, embroidered moons and stars. Rings glitter on nearly every finger, amethysts, garnets, and a chunky turquoise she swears is enchanted. Everything about her says: *I belong to this town, and I am at home here.* She's timeless, a little eccentric, and entirely unforgettable.

"The vines signal love and renewal," she says, planting them firmly on top of the counter as I wince. She doesn't even notice the dried leaves that rattle onto the floor. "I'm sensing you have both on the horizon, Willa."

"Mom, why are you bringing in outside things?" I wince, digging into my resilient politeness at her eccentricity. But this is what happens when you have a witchy mother. They *know* things.

My mom just smiles, hugs Rowan and then reaches to pull

me into a hug, as well. "A little magic never hurts anyone, except the boring ones," she winks at me.

"I am not boring," I say as I swipe up the wisteria leaves into my hand.

Rowan arches a brow, her lips twitching. Before she can say anything, I shoot her a warning look, and she chuckles.

My mom laughs. "Not boring? Darling, you wouldn't know fun if it hit you like a broomstick. You hide out in your bookstore and hardly ever leave. You practically have to *schedule* fun. If that isn't boring, I don't know what is."

"Introverted," I correct, brushing the dried petals into a neat pile. "It's called being a homebody."

"Mm-hm." Lilith tilts her head, her hair spilling over one shoulder in a cascade of silver waves. "You're becoming a spinster with cats."

Rowan snorts. "She already has the tragic spinster vibe. Just missing the cats."

"Excuse me?" I glare at both, though my lips threaten a smile.

Lilith plants her hands on her hips, rings glittering. "I am simply saying, my darling daughters, that life is short, and you should be living it as though it were dipped in honey and rolled in cinnamon sugar."

Rowan leans against the counter, smirking. "You mean like Ivy? Trying out job after job?"

Lilith waves a hand as if brushing away a gnat. "She's figuring out what makes her happy." Her eyes sparkle with mischief as she looks between us.

Rowan rolls her eyes, but she's smiling. "That's one way of putting it."

I try to hold firm, but Lilith's infectious grin threatens to break me down. "You're impossible," I mutter.

"And you," she counters, reaching out to tap my nose like

I'm still a little girl, "are delicious when you're ruffled. Don't waste your life on order when chaos is so much more fun."

This is exactly what it was like growing up in the Maren household. Chaos and comfort mixed into something like home. And I love it.

When the store finally clears out for the night and everyone is gone, I flip the closed sign, lock the door, and get my homemade chamomile tea. My good life doesn't require much, just a steaming mug of tea, a good book, and some quiet solitude in my favorite place.

I pull a cracked wooden ladder from the shelf, flip open a hidden latch, and climb up to the small loft with windows catching the moonlight over the harbor. Here is where my quiet solitude reigns. A plush armchair and worn quilt wait for me by a small reading lamp, as if ready for me and waiting for the day to end. A cozy bed, stacks of books, a tiny kitchen, and a bathroom. It's all I need, and it's mine.

This is also a perfect view of the Holloway place and the harbor just beyond it. The dark shutters tug at me again. Is he really back? I so badly wanted to ask Donna more, but Donna is not the one to ask. Donna is wonderful, but a big matchmaker, and almost as bad as my mom. Those two together are just about impossible when they get an idea.

I sip my tea and imagine what would happen if Tate showed up, knocked on the door. What would I even say to him? Maybe we'd talk, and he'd be nice. Maybe he'd be better and not the broody fisherman man he was when he left Wisteria Cove. Maybe he's changed. Or maybe he's not even here at all, and Donna is mistaken.

The harbor outside is calm, the moon silver and reflecting across the dark water. A lone gull shrieks. My eyes seem to play tricks on me, as I think for a second I see a single upstairs light flare and fade. Maybe a coincidence, maybe not.

I feel mostly peaceful, other than the thought of Tate Holloway being back in town after all these years. I haven't exactly been pining for him. However, it is hard when his house is still there and serves as a constant reminder.

I light a small candle on my table for hope, lay out a leaf for fall rootedness, and sea salt for openness.

Yes, my life is full. Cozy, fun, and I am happy. But deep down? I'm deeply lonely.

I miss him.

Chapter 2
Tate

The late-night salty sea air hits differently in Wisteria Cove. It's almost sharper here and full of ghosts that I feel deep in my chest before I even hit the harbor. But deep down, it still feels like home. And I have missed it, despite the empty grief that fills me when I think about the memories here.

Wisteria Cove probably hasn't changed. I would bet the same old crooked street signs are still there that the town refuses to update. The houses that line the coast are still sea-scarred and clinging to the edge of the cliffs like they're just daring a storm to come for them.

I drag my duffel higher on my shoulder, pausing on the dark corner when I see my house sitting up ahead, dark, familiar, and weathered. The house looks as if it's been holding its breath, waiting for me to step over the threshold again and bring her back to life. Like it's clinging on for life, like I feel like I have been for the past few years.

I had old Pete Delaney, the old, retired harbor master, checking in on the house in my absence. He made sure the yard was maintained for me. I was glad he agreed to help because he keeps to himself, and I knew he wouldn't talk about me or tell anyone where I was. Still, he had no problems updating me on the comings and goings around Wisteria Cove. At first, I didn't want to hear it, didn't want to know. But then I got homesick and looked forward to his updates.

And I specifically looked forward to the updates on Willa Maren. Her bookstore took off, and it sounds like it's been successful. Last he mentioned, she was 'single and ready to mingle,' which I hated hearing. I don't want her to mingle with anyone. But I also realized that me being gone for two years and her not dating anyone wasn't realistic.

But I don't like it at all.

I stare down the dark street, and suddenly my shoulders feel lighter. I'm home, and while I thought it would feel heavy coming back here, it doesn't. It feels like nothing has changed, yet somehow everything has changed.

Admittedly, I left without saying a word to almost anyone. I figured it was better that way. Easier. Okay, probably just easier for me, but I needed to do it. I needed to leave this place. I felt like every day I was drowning, and I kept having recurring dreams that if Willa and I stayed friends, she'd drown, too. The dream involved us on a boat during a storm. Now, a good therapist would say that is the trauma of losing our dads at the same time. But grief has a funny way of messing you up and putting you back together again when you're ready. And I'm finally ready to come back. I just don't know if I can call this place home anymore or if this is truly where I'm supposed to be.

I stayed and tried to make it work for a while after my dad died. For a long time, I told myself he was still out at sea fishing and just on a long trip. But after a few years, I knew he was never coming back. As I continued having to face the pitying looks, the whispers, and the way the salt air felt heavier in my lungs, it became too much. So, I left.

I took every deep-sea fishing job I could, one after another. Alaska. Nova Scotia. Even Iceland, once. The further I got from Wisteria Cove, the better.

Months went by, and before I knew it, years. The only things I focused on were the next haul and the next port. I lived for the salt on my skin, wind in my face, and calloused hands. Fishing made sense. Fishing didn't ask me to explain why I couldn't breathe in Wisteria Cove anymore. But I knew it would never be permanent. The sea could never be home.

And now I'm back because...well. There's nowhere else to go. My mom is living down in Florida with her new husband and stepkids, and I'm not the biggest fan.

Pete called a few weeks ago and said the house was becoming too much and it needed repairs before the weather turned again, and that I needed to come back and take care of my own damn property. He means well, but I think he misses me, too. When my father died, he stepped in and was like a father to me. I love that guy. We've checked in every week, and his updates have meant a lot.

At first, I told myself I'd only come back long enough to fix the place up, then go back out again. That was the plan. But the second I stepped off the fishing boat and set foot onshore, something shifted. I could feel the pull drawing me straight here.

Some call it a spell, or some other folklore witchy stuff. But there is a pull here. Wisteria Cove will pull you in. It'll make you feel something for a place, even if you want to leave. But this time it's not just Wisteria Cove. It's her.

I glance over at the place I've thought about every day for years. Wisteria Books & Brews.

She had just opened it when I left. If I close my eyes, I can still feel and see the memory of her unpacking new books and stocking her shelves with a gleeful smile on her face. A smile I loved to see and I've missed deep in my soul. There were some days I'd give anything to see that smile again.

I never called her. After a while, so much time had passed, I knew she was better off forgetting me. I could never be the person she deserved and needed me to be. But the longer I was away, the more I couldn't get her out of my memory.

It's practically still in the middle of the night, and likely no one is awake in this town yet. But in a few hours, Wisteria Cove will hum with life. It's like autumn itself has taken over the old storefront, and the bookstore and coffee shop look less like a business and more like an invitation into someone's home.

But, then again, Willa did always have the gift of making everyone feel seen and welcome.

Steam has fogged the large front window of the store. A wreath of dried sage, oranges, rosemary, and lavender hangs over the door from a ribbon the color of burned copper, swaying gently in the harbor breeze. Tiny pumpkins dot the windowsills and fill mismatched baskets on the outdoor tables. Cornstalks lean against the weathered clapboard siding, and bundles of cinnamon sticks with twine hang from brass hooks under the window overhang. A bell hangs from the dark wood, worn smooth by time and hands, waiting to be jingled at every arrival like it knows it's part of the ritual of coming here.

She really did it. She told me when we were kids she was going to open her own bookstore and coffee shop, and even had this place picked out. When it went up for sale, she grabbed it. I never doubted for a minute that she'd make this place what it is today.

A chalkboard sign sits off the stoop, its edges scuffed and smudged with chalk dust, reading in curvy handwriting:

Today's special:

Butternut squash soup + turkey with brie, and cranberry
Apple cider scones
Pumpkin Spice + Everything Nice
Cozy Vibes and maybe a little magic

Cute. Inside, I peek in through the condensation on the window to see worn and mismatched tables just begging to be crowded with locals leaning in over their mugs and books stacked on every surface, waiting to be read. Well-worn quilts hang over chairs like they belong there as much as the people do.

This is all hers. It's cozy, familiar, and beautiful, every detail.

Even out here, the scent reaches me. Cinnamon, roasted coffee, melted butter, toasted bread, and something else that I can't put my finger on...

Then I realize—it's her scent. Willa's. And that makes my heart clench. I don't see her, but I imagine she'll be in there baking before too long.

It's stupid how my chest tightens just thinking of seeing her. Just feeling her in every detail of her shop really gets to me. I can't imagine how I'm going to feel when I finally see her. It feels like we are in another lifetime, I've been gone so long.

If anyone asked, I'd always said Willa and I were friends. Just friends. That was the safe word for it, the one that kept people from looking too closely.

But the truth was, there was always something simmering between us. A spark that never really burned out, no matter how much time or distance got shoved between us. She'd walk into a room, and the air would shift, like even the walls knew she was there, and I felt it every time.

We never crossed the line, though. Maybe because I didn't want to risk ruining what we had. She was the one person I could talk to about anything, my frustrations, plans, the weight of growing up in this town with a mother like mine. Losing that and *her*? That scared me more than anything.

And Willa's always been good at tucking her feelings behind a wall of smiles and witty comebacks. If she ever wanted more, she never let me see it. And God knows I looked. I'd catch her glancing at me, and for a heartbeat, I'd swear there was something in her eyes. But then she'd blink it away, change the subject, and I'd tell myself I imagined it.

So we stayed friends, except I never forgot how close her laugh could come to undoing me, or how much I wanted to reach for her hand and never let go.

I finally step into the house, and the chill hits me first, cold and damp, heavy with that faint, briny scent of salt air that's seeped into the wood after all these years.

The place feels smaller and hollow, like it's been holding its breath since the day I left. Dust clings to every surface, and the floorboards creak under my boots, groaning like they resent my return. It smells stale, and I know it'll take more than just an open window to wake this house back up. I have my work cut out for me.

But there's a small mercy waiting, too. Pete's left a lamp on in the corner, its golden glow softening the edges of the emptiness. A stack of clean linens sits neatly on the old bed, folded with a kind of quiet care that almost undoes me. I set my duffel down with a thud and let out a long breath, feeling the weight of this place settle into my bones.

It's mine, technically, but it doesn't feel like home. Home will never be here. This is the place where bad memories live.

After a long hot shower, I change into a clean T-shirt, make the bed, and stretch out after a long day. The sheets have a faint scent of detergent and salt. And kindness, if kindness had a smell.

Sleep takes me fast, grateful and heavy, even as the house creaks and sighs around me like it's remembering.

* * *

It's barely nine a.m., and I've already been lingering outside her bookstore long enough for the seagulls to give me side-eye. I probably look like some love-struck fool, loitering on Main Street, too damn chicken to actually walk in and face her.

I know exactly what people will think, I've already heard the whispers. Felt the weight of Old Pete's stare down at the docks this morning when I was checking in, like he was already questioning when I was going to go see her. Everyone thinks I came back for her.

Maybe part of me did.

But mostly...I'm just tired. Tired of running. Tired of pretending this town doesn't still have its hooks in me, no matter how far or how long I stay gone.

I rake a hand through my hair, fingers snagging in the curls, and shove my old Red Sox cap down tight. It's not much, but it feels like a little armor between me and everything waiting for me on the other side of that door.

When I catch my reflection in the window of Wisteria Books & Brews, I barely recognize the man staring back. I look and feel older, harder. My jaw is shadowed with a few days of scruff, too short to call it a beard, too careless to bother shaving. The sun and salt have left their mark; my skin's darker now, bronzed from summers spent hauling nets under an unforgiving sky, weathered in ways it never used to be.

Beneath the brim of my cap, my hair's grown longer, darker, more chestnut than the sandy brown it used to be when I was a kid. My eyes look sharper, tired maybe, like I've seen more than I should have by thirty.

The boy who used to laugh too loud in this town, who carried around a spark of recklessness, is gone. In his place is someone leaner, harder-edged, someone carved out by tide and storm. And for a second, I wonder if Willa will see the difference. If she'll see me at all.

I catch a glimpse of her, her dark hair pulled up loose, her mouth curved into that soft half-smile that always made my chest ache. She's laughing at something one of her customers is saying. Her sisters Rowan and Ivy are perched at the counter. Probably nothing has changed with them, either.

And Willa...God, she looks good. Softer but stronger. Comfortable in her skin in a way she wasn't when we were kids, like she's grown roots deep into this place, into this life. Like she belongs here. And I...I don't. I should turn around and go back to the house and get started on the damn repairs and pretend I'm invisible. But my feet won't move.

Then the bell above the door jingles, loud enough to cut through the soft hum of conversation, and before I can even think about it, I've stepped inside. Warmth rushes around me. The smell of coffee, books, candles, and cinnamon. Laughter and voices, chatter and life. Her life. And every single person in that shop goes still the second they see me. And then Willa turns. She freezes, just for a second, eyes locking on mine.

Deep, warm eyes that still feel like they can see right through me, even after all this time. Her mouth parts like she's about to say something, but she doesn't. She doesn't look surprised to see me. Nor does she look happy.

I force myself to speak first. But it comes out low and rough. "Hey, Willa."

Chapter 3
Willa

The morning has settled into that perfect golden lull that happens late afternoon this time of year. The shop is humming softly, warm with the scent of cinnamon and roasted coffee and faintly sweet, dried orange from the garland strung over the windows.

The door sways gently every time the wind pushes against it, and the sunlight slants just right across the old oak floors, catching on a few scattered crumbs I haven't gotten to yet. It's cozy chaos today, my favorite kind. Rowan's perched at the counter with her tea, methodically labeling her newest batch of tea blends with that minimalist, witchy aesthetic she insists on. Ivy is cross-legged in one of the mismatched armchairs, one boot kicked off, her tangled hair escaping from her beanie, working her way through a half-eaten pumpkin scone as she flips the pages in a new romance novel.

And right now, as the last customers finally drift out, leaving behind only the faint smell of lavender tea, it's just us: a rare moment where Wisteria Books & Brews belongs entirely to the three chaotic forces of nature otherwise known as the Maren sisters.

"Sooo," Ivy says, her smile as bright as the bakery case, "Guess who's the new official employee at the Doggy Daycare? The owner told me I radiate positive energy. All the dogs love me."

"Oh, you definitely radiate something," Rowan says, not looking up as she adds another label.

"Dogs just... sense I'm their person," Ivy says, taking a bite of her scone.

"Or they just know you've always got treats in your pockets," Rowan says with a smirk.

I snort-laugh, grabbing a rag and moving behind the counter to tidy up. My heart feels light and warm. This simple rhythm between us is something I'll never take for granted. I built this life, and I love it.

It makes me wonder what Tate would think of this place. Would he even care? And do I even care? Wisteria Books & Brews barely existed back when Tate Holloway ghosted this town like he was better than all of us. He left like none of us even mattered. That jerk left without calling or anything. I didn't just survive. I thrived and built something freaking cool as hell here.

I slip a dish towel over my shoulder, stacking a few mugs near the sink, when Ivy pipes up again.

"Hey," she teases, "remember when you used to pine over Tate Holloway like it was your full-time job?"

Rowan chuckles, and I roll my eyes. I hate it when they try to read my mind.

"Oh, yeah. Tate," she says in a high-pitched voice. "I just love you Tate, I still love you and pine for you when I'm all alone in my bookstore," she says as she makes kissing noises and faces to go with it. Nice.

"Oh, please," I say, deliberately casual, pretending to be

insulted. "Give me some credit. I'm far too busy for that nonsense."

I glance over at them with a grin, feeling a little too comfortable, a little too free to let my mouth run now that I know we're alone.

"Besides, you remember what he was like back then," I continue, waving a hand as I lean against the counter, enjoying the rhythm of this conversation. "Always brooding around town, thinking his quiet scowls were irresistible, which, okay, fine, they kind of were."

Both Rowan and Ivy nod and grin.

"And do I need to remind you how he just up and left?" I ask, my voice pitching up as I snap a stack of napkins into place. "No goodbye. No note. Nothing. Just Houdini'd right out of here. Honestly? Classic romcom villain move. He probably thinks he's this sad Taylor Swift song, but he's just a guy who ghosted us all."

I'm halfway through my dramatic performance when I notice Rowan suddenly freeze mid-labeling.

Her pen hovers inches from the jar, eyes locked on a point somewhere directly behind me.

Then Ivy chokes on a laugh that sounds half like panic, half delight.

And that's when the butterflies hit my stomach, because I know this look and sudden hush. This stillness that only ever means one thing. I let out a long sigh, my heart thudding hard against my ribs even before I speak the words I know are true. "He's behind me... isn't he?"

Neither of my sisters answer. They don't have to. I swear the air itself shifts as I turn slowly, deliberately, unwilling to rush this moment because whatever it is, whatever I find standing in that doorway,

And there he is. Tate Holloway. Framed perfectly in the

doorway of my shop, a world I built after he left, and yet somehow looking like he belongs here all the same.

Ball cap pulled low, sun-faded Red Sox logo shadowing those dark green eyes that used to undo me with a glance.

His hair is longer now, dark waves brushing his collar, a little wild, a little unruly, and unfairly perfect.

A neatly trimmed beard sharpens the lines of his jaw, making him look older, rougher... but even more devastatingly handsome. And I'm not even sure how that is remotely possible.

"Well, I called it. He's still hot..." Ivy whispers loudly, and everyone hears it.

His broad shoulders fill out a worn flannel shirt that's rolled up at the sleeves, revealing strong, tan forearms. Jeans, faded and soft, molded perfectly to lean hips. Boots scuffed from years at sea, planted squarely on my not-yet-swept floorboards.

My first thought is, damn him. He looks good.

My second thought is, No. Absolutely not. I am not letting him just waltz back in here after treating me like that and then looking like this.

And my third thought is completely inappropriate and will not be named.

The air feels thick, electric, as he lifts his gaze and meets mine, those green eyes locking on me like no time has passed at all, like I'm the same girl I was when he left.

But I'm not. I built this place. I built a life. It's not like it was before, with the girl waiting on the dock for a boy who never came back. Tate is grown now, and so am I. We're not kids anymore. We're adults with lives. I don't even know him.

His mouth tips into the barest shadow of a smile, just the faintest curl at the corner of his lips, enough to send my stomach flipping even though I do not want it to.

"Hey, Willa," he says, low, rough, and soft all at once. Like that's all he has to say. Like those two words can just smooth over two years of absence.

I square my shoulders automatically, armor snapping into place, and give him a slow once-over, deliberately unimpressed.

"Well," I say coolly, even though my pulse is racing so fast, "look what the tide dragged back in."

Ivy lets out an audible gasp-squeak behind me, but I don't break eye contact with Tate. Because I can't, he's standing there, flesh and blood and scruff and flannel and boots, right in the middle of this life I built without him.

"Place looks nice," he says, letting his gaze drift slowly around the shop like he's trying to memorize it. "I hardly recognize it from when you opened."

His expression softens as he takes it all in the books, the mismatched chairs, the autumn garlands, the candlelight, the warmth. I wonder what he's thinking.

"That's because you haven't been here," I state the obvious, crossing my arms as I lean against the counter, heart hammering, voice clipped and steady.

The silence between us stretches and feels electric. Like static crackles between us. The tension is so thick.

Then he nods, slow and measured, that tiny smile flickering again like he's not sure if he should smile at all. "Guess I deserve that," he says.

Rowan clears her throat behind me, breaking the moment just slightly. "We'll, uh... leave you to it," she says, rising gracefully from her stool and grabbing Ivy by the arm.

I glare at both of them. Traitors.

Ivy, of course, is grinning wildly, practically vibrating with delight. "Good luck," she stage-whispers as Rowan drags her toward the back door.

The door clicks shut behind them, leaving a silence that feels heavier than it should, broken only by the faint murmur of the wind rattling the windows and the soft hum of the ice machine. And just like that, it's only me and Tate. *Alone.* My mom is in the back somewhere, but knowing her, she left me to my fate with Tate, too.

Tate clears his throat, shifts his weight, then tips his head toward the chalkboard menu.

"Are you still open for dinner?" he asks casually, like we haven't just been staring each other down as though we're in the middle of a Western showdown.

I stare at him, weighing my options, but deep down, there's no real choice. I could never send him away. Not when I still see the grief lingering inside the man, the one who lost everything.

"And I'd love a coffee, if you've got any. Black."

Black, of course. Just like he drank before; that much is the same, at least. I'm sure there's so much about him I don't know anymore.

I grab a mug from the rack, forcing my hands to stay steady as I set it beneath the spout.

"Black," I echo, glancing over my shoulder with a dry look that I hope doesn't reveal my nerves. "Like your soul."

That earns a low chuckle from him, warm and rough, and it does something awful to me, makes my pulse skip, makes the air between us feel too familiar, too easy, too much like...before.

"Fair," he says. "I see you're still mad."

"Nope," I clip. "I'm fine."

He gives me a look that says we both know damn well I'm not fine.

As the coffee brews a fresh pot, I run through what I can pull together for him from what we have on hand.

"Turkey sandwich with cranberry relish?" I ask briskly, reaching for the bread.

Tate nods and says quietly. "Sounds good. Thank you."

Before I can say another word, the back door swings open

and my mom sweeps in, a gust of cinnamon-scented chaos trailing behind her. Her velvet shawl is wrapped loosely around her shoulders, long silver earrings swaying, and her hands are full of herbs she's undoubtedly been "foraging" for again.

Her sharp gaze flicks from me to Tate in an instant. My mom misses nothing. Her intuition is almost spot-on. "Well, well," she says, a sly smile curving her lips as she saunters forward. "If it isn't the prodigal son home from the sea."

Tate laughs, a real, full-bodied laugh that pulls a startled glance from me because I can't remember the last time I heard it, much less directed at my mother. But the two of them always had a special bond. His mom April wasn't always the best mother to him, and he got what he needed at our house when he needed it. My mom has always loved Tate.

"Lilith," he says warmly, pulling off his ball cap and raking a hand through that too-long hair. "Still terrorizing the town, I see."

"Always," she replies, stepping right up to the counter next to him, leaning her elbows on the wood. Her bracelets jingle with every slight movement as she tilts her head and studies him in that way she has, like she can read straight through your ribcage into your heart. It makes most people uncomfortable, but not Tate. He smiles at her and tilts his head at her as if he's giving her permission.

"You look tired, Tate Holloway," she says softly, no pretense now, no teasing. "More tired than you should be. What've you been running from all these years?"

I freeze at the kitchen counter, my breath caught because... leave it to her to ask the exact question I didn't dare ask myself. She never shies away from asking the questions everyone else is thinking. Her inside thoughts usually come out to play.

But Tate doesn't bristle or brush her off or retreat. Instead, he exhales slowly and taps his knuckles once on the counter, eyes fixed somewhere in the middle distance. "Every damn thing," he says quietly.

She hums and nods, not smug or satisfied, just understanding. She reaches across and squeezes his forearm gently, her bangles clinking. "Well," she says after a pause, straightening again with a small smile, "you'll need food in your belly before you face your demons. And my daughter makes an excellent turkey sandwich."

"Already working on it," I mutter, half amused, half horrified at how easily they're slipping into this old rhythm like nothing happened.

But what he said gutted me. His vulnerability was raw and unexpected.

By the time I set the plate in front of him, he's settled in like he's never been gone.

Lilith perches beside him, chatting easily about whatever town gossip she's picked up this morning, her laugh low and warm. And Tate...he's laughing too.

Not just polite chuckles, but real, deep, genuine laughter, the kind that used to curl low in my stomach, back when I let it affect me, back when we were kids, and I thought we had forever.

And it truly stuns me how easily he fits back in here, as if these past two years were nothing more than a brief detour. Like this is still his world. Like I'm still his Willa. Only I'm not. He made it very clear when he never reached out during the past few years that I didn't mean anything to him.

He sips his coffee and wipes his fingers on the napkin I've provided, leaning in to say something that makes my mom snort with laughter.

I hover behind the counter, watching them, arms crossed, pretending to wipe a non-existent smudge from the espresso machine, heart pounding even as I remind myself that I will not get pulled back in by that smile and those green eyes. Not a chance.

But God help me, he looks really good sitting there with his broad shoulders hunched slightly over the counter, calloused fingers curled around the mug like this seat's been waiting for him all this time.

And somehow, that infuriates me more than anything. Because if he feels so comfortable here now, why didn't he stay, then?

Chapter 4
Tate

I don't know how many screws I've driven into this damn porch today, but I can tell you one thing: none of them are fixing what really needs fixing. Not the thing between me and Willa. I didn't think coming back here would be easy, but I didn't expect her to be so angry and indifferent. She looked like she was seething yesterday. Lilith and her sisters were happy to see me, but Willa definitely was not.

I pause, leaning back on my heels to wipe sweat off my brow with my forearm. The sun is relentless, baking the tops of my shoulders on this warmer-than-usual fall day. My cap is turned backwards, hair damp beneath it, and my shirt's long gone, draped somewhere over the railing I'm trying to replace.

The boards creak beneath my boots, and I remember her laughter right here, years ago. I remember the paint splattered across her cheek when we first fixed up this porch together, the way she teased me about my terrible brush strokes. That light in her eyes. God, I was stupid to think walking away was the right thing to do. I left before we could ever really be something. She was my best friend. She was supposed to be my everything. We both knew it. And I threw it all away because I was scared.

My drill stills, and I can almost hear her saying, "You promised you'd never leave, Tate."

Yeah, I broke that promise so thoroughly, I'm surprised this porch didn't fall apart in my absence.

The sound of a car pulling up yanks me out of my guilt spiral. It's an old pickup, Rowan's.

She steps out before I can even stand, arms crossed over her chest, sunglasses keeping me from seeing her eyes, her stride purposeful. Rowan's always been the most no-nonsense of the sisters, direct, sharp, fiercely protective of Willa. And right now, she's a woman on a mission.

"Rowan," I nod, trying to muster a casual tone. She's having none of it.

"You busy?" she asks, already walking straight up to me.

I have a feeling that even if I was busy, this conversation would be happening regardless.

"Just fixing things," I answer, as if that explains anything. As if this sweat-soaked apology project counts for something.

She leans against the post I just fixed, eyes narrowed behind those shades. "You know you have a lot more to fix than this railing, right? You didn't only hurt Willa when you left. We all missed you, Tate."

Okay, so we're just getting straight to it. These Maren sisters don't mess around, especially Rowan, who is known for being the toughest of all of them. My throat tightens, and I grip the drill a little harder, but I say nothing. I know she's here to let me have it, so I'll take it. I deserve it.

She doesn't wait for a response but rolls right on. "You hurt all of us, Tate. You left a crater, and it wasn't just her picking up pieces."

I nod slowly, eyes cast down. "I know, and I'm sorry."

Her voice softens, not by much, but enough that I feel it like a squeeze around my ribs. "Willa...she's strong. She won't admit it, but when you left? It broke her." She pauses, lips pressed together like she's holding back more. "And when she broke, it broke all of us, too. And you're an asshole for that, Tate."

The air between us is heavy now, loaded with everything unsaid, and I swear it's harder to breathe.

"I know I have a lot to fix," I manage, voice low, thick.

She sighs, steps forward. "I won't pretend I'm not mad at you. I am. Hell, I could throttle you right now." She reaches out suddenly, surprising me, and pulls me into a fierce hug, tight and no-nonsense.

"But we missed you, Tate," she whispers. "And I'm glad you're back. Even if I still want to kill you a little."

I freeze for a heartbeat before hugging her back. When she pulls away, there's a shimmer in her gaze, steel and softness wrapped up together. Classic Rowan.

"Be good to her," she says. "Earn her trust back. You better fix this."

And just like that, she's gone, strolling back to and climbing in her truck. The engine rumbles as she pulls out and turns down the road.

I stand there, feeling more feelings than I have in years. And I'm kicking myself for leaving and staying gone. When I left, I felt like I was an outlier. I didn't have family here anymore. Just ghosts. And I told myself that I needed to go away.

By the time the sun slips lower on the horizon, I've got the railing solid, a lot sturdier than when I started. It's barely a dent in all that I need to do, but it's something.

The sweat rolls down my back as I put everything away, my muscles tight and tired in that good way, where the physical exhaustion almost makes you forget the exhaustion. Almost.

I stretch my back, wiping sweat from my temple with the edge of my wrist, and lean against the porch to admire my work. And then I feel it, that tingle at the back of my neck. I know before I even look up. There she is. Willa, standing at her upstairs window, half hidden behind sheer curtains, is watching me.

My heart lodges in my throat. She's beautiful in the golden light, hair loose, face unreadable from this distance, but I swear her gaze is burning holes straight through me. I can't help myself.

I grin. A slow, crooked, lazy grin, the kind that used to make her laugh and roll her eyes all at once. And just like that, she looks away. Pretends she wasn't watching. But she was.

I stay rooted there for a second longer, heart pounding, grinning like an idiot at nothing now.

Then I turn back to my tools and finish tightening the last railing bolt, because this isn't about rushing. Not this time. As twilight falls, I gather my tools and pause at the top step of the porch.

I sit on the steps for a while, elbows on my knees, watching dusk settle over the street. A neighbor bikes past and calls out with a grin, "About time you came home, Holloway!"

I laugh softly, lifting a hand in acknowledgment. Yeah. It was time.

As night falls, I close my eyes, leaning back against the porch post. The smell of her favorite candle drifts down from the open window above, a vanilla scent I haven't smelled in years but know by heart.

God, I missed her. And I'm not leaving again. I left because I thought she deserved better than me. All I did was make her carry the pieces I shattered. Not this time. I open my eyes, looking up at her window once more.

I whisper to the quiet night, to myself, to her, even if she can't hear it: "I'll fix this. Every board, every brick, every damn thing I broke. I'll fix it all."

And as I pick up my shirt and sling it over my shoulder, I feel it deep in my bones. This isn't over.

It's just the beginning.

* * *

I'm still asleep the next morning when my phone rings. I answer it, blinking with surprise at the caller.

"Hey, Lilith," I say, rubbing the sleep from my eyes.

"Tate," she begins, sweet but sharp, like she always is. "I hate to bother you, honey, but my kitchen sink is leaking something awful. It's practically flooding the entire place."

There's a pause.

"And honestly, I think you owe me some neighborly help after disappearing without a goodbye for years?"

That earns a tired smile from me. Lilith doesn't miss a chance to twist the knife, even if she does it with a friendly voice.

"I'll be right over," I tell her.

I walk down Main Street, hands shoved in the pockets of my worn flannel, boots scuffing against cobblestones as a cool breeze sends a swirl of leaves skittering past. Wisteria Cove doesn't just decorate for fall; it becomes fall. Every porch is drowning in pumpkins and cornstalks, wreaths of orange, crimson, and brown leaves, along with dried herbs, hanging from every door. Businesses decorate their storefronts, competing for the most elaborate decorations. The whole town smells like cider, wood smoke, and nostalgia. Even Wisteria Books & Brews has gone all in, and honestly, it's my favorite of them all.

Everywhere I look, it's cozy fall chaos: lanterns strung between lampposts, corgis in witch hats, with scarecrows propped up. Wisteria Cove never did simple, and God, it's beautiful. There's no other place in the world like fall here.

By the time I reach Lilith's old Victorian, painted that deep plum color with herbs drying from the porch beams and her willow tree draped in flickering amber lanterns, I already know I'm not here to fix anything that's actually broken. Her place is as perfect as ever, leaning fully into its witchy splendor, like the entire yard has been waiting all year for this exact season. I pause under the branches, breathing it all in, and can't help but smile. This town wraps around you whether you want it to or not. When Lilith appears at the door before I can even knock, a sly smile on her face, I shake my head. I missed her. But coming home also reminds me that I lost my father and my mother. Technically, Mom is still alive, but she has never been as warm and welcoming to me as Lilith.

Her house is exactly as I remember it: warm, cluttered, smelling faintly of cinnamon and something baking. A wreath with dried flowers is on the door.

When she holds open the door for me to enter, Lilith is wearing an apron dusted with flour, her long silver hair twisted into a neat bun. She looks like the small-town matriarch—only make her a witch. Those eyes have a way of seeing straight through me. She's full of intuition and heart. There's no one I've ever met like her. She has a way of making you feel seen and heard.

"Thanks for coming, sweetheart," she says, ushering me inside. "The sink's over there. It's leaking from somewhere underneath, and I just don't know what to do."

I crouch down and open the cabinet door. Barely a drip. I twist the pipe gently. Tight. Dry.

"Lilith...this isn't leaking," I say, confused.

She waves her hand in the air. "Oh, it was yesterday. I swear it was. Maybe it fixed itself overnight."

She smiles too innocently, leaning on the counter as if that'll distract me.

I smirk, shaking my head. "You made this up to get me over here, didn't you?"

Instead of denying it, she shrugs. "What can I say? You're not exactly easy to pin down these days, Tate. No one knows when you'll be gone again."

It's impossible not to chuckle at her ridiculous honesty. I close the cabinet and stand, wiping my hands on the towel she's suddenly offering me.

"Coffee?" she asks.

She's already pouring before I can answer.

"I feel like I should charge you for this service call," I tease.

"Oh, please. You owe me just for breaking my daughter's heart. And mine."

I wince at the jab. Even though her tone is playful, it lands. Lilith doesn't let much go unsaid.

The coffee is strong. We sit at her little kitchen table, and she watches me like I'm a kid who's come home from college, half proud, half suspicious.

Her kitchen is cozy, with jars on shelves containing teas and herbs. I've always felt at home here in the Maren kitchen. Lilith pours herself into everything she does. And every meal she's ever made me in here was nothing short of incredible.

She stirs her mug and murmurs something, then says, "So, what are your plans now that you're back?"

I take a breath, weighing my answer. It's a simple question, but I know it's not simple for her. Or for me.

"I don't know yet," I admit. "Fix up the old place. Maybe stay through fall. I haven't thought much beyond that."

Her brow arches. "Mm-hmm. And Willa?"

That name on her tongue hits different. Soft and sharp at the same time. Like a match striking. "What about Willa?"

"Are you planning to fix things there, too?" she asks bluntly.

I sip the coffee slowly, buying myself a second.

"Honestly? I don't know if I can, but I'm going to try. She's not exactly eager to forgive me."

Lilith nods in agreement, leaning back in her chair and studying me.

I run a hand over my jaw. "I messed up."

Lilith leans forward now, elbows on the table. "Why did you come back?"

That one catches me off guard, not because I don't have an answer, but because I'm not sure how honest I want to be with Lilith right now. What is it with Maren women confronting me, anyway?

I swirl the coffee in my mug and then set it down carefully.

"I missed it," I say quietly. "This place. Her. Everyone. All of it."

Lilith softens at that, her eyes warming. "Well...good. Because this town hasn't been quite right without you, Tate, whether Willa admits it or not."

I look around her kitchen, the black lace curtains, the pumpkin centerpiece on the table, the cinnamon sticks in a jar by the stove and realize how much it really hasn't changed.

It's as if Wisteria Cove has been waiting for me to come back and pick up the pieces.

Lilith's watching me again with that look, the one that says she sees every thought running through my head.

"I missed you, Lilith," I say finally, smirking. "Even your meddling."

She laughs then, rich and full. "Oh honey, I know. But I figured a little motherly meddling never hurt anyone. Plus, I missed you something fierce."

I shake my head, stand, and drain the last of the coffee. "Well...consider me officially meddled with. And you can call me to hang out and not pretend you need me to fix anything. But I will always help you fix things if you really need it."

She follows me to the door, pulling me into a quick hug before I leave. "Willa's stubborn," Lilith says with a small smile. "But she's got a good heart. She just needs time."

I nod, because I know that's true. And maybe—just maybe—time will be enough. Still, loving her from a distance is the only thing I've ever really figured out how to do. I don't know if Lilith's words are meant to reassure me, but they do. Enough to stay. Enough to keep hoping that maybe what I feel isn't just mine to carry.

I have no doubt Lilith's working whatever quiet magic she can to see that Willa and I end up together again. That's just how she operates, pulling strings behind the scenes, always two steps ahead. But after the storm, after my dad went missing, my mom drifted away from her. Something happened between them that night, something I was too young to understand, and whatever it was, it built a wall I couldn't see over. The mother I had before the storm and the woman who emerged after? They weren't the same.

"Okay," I murmur as I step outside, the cool autumn air sliding over my skin, crisp and clean, sharp with the scent of fallen leaves.

I pause on Lilith's porch, breath misting in front of me, feeling the tug of this town, the history, the secrets, the way Wisteria Cove never quite lets you go.

And for the first time in a long time, I wonder if I even want it to.

Chapter 5
Willa

This is fine. Totally fine. I do not have feelings for Tate Holloway. I absolutely, one hundred percent, do not have feelings for Tate Holloway.

And if this entire town thinks otherwise? Well...they can keep their opinions to themselves. And I won't be giving them any pumpkin scones if they give me any crap about it.

Okay, I won't withhold the scones, but I don't like that everyone is so happy and forgiving that he's back. And I'm over here just floundering like a floppy fish loose on the dock. I feel awkward around him. Like I have zero chill at all.

It happens every morning now. I can't even take a peaceful walk along the harbor without running straight into reminders of him. Or him.

It's kind of like if you think about a specific color and car. Then you see it everywhere you look. And you probably wouldn't have noticed that car before. But then suddenly it's everywhere you look. Yeah, that's how I feel right now.

Sigh. Now, he's everywhere. He's at my house, chatting it up with my mom. I see that he's been working down at the dock again, like old times. It's a full-time job right now to pretend I'm not affected by him being back in town. But I am. I take a walk every day on my break and take in the fresh autumn air. And somehow, I usually end up near him or seeing him.

And here he is.

The scruffy kid who once ruled these docks with cocky smirks and boyish charm has vanished, replaced by a man who carries himself like he's weathered every storm and come out stronger. Broad shoulders, sun-warmed skin, that steady gaze that pins me in place. Just one look at him, and it's not just my knees that go weak. It's every part of me that remembers exactly how dangerous he's always been to my heart. He has the power to destroy me piece by piece. And he has before.

Tate's on the dock, sleeves shoved up to his elbows, forearms flexing with every crab trap he hauls onto the decking like it weighs nothing. The low Red Sox cap shadows his face just enough to make him look annoyingly sexy, as if he belongs on the cover of some salty New England fisherman calendar. The morning sun slices through the harbor mist, turning the water to silver glitter, but all I see is him.

He works with a steady, practiced efficiency, shoulders broad, back straight, that quiet determination he's always had, but it's different now. There's a calm confidence about him, like he's completely at home down on that dock. And holy hell, that skin...tan and weathered and stretched over muscles I'm definitely not supposed to be thinking about.

He hasn't even looked my way, probably doesn't realize I'm standing here at all, but every movement he makes feels like it's just for me. It's doing dangerous things to my ability to function like a normal human being.

Yeah. This is going to be a problem.

I clutch my coffee tightly as I turn and walk faster, willing my pulse to calm down on my way back to the bookstore.

I glance around and see people watching me and glancing

over at Tate. It's as if they're waiting for a reaction. I swear this town is conspiring to ruin me.

And speaking of conspirators: Donna Bennett is staring at me with a knowing grin from the bench along Main Street facing the harbor, knitting needles clicking like tiny weapons. She's probably already adding me into one of her small-town romance books with Tate.

"I saw you watching our Tate, dear," she calls out at full volume. "You two have so much chemistry! You know what clears the air between two stubborn people? Breaking a bed frame! Works like a charm!"

My face burns hotter than my latte. "Donna," I mutter, glancing around to see if anyone else heard.

Spoiler alert: everyone did. Ben from the bait shop is openly grinning. He looks like he wants to start clapping.

Great.

By the time I storm back into the bookstore, I'm muttering under my breath.

"Rough walk, sis?" Rowan asks, amusement curling around every word.

I glare at her. "Your favorite town busybody just suggested I break a bed frame with Tate Holloway to 'clear the air.'"

Ivy looks up from behind the counter, where she's taping up a new "AUTUMN SPELLS & STORIES" sign that she designed. "Donna again?"

"She's practically your PR manager at this point," Rowan says, leaning dramatically on a display table.

"Then she's fired," I mutter.

The bell above the door jingles for the hundredth time today as another group of tourists floods in, all bright eyes and camera phones, whispering like they're on safari.

One of them points right at me dand stage-whispers in awe, "That's one of them! A Maren sister!"

This never gets easier, but I do my best to be friendly. Usually, I don't even have to try. Normally, I thrive on the noise, the bustle, the constant stream of chatter in and out of the shop. I've always loved welcoming strangers, swapping stories with tourists, laughing with locals who linger over coffee.

But today? My mood's all twisted up like a messy knotted fishing net. I paste on a smile, even as every nerve in me feels prickly and out of sync. Thanks to Tate showing up out of nowhere, looking like every broody sea-soaked daydream come to life, and the entire town deciding my love life is a community project, I'm out of sorts. It takes effort just to keep my voice light, to keep the edges of my irritation tucked away.

And that only makes me crankier. Because when being friendly becomes work, I start to feel like I'm losing the very thing I've always loved most about this place. I plaster on my best polite smile and shuffle behind the counter before I say something snarky that ends up on Yelp.

The bell above the door jingles again like it's laughing at me, and more tourists pile in looking for books and drinks.

Inside the shop, cozy chaos is everywhere. When I left for my break, the place was slow.

The bookstore is full now, tourists everywhere, taking photos, hovering near the 'Local Legends' display, whispering about the 'mysterious Maren sisters.' A few of them glance at the display and back at me, and I see another lady slide her phone out of her purse and hold it up to take a photo.

Great. Just what we need. I take it all in stride, though. It's weird, but this time of year is always busy and full of tourists. They help out our town, despite it being creepy.

Behind the counter, Ivy looks far too pleased with herself as she rings up another tote bag full of books and chats up the customers. This time of year, we need all the help we can get.

We've been saving up to expand next door, where Rowan plans on putting an apothecary shop.

And then there's my mother, Lilith. She's behind the bakery case, apron dusted with flour, proudly sliding a tray of pumpkin scones into the glass bakery case, as if she's hosting a Food Network special.

People will quickly buy out every one of those scones, judging by the forming line.

"Oh, Willa," my mom says far too casually, "Did you know Tate Holloway loves these pumpkin scones? You should take him some before they're all gone. He must be starving after unloading traps all morning."

I stop in my tracks. "Mom," I warn.

"What?" she asks, feigning innocence, drizzling icing onto the scones. "It's just neighborly hospitality."

She has a sparkle in her eye that says she's up to something. I'll be keeping a close eye on her. Closer than ever now. She's scheming. I can feel it. I stare at her for a while and squint my eyes until she looks at me, shrugs her shoulders, and grins.

The afternoon hums right along, refusing to slow for anyone, least of all me. The sun drifts lazily over the harbor, casting everything in a golden haze that makes the pumpkins on every porch glow like lanterns and the falling leaves swirl like they're part of some slow, deliberate dance. Somewhere down the street, wind chimes tangle in the breeze, and the distant clatter of people out walking echoes. But no matter how beautiful the day is, it just keeps pulling me with it, tasks unfinished, errands waiting, feelings I'm not quite ready to name piling up right alongside everything else. And through it all, I catch myself glancing toward the dock again, where Tate was working, unaware that he's taking up far too much space in my head. The three of us, me, Ivy, and Rowan, are deep in a ridiculous argument about how to rearrange the store to handle the tourists and make more space.

"Rowan, we can't just dump the romance section in with the horror," I protest.

"Why not?" she counters. "Some plots overlap. Stalking, obsession, bad decisions. It makes sense to me."

Ivy snorts. "She's onto something here. It's all basically one genre anyway: red flags and bad decisions with or without a knife."

I laugh. "You're both hilarious."

"Says the three of us, whose dating lives are basically horror stories anyway." Rowan jokes.

"Hey!" Ivy protests but then closes her mouth when Rowan gives her a pointed look. She has an on-and-off-again boyfriend, but he's a jerk, and none of us like him.

We all have nicknames for Derek, depending on the day and whatever he's done to Ivy. Last week he was Bruno. Because we don't talk about Bruno.

Last week Rowan referred to him as Caillou because he's going bald and he acts like a whiny child.

It's funny because it's true. Derek is not good to Ivy, and we're all just basically waiting for her to see what we see. And yeah. We might as well shelve ourselves right between thrillers and tragic comedies.

Outside, another tourist couple poses for a selfie under the bookstore sign like we're some glossy travel guide stop, and for half a second my mood wants to turn grumpy. But I catch myself. That's not fair. They're sweet, smiling, holding onto each other like the world is something to celebrate. People like them keep the lights on here, spreading pictures of Wisteria Books & Brews across their feeds and drawing more curious souls into my shop.

Normally, I'd be out there waving, maybe even offering to snap the photo for them. I love that part, the steady stream of people who walk through my door with stories from places I may never see. Usually, it fills me up. Today, though? Today it feels like work. And I know exactly why. My emotions are all jumbled, turned upside down by a certain broody fisherman and the meddling chorus of townsfolk who seem more invested in my love life than I am. It's unfair, I know, to let my mood color how I see people who are only here to enjoy themselves. And realizing that makes me crankier still, because friendliness is usually effortless for me. Warmth is supposed to be my gift, not something I have to summon.

So, I take a breath, shake it off, and remind myself: none of this is their fault. My chaos is mine to carry.

"Willa, you've become one of the town's famous landmarks," Ivy says, grinning. "Right between the lighthouse and the saltwater taffy shop."

I turn and smile, "I am glad people are coming here."

"And you're going to need to order more books," Ivy says, reaching out to tug gently on the sleeve of my cardigan. "Besides...we all know you've been extra cranky because a certain broody fisherman is back."

My stomach flips. "Excuse me?" I say, pretending not to be bothered.

Rowan leans back dramatically in her chair. "It's so obvious. Maybe you should just kiss and make up, or we'll have to shelve your love life in the dramatic works section."

I open my mouth to argue, but before I can, my mom sweeps into the conversation like she's been lurking in the shadows, just waiting to drop her next bomb.

"Speaking of Tate," she says, balancing another fresh tray of pumpkin scones like some flour-dusted witch, "He'll probably stop by. When I dropped by the harbor earlier, with the scones you refused to deliver, he mentioned needing a book to read."

"Mom! Stop it," I groan. I doubt that is true. She's just messing with me.

"What? Just helping you sell books," she says innocently.

There's absolutely nothing innocent about it.

I'm stacking a new shipment of candles on the front table when I hear the bell over the door jingle. Before I can even look up, Rowan's voice floats in, syrupy and smug. "Well, well, well... speak of the flannel-wearing devil."

I don't have to turn around to know who she's talking about. I can feel him behind me, like gravity just shifted slightly toward the front of the shop.

"Who?" I ask anyway, feigning indifference as I straighten a row of amber glass candle jars labeled Witch's Hearth.

I glance up, and he's sliding onto a stool. His eyes meet mine and soften. "Hey, Willa."

My mom joins in from her usual perch at the counter, warm and teasing. "He's got that whole lumberjack grump thing going for him now, doesn't he?"

My cheeks heat instantly, but I keep my back to them. "Mom, he can hear you. Do you all have anything better to do?" I mumble, adjusting the candle display like it's suddenly the most important task in the world.

"Oh, we're doing exactly what we should be doing," Ivy pipes up from the other end of the shop, smirking. "Speaking of...it's time for my break. You'll need to help Tate with his order."

I straighten my apron and head over to the coffee shop and face him.

His Red Sox cap is pulled low, beard a little more scruffy than the last time I saw him, sleeves shoved up to reveal those infuriatingly perfect forearms I could run my fingers up. He's leaning against the counter like he owns the place, and despite myself, my eyes linger a little too long on the way his jeans sit low on his hips, and the hint of sun at his collarbone.

He takes off his cap and runs his fingers through his hair, still damp from a shower.

My mind wanders to him in the shower.

Get it together, Willa.

My mom grins at him, ever the instigator. "So, Tate, what's new since you've been back?"

He just shrugs, easy and casual. "Not much. Buying a truck and fixing up my dad's old fishing boat. Planning to work it again."

My heart drops when he says this. It's like a light switch flips.

"Oh, so you decided to stick around?" Lilith asks.

He shrugs, but his eyes never leave me, as if he's waiting to see how I'll respond.

The words hit me like a cold splash of harbor water. Fixing up his dad's boat. Working it again.

Suddenly, my throat goes dry, and a pit opens in my stomach. Because I know exactly what that means. Long days, early mornings. Cold, choppy seas. Not everyone who goes out comes back. Just like our dads. But I say nothing. I shove the worry deep down, like I always do, tuck it away behind a carefully constructed smile. I turn toward him, keeping my expression neutral, cool, even bored, and force myself into "regular customer" mode.

"Let me know if you need anything," I say deliberately casual, my tone light but my insides twisting.

He lifts his chin in acknowledgment, his gaze catching mine for half a second, just long enough for my stomach to flip before I look away. He wanders across the room to browse the books but him being here has me feeling like an awkward teenager.

My mom leans across the counter, chin in her hand. "He's all grown up, Willa. When did that happen?"

"Didn't notice," I say flatly, moving behind the register and pretending to rearrange receipts that absolutely do not need rearranging.

But of course, Rowan can't leave it alone.

"She's lying," she singsongs, bumping my hip with hers as she slides in next to me. "She noticed, and she's been noticing. Haven't you, Willa?"

I grit my teeth, keeping my face carefully blank. "Nope."

Ivy snorts from the corner. 'You're practically vibrating, sis. You haven't looked this flustered since you realized someone bent the spine on your favorite book, and you still haven't been able to forgive them.'"

My mom chuckles. "He's got her all tangled up, and he doesn't even realize it."

And that's the worst part. Because he *does* know it. I've seen it in the way he looks at me.

He's here like he hasn't haunted my thoughts every single day since he left, like he didn't just casually announce that he's going back out on the water. Like that doesn't terrify me in ways I can't even explain to them, to anyone. We live in a fishing town. People work the boats here. And up until now it wasn't something that was close to me anymore. Until he announced that and now, I don't even know what to do with that. I know he just got back from fishing.

Old Pete and I had a secret pact. He'd tell me if anything was wrong. And he would always just say, "All is well." But that doesn't mean I didn't worry. I never stopped worrying.

So I do what I always do, I ignore him.

I ring up a customer's coffee as if it's the most pressing task in the world. "Here you go," I say cheerfully, handing the change over, though my heart is pounding hard enough to shake my ribs.

The words stick in my chest. Too late, I think. I've been trying to convince myself for years that he doesn't matter. But he does.

Across the room, Tate's busy browsing the shelves, running his fingers absently along the spines like he has nowhere else to be. Like he's home again and doesn't realize he's making every nerve in my body feel like it's on fire.

I let my gaze flick toward him one last time, and my heart sinks all over again. Because even now, even after all this time, I'm still tangled up in him.

But I won't show it. I can't show it. Instead, I paste on a smile, turn back to my sisters, and toss out the only armor I have left: sarcasm. "You all need hobbies," I say breezily, though my insides feel anything but breezy.

They laugh, and the teasing continues, but my mind is far from the chatter.

Because that pit in my stomach? It's not going anywhere. Not when he's going back out on the water.

And not when my heart is clearly too stupid to understand that loving a fisherman means learning how to live with that dread. So, I'll just keep trying my hardest not to love him.

Chapter 6
Tate

"I've told you, Tate, we're buying a vacation home," my mother says, her voice crisp enough to cut glass.

I pace the living room, thumb pressed tight against my phone, my bare feet making slow, restless tracks across the cool wood floor. "Yeah," I say, because I'm not sure what else she wants from me.

She doesn't ask about the house or the boat. Doesn't ask how I'm settling back into Wisteria Cove. Just keeps talking about her new husband, stepkids, and their perfect lives.

I drop onto the edge of the couch, elbows on my knees, and stare at the framed photo of the harbor on the wall from back when the water felt like home, before everything got complicated. My jaw tightens until it aches, a dull throb spreading up to my temples.

She laughs at something she's saying about dinner parties and spa days, a sound too bright, too far away. It lands in my chest like a thud. Heavy and cold. I can't remember the last time she asked about me or if I was happy.

When I finally hang up after she's rattled on about everything in her life, the quiet slams into me. I head down to the one place that

51

feels right to me. The place where it all makes sense. And the place where I can still feel my dad. The Wisteria Cove harbor. The dock creaks under me, the ropes groan, and Dad's old boat sits there, beat-up and tired. Just like me. *April Showers*. Named after my mom. He was so proud of that boat, and he loved her so much. And it doesn't seem right to still have her name on something so important to him. Not when my dad and I are no longer important to her. She has a new family and has made clear what is important to her now.

I stand slowly, jam my hands into my jacket pockets, and start walking. The harbor path stretches out in front of me, winding along the shore where the salt air cuts sharply. The town is quiet this time of day, just a few gulls circling lazily above and the occasional sound of waves slapping against the rocks.

I don't know where I'm going. I just need to move and to shake the lonely ache out of my chest.

Then I see her. Willa. She's coming toward me on the path, arms crossed tight over her chest, head down like she's lost in her own world. But even from a distance, I feel it, that invisible tether between us tightening with every step.

She slows when she spots me. For a second, I think she's going to turn around. But she doesn't. She keeps walking until we're side by side, close enough that I catch the faintest trace of her warm skin, soap, something soft and familiar that nearly undoes me.

Neither of us speaks.

We fall into step, walking in silence as the harbor stretches out beside us, mist curling over the water. The air feels heavy with unspoken things. The wind tugs at her hair, pulling it loose from the knot at the back of her head, and she doesn't bother fixing it.

When we reach the overlook, we both come to a stop. The

water below glints silver in the fading light, boats rocking gently at their moorings.

She stares straight ahead out at the water when she finally says it. "Why?"

That one word is enough to knock the breath out of me.

I look at her, but she doesn't meet my gaze. I know exactly what she's asking. Why did I leave? Why didn't I say goodbye? Why now?

I clear my throat. "I couldn't be who you needed me to be. And I couldn't stay here. Not then."

Her jaw tightens, and she finally turns to me, eyes flashing with hurt and anger. "Then why are you back, Tate?"

I don't have a good answer. None of them feels right or enough.

Before I can speak, she takes a step back, her voice sharp and breaking. "You left without saying anything. No calls. Nothing. You could have sent a message in a bottle, Tate. *Anything*. But you didn't."

Her anger hits me square in the chest, but underneath it, I feel the hurt radiating off of her. The crack in her voice nearly shatters me.

I take a step toward her, closing the space between us. She stiffens, but she doesn't move away. I can feel her breath now, short and fast, see the way her lashes lower when my hand almost reaches for her.

"I know I hurt you," I say quietly. "I'm sorry. You deserved better than that."

"Damn right I did," she snaps, but her voice is softer this time.

The wind picks up, swirling around us, carrying the sharp scents of salt and wood smoke. I want to say more. I want to tell her everything I never said before I left. But all I can do is look at her, the girl I left behind, now very much a woman, beautiful and burning with fury.

Somehow, impossibly, she steps closer. Just enough that her hand brushes against mine, fingers grazing like a spark catching kindling, and for one breathless second, neither of us pulls away. The pull between us is magnetic, inevitable. My heart thunders, and I tilt my head down, just enough to catch her scent, to breathe her in like she's oxygen after years underwater.

Her gaze flicks up, meets mine, and I swear she sways toward me.

And then she pushes me, a firm hand on my chest, shoving me back a step. "No," she says, her voice shaking. "I'm not doing this."

The invisible wall that feels like it's made of steel slams back into place between us. The warmth between us snaps like a rubber band. She turns on her heel and starts walking fast, her boots crunching over gravel, her hair whipping behind her. I watch her go, chest aching in a way that feels familiar and fresh all at once.

But just before she disappears around the bend, she hesitates and stops. Turns her head slightly, as if she might look back and say something.

My breath catches. Then she shakes her head and keeps going, disappearing into the fog.

I stand there for a long moment. The wind cuts colder now, the harbor quiet but for the creak of the boats below.

I sink down onto the bench by the overlook, elbows on my knees, head in my hands. What the hell am I doing?

The fog drifts in thicker now, curling around my legs, heavy and damp. And just as I think I should get up, go home, figure out what the hell to do next, I spot something on the bench beside me.

A single maple leaf, bright red, lying there like a sign. Like a message. I think about what she said about not even sending a message in a bottle.

I pick it up, turning it between my fingers. Yeah. We're nowhere near done.

* * *

I head straight for Dad's old boat, its weathered hull like a ghost waiting for me. The rust on the railings is worse than I remember, the lines are tangled, and everything needs work. Maybe that's why I'm drawn here tonight, because fixing this wreck feels easier than fixing myself.

I think about what happened that night. My dad went out with her dad to help and never came back. I think about what if he hadn't gone. What if he were here right now, working on the boat with me like we'd planned?

I roll up my sleeves, grab a brush, and get to work. Salt and rust flake off under my hands, but the ache inside me doesn't budge. Each stroke brings back memories, like Dad standing right where I am now, barking orders, laughing when I tripped over the lines, his voice gruff but never cruel. He wanted to teach me everything he knew.

I pause, brush my hand over the weathered wood, then step into the tiny cabin where the smell still reminds me of him. Salt, diesel, and old cigarettes. Taped to the wall by the bunk is a sun-faded photo I left there years ago: Dad at the helm, arms crossed, squinting into the sun. He looks larger-than-life and completely unreachable. He loved being out at sea.

I lean my shoulder against the frame and murmur, "I don't know if I can do this right, Dad, but I'm trying."

And God, I am trying.

The sound of boots on the dock snaps me out of it. I turn to see old Pete leaning casually, grinning like he's caught me talking to ghosts.

"You're doing fine, kid," he says, tipping his cap back. "That boat always needed a stubborn hand."

I huff out a laugh. "I don't know if stubborn's gonna be enough."

"Oh, nobody is more stubborn than you," Pete ambles closer, hands in his pockets. "But, you always had a good heart. Your dad would be so proud of the man you've become today."

His words land heavy. I nod and am grateful for them.

He claps me on the shoulder, warm and solid. "Don't work yourself to death tonight. Harbor'll still be here in the morning."

I stay another hour, scrubbing until my arms ache and my fingers sting. The deck looks cleaner than it has in years, but inside, I still feel like a mess. The tide laps softly at the hull as I gather up a battered bucket of tools and call it for the night.

On my walk back through town, I catch sight of Mrs. Ellery on her porch. The basket in her arms is almost as big as she is, loaded with pumpkins, mums, and what looks like half the produce section from the Wisteria Cove Grocery store.

She's balancing it awkwardly, teetering on the top step, and I don't even think before setting my bucket down and jogging over.

"Here," I say quietly, taking the basket from her arms. "Let me help you with that."

She peers up at me, sharp-eyed as ever despite the soft knit shawl wrapped around her shoulders. "Well, look at this. Tate Holloway, back from wherever you ran off to. Thought you'd forgotten all of us."

I chuckle under my breath, adjusting the basket in my arms. "Nope, I didn't forget."

She unlocks her front door and steps inside, waving me to follow. Her porch smells like dried herbs, and her tiny front room is exactly as I remember it, overstuffed chairs, stacks of books, knick-knacks crowding every surface. When I was a kid, she always had fresh cookies for all the neighbor kids.

I set the basket down gently. "You always decorate early for fall."

"Early?" she snorts. "It's never too early, Tate. Town's late by my standards."

I smile. "Fair enough."

She eyes me carefully, crossing her arms. "Back for good this time?"

The question hangs between us longer than it should. I want to say yes. I want to believe it. But, I also don't want to let anyone down again if it doesn't work out here.

"Trying to be," I finally say, because it's the only answer I've got.

She softens, patting my arm gently. "Well, this place has a way of making you stay...or breaking your heart all over again."

The truth in her words makes my chest tighten.

She doesn't ask more, simply offers a knowing smile before disappearing into the kitchen. I take my cue and step back out onto the porch, closing the door softly behind me.

The walk back to my house is quiet, the streets empty and lined with flickering lanterns strung between lampposts, and the scent of wood smoke drifts on the breeze, mingling with the briny tang of the harbor air. The whole town feels like it's holding its breath, and maybe so am I.

I can't stop thinking about Willa. The sharpness in her voice, the fury in her eyes, but also the way her fingers brushed mine. The heat between us existed even when she was telling me to go to hell.

I glance back toward the harbor path, my boots scuffing to a halt. The place where we stood earlier feels charged, like I could almost see her standing there again, hair blowing wild in the wind, mouth tight with anger and something else she won't say.

I shove my hands in my pockets and exhale slowly. I left this place thinking I could outrun all of it, my grief, my guilt, my feelings for her.

But tonight proves it: I outran nothing. It was all waiting for me right here.

I walk the rest of the way home slower than before, each step weighted with the truth I can't avoid anymore.

I'm still in love with her. Always have been. I always will be.

Chapter 7
Willa

Some nights I wonder if I could have written just one letter to explain why I left, if it would have made any difference. Then I think: you deserved more than a letter. You deserved to have me to stay...and I couldn't. I'm sorry. So now I'm going to show you.
                                                                   -Tate

The bookstore smells like coffee and old paper when I climb down from my little loft above it. My hair's still damp from my shower, and I'm tugging my cardigan tight around me when I stop short at the bottom step.

Rowan, Ivy, and my mom are all gathered at the front counter, huddled over something like it's a precious artifact.

"Uh...what's going on?" I ask cautiously, but my eyes are already zeroing in on a glass bottle, stoppered with a note inside.

Rowan looks up first, practically glowing with mischief. "You've got mail," she says, tipping her chin toward the bottle. "It was on the front mat this morning. Just sitting out there, it looked like it floated up from the harbor."

Ivy grins, crossing her arms. "Were you aware that you have a secret admirer?"

Lilith lifts the bottle gently, turning it in her hands. Her eyes gleam as she speaks softly, "Oh, I bet we all know who it's from."

My pulse stutters. Before I can reply, the memory rushes back, sharp and uninvited, of me standing in front of him just days ago, voice shaking as I hurled the accusation: *"You left without saying anything. No calls, nothing. You could have sent a message in a bottle, Tate."*

God. Did he actually listen to that? Did he...?

Rowan's watching me closely now, her grin turning sly. "You okay, Willa? You look like you've seen a ghost."

I force a shrug, stepping forward and reaching for the bottle with careful fingers. "Maybe it's just some tourist messing around." But my heart knows better.

My mom's voice lowers, soft but strong. "Some people call us witches; I call us healers. Your father was my protector. He always was. He used to do romantic things like this, too," she says, gesturing gently to the bottle. "Little gestures. Small magic touches. He believed healers need protectors...someone who stands between them and the wrong people. Someone who makes them feel safe enough to open their heart."

I turn the clear bottle and look at the cream paper inside.

My mom's gaze catches mine, steady and piercing. "And that's why Tate's good people," she adds quietly. "You might not want to hear it right now, but it's true. He's a protector, Willa."

The words hit somewhere deeper than I'm ready to admit.

Ivy leans forward, eyes sparkling with curiosity. "Well? Are you going to open it, or should we all stand here dying of suspense?"

But my hands are trembling a little as I pull the cork free and slide out the note inside. The paper is soft, tied with twine that comes loose under my fingers almost too easily.

I unfold it carefully, reading first in silence as my throat tightens, then aloud, because I know they're all emotionally invested, all leaning in, hanging on every word.

> Some nights I wonder if I could have written just one letter to explain why I left, if it would have made any difference. Then I think: you deserved more than a letter. You deserved to have me to stay...and I couldn't. I'm sorry. So now I'm going to show you.
> —Tate

The shop falls silent. Even Rowan has nothing to say for once.

I stare down at the paper, heart pounding, because I do remember my dad doing little things for my mom like this, little gestures that spoke louder than words. Romantic, yes... but deeply intentional. Thoughtful in a way that hit right where it hurt. That's when it hits me that Tate does remind me of our father. And I remember that he grew up alongside him, too. He probably misses him as much as we do. Just like we miss Phil.

Ivy exhales slowly, shaking her head. "That's...kind of devastatingly romantic."

Rowan hums in agreement under her breath. "It's swoony, that's what it is. He really just left you a message in a bottle."

But I can't say a word. Not yet. Because this is breaking through every wall I've carefully built around myself since Tate left, and before that, when my dad died.

I slip the note into my apron pocket quickly, too quickly, as if I can shove my feelings in there, too, and pretend they're safe and contained.

My mom's words echo in my mind: *Healers need protectors.*

And suddenly I'm wondering if that's exactly what Tate always was. My protector. But then I think about how he's gone through so much, too. And where was I? Maybe he needed a protector, too, and I wasn't there for him enough, and that's why he left.

Now I want to know. No, now I *need* to know. I need to talk to Tate.

* * *

Unfortunately, with the busy day of bustling tourists buzzing in and out of the store, I haven't had the chance to go find Tate. He hasn't come into the shop, not even to loiter at the counter like he has been, and between refilling coffee orders and helping leaf-peepers pick out paperbacks, I haven't had a moment to even think about him... except, of course, I do think about him. Constantly. And I keep staring at that bottle behind the counter, and then my hand drags over the crinkle of the note in my apron. And I would never admit it to my sisters and mom, but yes, I have taken it out and re-read it several times when no one was looking.

And now, just as the sun's setting and I'm locking the door, I'm dreading what's next. The town meeting. The annual Harvest Moon Festival planning session, better known as a thinly veiled ambush where the most "available" locals get volun-told for everything. And it's run by no other than my mother, so she thinks nothing of volunteering me and my sisters for everything. She's done it since we were toddlers, and it's become a family event, so to speak.

I step into Town Hall and immediately feel trapped: every folding chair full, every town elder ready with clipboards, and the unmistakable scent of coffee, cinnamon cookies, and muffins on a folding table, and impending obligation hanging heavy in the air.

Rowan and Ivy are already here, seated in the back row, with matching smirks when they spot me. They know exactly what's about to happen. We're going to be helping in any way my mom needs us.

At the front of the room, Donna and my mom, Wisteria Cove's unofficial queens of community organization and small-town guilt trips, wave me up front. "Willa, darling! There you are! Come sit right here next to us."

Oh shit. No.

I must look like a deer trapped in someone's headlights, and I hesitate for half a second before Donna pats the empty seat beside her again pointedly and I know that I'm not getting out of this. I sigh and weave through the crowd to sit beside her, smoothing my cardigan over and bracing myself.

I'm saying no this year. No volunteering. No getting dragged into this madness. I have a bookstore and coffee shop to run and an emotional mess with a broody fisherman I am trying very hard to ignore.

And then, because this is just how my luck works, Tate walks in. Late. Ball cap pulled low. His faded jeans are worn and perfect. His sleeves are shoved up, and forearms casually flex as he leans against the back wall, arms crossed with another of his worn and soft-looking flannels over a white T-shirt.

His gaze flicks to me immediately and lingers for just a second too long, sending an irritating and completely involuntary flutter straight to my chest and down my body. I force myself to move, turning to sit reluctantly by Donna, unsure of what my punishment is about to be.

The moment I lower myself into the chair, a shiver ripples through me. Not from the draft sneaking under the door, but deeper, stranger, like someone just brushed cold fingers along my spine. The air thickens, scented with the faintest trace of woodsmoke and something sharper, metallic, like the snap before lightning strikes.

It prickles across my skin and makes the tiny hairs on my arms lift. My senses sharpen, as if every whisper, every shuffle of paper and creak of a chair echo louder than they should. I've felt this before. It's my gift tugging at me, my own private weathervane. Something is coming. Change, big and unshakable. The kind that rearranges more than just calendars and agendas.

Donna claps her hands cheerfully, the sound bright and oblivious against the hush of my nerves. "Now that we're all here, let's begin!"

She breezes through a few updates, shares reports about town traffic and tourism (up twelve percent thanks to the changing leaves, apparently), her voice rising and falling in a rhythm that doesn't match the pulse in my chest. By the time she clears her throat dramatically and reaches the agenda item labeled *Harvest Moon Festival Chairperson*, the tingling sensation is nearly humming through my bones.

I don't need her to say it aloud. I already know. This is where everything shifts.

"Of course," Donna says with a bright smile, "we have a very special situation this year! Our dear Lilith, who usually chairs the festival, has unfortunately decided she's not able to chair this year."

A murmur of sympathy ripples through the room. My mom, who wears a smirk on her face, nods.

"So," Donna continues, her smile widening as her gaze settles right on me, "we'll need capable hands to take the lead. And I am so delighted to announce that our Lilith has gotten Willa Maren and Tate Holloway to co-chair this year's festival!"

What the hell.

The entire room erupts into applause. Actual applause and a few whistles. My stomach drops.

Rowan claps loudly from the back row...*traitor*. And Ivy follows it up with a sharp wolf whistle. Even my mom nods approvingly, her expression smug and witchy, like the mastermind she is behind all of this.

I'm frozen for a beat before I scramble to recover. "Donna, wait—I didn't agree to—"

But Donna is already talking over me, completely undeterred. "Now, now, Willa, we all know the festival happens right in front of your lovely bookstore and coffee shop. It's practically your front yard! And we couldn't ask for a more perfect team than you and Tate. You'll both make sure everything shines!"

I turn my head slowly toward Tate, willing him to intervene, to object, to save us both, but he doesn't. Of course, he doesn't. He's leaning casually against the wall, arms still crossed, looking entirely too entertained by my panic. When our eyes meet, he tilts his head slightly, almost like he's saying: *go ahead and fight this...but you won't win.*

My mom chimes in next, her voice warm and cheery. "You two'd be doing me a big favor. I hate not being able to see this through. I just couldn't make it happen this year."

I scoff and resist rolling my eyes. My mom looks no older than forty-five and is spry as a squirrel.

And that's it. Because no one says no to Lilith Maren. Especially not me. Especially not when half the town is now clapping enthusiastically, murmuring to each other, and already crafting a new chapter in the Tate and Willa saga.

Someone from the back calls out, "They'll finally work things out while planning!"

The whole place laughs. My cheeks burn. Tate finally pushes off the wall and strolls forward. He stops next to me at the front of the room, standing far too close, smelling far too good, and projecting that quiet confidence that's been undoing me since the minute he came back.

"Guess we're partners again," he murmurs, low enough only I can hear.

I stiffen. "Don't get used to it."

His mouth curves into that crooked, almost-smile that makes my breath catch for a stupid half second. "Oh, I'm counting on it," he says, eyes gleaming.

Donna claps again, delighted. "It's settled! Willa and Tate are our fearless leaders for this year's Harvest Moon Festival! We're in good hands, everyone."

The applause starts back up, the crowd leaning in, smiling, chattering, and the energy in the room shifts, not just with excitement about the festival but about us. The gossip mill is already in motion. Every eye will be watching us now, even more so than they already were.

Tate leans in just slightly as the noise swells, his voice so close to my ear that it sends a shiver down my spine. "Looks like we're going to be spending a lot of time together, Willa."

I shoot him a glare I don't quite feel, my heart beating far too fast to pull it off properly. "Don't think this means we're friends again."

His grin deepens. "Wouldn't dream of it."

But inside, I can feel the ground shifting beneath me. Because now the whole town is watching.

And I already know this will unravel every carefully constructed wall I've built since the day he left.

* * *

By the time I reach the bookstore door, my heart is racing, and I'm desperate for quiet. The meeting was chaos, everyone watching us like we're some town-sponsored romance story they're all rooting for. And now...I just need a second to breathe.

But then I hear his boots on the sidewalk. I close my eyes for a moment, waiting for them to continue, but they stop.

I spin around just as Tate steps up to the door, hands in his jacket pockets, looking calm. Like this is all fine. Like my whole world isn't spinning out of control. Like a freight train flying down the tracks, and the tracks aren't stable.

"Really?" I snap. "Your house is over there Tate."

I soften some when I remember how I felt earlier and wanted to find him to ask about the bottle.

He shrugs, stepping a little closer. "Figured we should talk."

"I don't have time for this!" I glare, arms crossed so tightly it hurts. "Why are you doing this? Why now? Everything was going great until you came back and messed with my head and my heart."

He doesn't flinch. He just steps forward again, closing the space between us until we're toe to toe, close enough that I can feel his warmth, close enough that my breath catches whether or not I want it to.

His voice is quiet, sure. "Are you sure it was all going great? Because I *see* you, Willa."

That soft, devastating line knocks the wind out of me.

"You look lonely," he goes on, eyes locked on mine. "Your smiles don't reach your eyes. You look tired. Worn out. Not the adventurous, happy person I used to know. We were friends, Willa. And to be honest, I always wanted more."

That cuts deep, and I hate that he's right about me being lonely. Really freaking lonely. Some nights, when the shop is closed and I'm in my loft for the night, the silence is too loud. I ache for a friend: my old friend, Tate. But then I remember that I wasn't the one who left, the one who didn't care.

And he always wanted more? I don't even know what to say to that. What does that even mean?

So I shove the words back at him before he can say anything else. "The girl you used to know is gone, Tate. You don't know her anymore."

His gaze doesn't waver. "Then let me get to know the woman standing in front of me now."

I blink hard, throat tight. But I'm not done. Not yet, and not even close. I'm not going down without a fight. "You can't just send me a message in a bottle and think that fixes everything!" I snap, voice cracking.

And the absolute nerve of him...he smirks, leaning in just slightly, close enough that I can feel the heat of him in the cool night air. His voice is low, teasing, but with that edge that always undoes me. "Which is it, Willa? You want me to send messages, or you don't?"

It's too much. All of it. The steady burn in his eyes. The half-smile he's fighting is like it might give him away. And the quiet, unbearable tenderness of him standing here when I'm clawing at every scrap of willpower not to feel a thing.

My chest squeezes, sharp and aching. The words slip out, softer than I mean them to. "You don't get to do this, Tate."

For a moment, he looks at me like he's memorizing something he's afraid he'll forget. Then his smile changes. It softens, turns sad in a way that feels like it's unraveling me thread by thread.

"I wish I knew how not to," he says. His voice is low, almost regretful, and then he turns, walking away with that slow, unhurried stride that makes me want to call him back.

The street feels too quiet without him. Too empty.

And somehow, that's the most dangerous thing of all. Because he *is* doing this. And I'm letting him.

It's only then that I notice it right by my feet.

A small glass bottle, the streetlight catching on it in the light, like a secret he's left behind just for me.

Chapter 8
Tate

I thought I knew what loneliness was until I saw you pretending to smile for everyone else. You don't have to pretend with me. Not ever.
—Tate

I'm crouched on the deck of my dad's boat, knuckles raw and grease on my forearms, trying to loosen a rusted bolt that refuses to budge, when I hear the soft patter of tiny feet. The little feet stop next to me on the dock. "Hi! Are you a pirate?" I look up, blinking into the late afternoon sun, to see a little girl in a sparkly purple jacket, pigtails flying, one front tooth missing, and the biggest grin I've seen in days. She's standing on the dock, arms crossed, like she owns the place.

Before I can answer, I hear a familiar low chuckle—that of my friend Remy, who owns the tree farm on the edge of town. He's also Donna's son and Finn's brother. A long-time friend of mine. "This is Junie," he says proudly, catching up with her and scooping her up easily. "She's five now. Thought it was time you two met properly again. I also might have told her you're a pirate."

I feel something twist deep in my chest. She was three when I left, had chubby cheeks and soft curls and was still toddling around. Now here she is, bright-eyed and chatty, looking at me like I'm cooler than I am.

"Hi Junie," I say softly, wiping my hands on a rag. "This was my dad's boat. I bet it has a pirate history."

She plants her little hands on her hips. "Daddy said you went away for a long time. Where'd you go? Prison?"

Remy chuckles behind her. "Not prison, kiddo, Tate's a fisherman. Remember what I told you? Tate and I are buddies."

Junie turns back to me, eyes wide. "Do you know where the treasure is? Every pirate ship has treasure."

I crouch down so we're eye level, the corner of my mouth tugging into a grin I haven't felt in a long time. "You're right. Only brave sailors can find it, though. Got a map?"

Her entire face lights up as she pulls out a wrinkled piece of paper drawn in crayon, with lines zigzagging everywhere. "I do! Daddy helped me!"

Remy crosses his arms and leans against the dock railing, watching his daughter with a tired fondness that makes my chest ache again. There's more weight on him now, lines around his eyes I don't remember, a quiet steadiness that wasn't there before.

"It's just me and her now," he says quietly, catching my gaze over Junie's head. "A lot has changed since you left."

I nod slowly, carefully. "I heard."

Remy and his wife split up. They had a very public divorce, and she lives in Boston. I've heard she hasn't seen or talked to Junie in a long time. And I can't really understand that. Old

Pete looks after Remy because he and Donna have been friends for decades. He isn't a fan of Remy's ex.

He nods too, but there's nothing bitter in his voice, just quiet acceptance. "We're doing okay."

Junie crouches near an old crab trap, tapping it like she expects it to pop open and reveal gold coins. "Why's this boat so rusty, Captain Tate? Did the treasure make it rusty?"

That makes me laugh out loud. "Exactly that. Pirate gold does that."

She giggles and spins in a circle, making up a song about rusty treasure and crab pirates.

Remy watches her for a minute, then glances back at me. "I heard you're planning on sticking around. That true?"

The question settles heavily between us, but there's no judgment in his voice, just curiosity.

"I think so," I say. "Yeah. I think I am."

His smile is small but genuine. "It'd be good if you did. Missed you."

I don't know why that hits so hard. Maybe because it's simple and honest. And real. And I need good people like that in my life. Maybe because I did miss this place, this life, even when I tried to convince myself otherwise.

"I missed a lot," I say, and it comes out rougher than I expect.

Remy follows my gaze as Junie climbs up on the captain's chair, pretending to steer the ship, humming to herself without a care in the world.

"Plenty of time to catch up," he says. "You'll have to come to one of our Friday pizza nights. Finn's a regular."

I nod, "Yeah, that'd be good."

Then I hear familiar voices from the dock.

Rowan and Ivy, arms linked, coffee cups in hand, strolling toward us. "Heyyy, Holloway!" Rowan calls out, loud enough for the entire harbor to hear. "You done pretending to fix that boat yet?"

Ivy grins, adding wiggling her fingers, playfully, "We're watching you, you know. Break our sister's heart again, and we'll feed you to the lobsters."

Remy laughs under his breath beside me. "You really picked the stubborn one. Rowan is...a little unhinged. Ivy is the sweet one. I guess you messed up when the sweet one is making threats at you."

"Yeah," I say, shaking my head, but smiling despite myself. "I definitely did."

Remy lifts an eyebrow. "Speaking of...how are things with Willa?"

I sigh, laughing under my breath as I lean back against the railing. "She's a hard one to win over. Not as welcoming as the rest of the town."

He nods, not missing a beat. "Yeah."

Junie jumps down from the chair and comes to tug at my sleeve, holding up two of my bottles, looking up at me earnestly. "Do pirates leave messages in bottles too, Mr. Tate?"

I freeze for a second, then laugh, crouching again so we're eye level. "Yeah. Sometimes that's how they say what they can't say out loud."

She nods, as if that makes perfect sense.

Remy claps me on the shoulder as he hoists Junie back into his arms. "Good luck, man," he says, eyes twinkling. "You're gonna need it."

They head down the dock, Junie waving enthusiastically over his shoulder, and I can't help but stand there watching them for a moment longer than I probably should.

Ivy and Rowan come up to where I'm standing.

Rowan nudges me with her coffee cup. "So...ready to co-chair a festival with our very difficult sister?"

I shake my head. "I've got my work cut out for me."

Ivy snorts. "Yeah, but this is how you can get her to talk to you. And nice touch with the message in the bottle by the way. I've caught her re-reading the note."

This makes me smile. Because for the first time since I left, this feels...right. Like I'm exactly where I should be, surrounded by people who know me, even the parts I tried to leave behind.

Even Willa. Especially Willa.

* * *

I wasn't planning on running into Willa tonight. But that doesn't mean she's not on my mind.

I've missed Marco's, and I just wanted pasta and maybe to sit in the back, enjoy a plate of something hot, and quietly figure out how I'm going to restore this boat and what I'm doing with my life. But when I push open the door, there she is, already at the counter, arms crossed, waiting for her takeout order. She looks lost in her thoughts despite Marco's busy arcade and families packed in at every table.

She hasn't noticed me yet. Then she glances up, and her eyes meet mine. And there it is, that spark, that flash of annoyance mixed with something else she probably doesn't want to admit is still there. She turns back to the counter like she's going to pretend she hasn't seen me. Classic Willa.

Marco, of course, notices everything.

"Ahhh, look at this," he booms, leaning over the counter toward us with a grin as wide as Main Street itself. "Two beautiful people ordering pasta at the same time. You know what this means, yes?"

Willa closes her eyes briefly, as if she's praying for strength. "Marco, please—" she starts.

But he's already waving her off, delighted. "It's a Lady and the Tramp moment!" he declares, gesturing between us. "Pasta dinner for two! I threw in extra! For the next great love story of Wisteria Cove!"

My laugh escapes before I can stop it, and Willa shoots me a sharp glare for encouraging him.

"You two! Come back soon for dinner together, eh?" Marco winks, sliding our takeout bags toward us with a flourish. "On the house tonight. My gift to love."

Willa mutters a half-hearted "thanks" and grabs her bag quickly, like she can escape this entire situation if she moves fast enough. I catch up easily as we step outside, the cool autumn air cutting through the heat of embarrassment that Marco left in his wake.

"That was something," I say, falling into step beside her.

She exhales hard. "This town...honestly."

But she doesn't walk away. She doesn't tell me to go.

Instead, we end up walking side by side down Main Street, paper bags in hand, heading in the general direction of both her bookstore and my house. The easy silence between us is strange, comfortable, but charged, and I can't help sneaking glances at her while we walk.

About halfway down the block, she hesitates. Then, almost grudgingly, she says, "I guess...you could come inside and eat. We could discuss the festival plans."

It's not an overly friendly invitation exactly, but it's not nothing.

I don't even pretend to play it cool. "Sure," I say, keeping my tone light even though my heart's thudding a little harder than it should.

When we reach the bookstore, I hold the door open for her. She unlocks it quickly, slipping inside, and I follow, only to realize there's already a small crowd gathered on the sidewalk watching us through the window, smiling as if they're watching a nineties romcom.

Seriously.

Even more townspeople are gathering. Pretending to chat with someone or sip coffee, but we can both feel their eyes on us.

"Unbelievable," she mutters, locking the door firmly behind us and pulling down the shade that doesn't quite give us privacy. "They're going to stare through the window the whole time."

I glance toward the window where they're watching, waving exaggeratedly when they catch my eye.

Willa groans softly and turns toward the back of the shop. "Come on," she says, jerking her chin toward a narrow staircase. "Upstairs. They can't see us up there."

I follow her up into her loft, and the second I climb inside, I'm floored.

This space... It's so her. Cozy, lived-in, full of books stacked on every available surface. String lights draped casually across the ceiling beams. A worn old sofa is tucked into a corner near the wide window that overlooks the harbor. Soft throw blankets, mugs on the windowsill, a candle begging to be lit on the table.

I feel like I'm stepping right into her mind, and it's warmer and softer than I expected. "This is...nice," I say quietly, taking it all in.

She glances back at me, cautious, a little wary, but I catch the faintest hint of a smile. "It's my cozy space," she says.

She sets her takeout on the small table near the couch and pulls out two mismatched plates, handing me one without meeting my gaze directly.

"Sit," she says, nodding toward the couch. "Eat. Discuss the festival. That's all."

"Of course," I say, doing exactly what she says but grinning, anyway.

We sit across from each other, pasta warm on our laps, and for a while we don't say much, just eat quietly while the sounds of the harbor drift in through the cracked window.

And down below? The townspeople slowly lose interest, one by one drifting away when they realize they can't see anything from down there.

The silence between us stretches out, but it's not uncomfortable anymore. If anything, it feels...right.

After a few minutes, Willa sighs softly and finally speaks. "I can't believe we're co-chairing this thing together," she says, shaking her head. "I was supposed to be avoiding you."

I chuckle. "You've been doing a terrible job of that."

She rolls her eyes, but this time, there's no heat behind it. And just like that, the frost melts slowly, carefully, and she lets her shoulders relax.

After we finish eating, she stands and carries the plates downstairs, and I follow.

"I'll make coffee," I offer, moving behind the counter before she can object.

She snorts, folding her arms as she leans back against the register. "You? Make coffee? This I have to see."

I fumble around with the coffee machine like an idiot, knocking over the scoop and spilling grounds everywhere, which earns me my favorite thing so far tonight: Willa laughing. Really laughing. It's bright and genuine and makes my chest ache in the best way.

"What kind of coffee maker is this? It's like a spaceship," I chuckle.

She steps in close, reaching around me to take over. Her arm brushes mine, and the air shifts instantly. Warmer. Closer. "Let me show you how it's done," she murmurs, voice soft but edged with amusement.

I'm close enough to breathe her in—cinnamon, soap, and Italian food—and the urge to lean in nearly undoes me.

But then, as she pours water into the machine, I say, half-joking but half-serious: "You have to come learn to fish."

She freezes.

Her smile falters slightly, and then she shakes her head.

"No," she says firmly, quieter and colder this time. "I will never go out on the water."

Her words land hard, sharper than she probably intended. But I don't flinch. I watch her, seeing the truth beneath what she's saying.

This isn't about fishing. It's about loss. And I get it.

So I lean in just a little, not enough to scare her, just enough so she knows I mean it when I say, "Okay... I'll just have to learn your world instead."

She hesitates, and for a heartbeat, I swear she almost softens completely, but then she straightens and hands me a steaming mug of coffee like that whole moment didn't just happen.

I take it anyway, smiling gently. "Thanks for the company," I murmur.

She doesn't say anything back. But she doesn't kick me out, either.

Instead, we fall into an easy rhythm, her jotting notes, me tossing in suggestions where I can. The clock ticks on, the air warm with the scent of coffee and cinnamon, the lamplight pooling golden over stacks of papers and books. For a few quiet hours, we're just there together, in her cozy little space, going over festival plans like it's the most natural thing in the world.

Yeah...we're getting somewhere.

Chapter 9
Willa

I may not have said it when I should've, but
here it is, plain as day:
I missed you every second I was gone.
Even when I didn't know how to come home...you
were home.
-Tate

I t's Friday night in Wisteria Cove, which means it's outdoor movie night on the green in the town square. The air smells like kettle corn, crisp apples, and cinnamon. String lights stretch overhead, twinkling like tiny stars between the oaks. A crowd has gathered, spilling onto picnic blankets and folding chairs, bundled in scarves and sipping hot spiced cider. Children dart through the grass, shrieking with laughter while candle lit lanterns flicker around the wisteria that grows around the town pergola.

Our small-town traditions that bring us all together are

something I look forward to. I keep looking for Tate but haven't seen him yet. I will admit that I'm looking, and I can't get him off my mind. I keep telling myself that it's just because we've been roped into the fall festival planning—which was mostly already planned. It's just my mom's way of getting Tate and me into getting together and talking. She's always had a soft spot for Tate and hates that we're not getting along. But are we not? I mean, I saw a hint of old Tate, and I miss him. But I can't trust him. He has too much power over my heart.

And there he is. Tate Holloway. Looking...well, like a dream. He's in a faded henley rolled at the sleeves, jeans worn and fitting him like a glove, and his usual well-worn Red Sox ball cap shoved low. I wonder if it's the same ball cap he used to wear when he and his dad would watch games together. That was one of their things they did together; they rarely ever missed a game. Whether it was at Fenway or on TV. If they were out at sea, they'd try to listen or call in for updates.

His smile is easy tonight, his eyes crinkling as he swings Junie Bennett into his arms like it's the most natural thing in the world. She's shouting, "Aye aye, captain!" and he spins her like a pirate's wheel, her curly hair catching the golden glow of the lights.

God help me, my heart stutters.

Beside me, Ivy lets out a low whistle. "Are your ovaries exploding right now? Because I think mine just did."

I snort, but I don't look away.

He's crouched low now, and Junie's showing him some plastic pirate coins she's found in the grass. He listens and laughs when she launches into a full story about how she's discovered buried treasure. He asks her questions and listens intently to her answers.

And for a ridiculous moment, I wonder if he wants a family

of his own. We never talked about that. We were young and just getting started in life when he up and left.

Then the thought hits me sideways, unexpected and sharp. The idea of him like this... but with someone else. Some other woman leaning her head on his shoulder, laughing at Junie's antics. I blink and look away quickly, heat blooming in my cheeks.

"Ivy," I mutter under my breath, "is it bad that the thought of him doing this with someone else makes me feel...feral?"

Her laugh is immediate and delighted. "Bad? No, that's just the Maren gene kicking in. We're professionally feral."

I elbow her, and we both dissolve into giggles just as Junie runs past us, wielding her plastic sword and dragging Tate behind her.

"That man," Ivy says, shaking her head, "he's dangerously hot. Too bad he doesn't have a brother."

I snort. "Where's Temu this evening?"

Ivy groans, though she's still laughing. "You're impossible. Derek's not...he's not *that* bad. At least not all the time."

"Wow," I say, sipping my coffee. "Glowing endorsement. You should put that on his dating profile."

Ivy rolls her eyes playfully, "Why are you calling him Temu?"

"Because Derek is not what you ordered," I tell her. Earlier today he told her to go to the movie by herself because he made other plans. He constantly disappoints her and leaves her hanging.

Ivy changes the subject, "How's the festival planning coming along? Still biting his head off at every meeting?"

"Yeah, well," I sigh dramatically, "we're just now at the point where I can be in the same room with him without committing murder."

"Coexistence is the first step to co-parenting," Ivy teases. "Even if the only child you share is this festival."

Before I can answer, my mom appears with two cups of cider, her silver hair braided back and a mischievous sparkle in her eyes. She's set up her "tarot card" tent just beyond the cider station tonight with candles flickering inside, velvet cushions strewn about. Half the town will rotate through her space before the credits roll on tonight's movie.

She hands me a cider and leans in conspiratorially. "Your heart knows before your mind catches up," she says, tapping her temple gently.

I groan. "Speaking of...nice ambush with getting Tate and me to co-chair the festival, Mom."

Her grin is unapologetic. "What can I say? I'm just looking out. A little shared purpose never hurt anyone."

"Shared purpose," I repeat flatly. "More like shared punishment."

She clinks her cup to mine. "All part of the process, darling. Just remember, you're your mother's daughter. Stubborn and smart. And," she winks, "your heart knows what it wants. Even if your mouth hasn't figured out how to say it."

I can't help but laugh, even as I feel that flutter again, the one that rises whenever Tate's near. I glance back toward him instinctively, and of course he's watching me. Not a casual glance, either.

His gaze is warm and steady, like he's been waiting to catch my eye all night. He tips his chin up in a silent greeting, a little smile tugging at the corner of his mouth.

Ugh. Stupid gorgeous Tate. I squeeze my legs together and try to look away, but it's really hard.

"Stop staring at him," Ivy stage-whispers beside me.

"You stop staring at him," I whisper back.

We both laugh again, arms linked as we sip our cider.

Around us, Wisteria Cove hums with life and charm. This is our place, a town where everyone knows each other's business, but also drops off soup when you're sick and leaves flowers on your kitchen table just because. There's comfort in the predictability: Friday nights mean movie nights where we all catch up. Saturday mornings mean farmer's markets and dinner nights with friends if you're lucky enough to get an invite. There's something about living here that makes the seasons feel special, like fall isn't just a season, but an experience. I have friends from other places, and when they visit, they say they've never seen anything like it.

Pumpkins line the steps of the bookstore. Candles flicker in every window. The bakery down the block is debuting its maple pecan loaf tonight, and I can already see a line forming. I'll be grabbing one for myself to have with my tea tonight when I read in bed.

And here I am, sitting with my sister, cider warming my hands, my cheeks flushed from the cool air and, I'll admit it: maybe from the way Tate Holloway keeps looking at me, too.

"Do you think he knows?" I murmur, watching him chase after Junie again, this time pretending to limp dramatically as she "attacks" him with her plastic sword.

"Knows what?" Ivy asks.

"That he's...so ridiculously good looking." I scowl.

Ivy's grin is wicked. "Honey, I think *everyone* knows."

Before I can respond, Tate catches Junie, tosses her gently into the air, and when he looks back over his shoulder, it's right at me. Again. Like he can feel me watching. And he winks.

Damn it.

My chest tightens, and Lilith's words echo in my mind: *Your heart knows before your mind catches up.*

Maybe it does. Maybe...just maybe...this town, this moment, this man, they're all conspiring to remind me that life doesn't have to be perfectly planned. And it doesn't have to be so lonely.

Sometimes it's just cider on a Friday night. Sometimes it's your sister laughing at inside jokes beside you and your mother handing you wisdom and a mug of cider.

And sometimes it's the realization that *maybe* Tate Holloway isn't the enemy I've been telling myself he is.

I take another sip of cider, smile to myself, and let the thought bloom fully this time:

All right, maybe he isn't that bad.

* * *

It's the next evening after work, at my mom's house, and if fall has a smell, this is it. Warm cinnamon, brown sugar, cloves, and the buttery scent of apple crumble baking in the oven. Her kitchen is comfortable chaos: flour dust swirling in beams of golden afternoon light, mismatched mixing bowls stacked high, and every available surface cluttered with measuring cups and spice jars.

She's got a fall-themed playlist playing in the background, and the vibes are perfection.

And at the center of it all? The annual Maren family bake-off.

Mom's idea of a "casual family gathering," which everyone knows is code for *cutthroat culinary combat.*

"I hope you brought your A-game, Willa," Ivy teases from across the farmhouse table, her apron dusted in flour, a smug grin on her face as she folds cinnamon sugar into her pie dough.

"Please," I scoff, cracking eggs like a pro. "I *am* the reigning champion. This pumpkin bread practically makes itself at this point."

Before Ivy can retort, the front door creaks open, and in

strolls Tate Holloway, looking all-too-smug, himself, in an orange and black plaid flannel rolled to the elbows and jeans slung low on his hips and carrying a six-pack of cider under one arm.

"What's *he* doing here?" I whisper ask, louder than I intend as I blow flour-dusted hair from my sweaty face.

My mom of course, claps her hands together like she's been waiting for this moment. "Oh, didn't I mention? Tate's my guest judge/competitor today."

Ivy snorts into her dough. "Correction: we're pairing him *against* you, Willa. You know...since you take this competition so seriously."

The room erupts in laughter and cheers as Tate sidles up next to me at the counter, plopping his cider down and rolling up his sleeves even further. He smirks at me, "Hi, Willa."

I just stare at him with a deadpan glance, pretending to be unimpressed.

"Careful," he murmurs, leaning close, his voice low and teasing, "wouldn't want you to crumble under the pressure."

"Funny," I say sweetly, elbowing him just enough to make him stagger a step. "Shouldn't you be out fishing or something?"

He grins, with that maddeningly charming grin that makes my stomach do stupid little flips. "Not when there's treats to be eaten."

And I don't miss the way his eyes never leave mine or my lips when he says it.

And just like that, the battle is on. By the time the apple crumble is in the oven and the kitchen smells like something out of a Norman Rockwell painting, I'm dusted head-to-toe in flour and so is Tate, though mostly because I've "accidentally" flung some at him when he teases my icing technique.

We're laughing, bickering over who makes a better caramel

drizzle, and somewhere between the cinnamon sticks and nutmeg, things shift.

He stills, gaze dropping to my mouth. For a long, suspended moment, he doesn't smile. Doesn't move. His expression is intent, heavy, like the world has narrowed to just me.

And then slowly, carefully, giving me every chance to pull away, he lifts his hand. My pulse stutters, and his thumb hovers for half a breath before brushing the corner of my mouth, rough and callused, the scrape of his skin making my stomach clench.

"You had frosting," he murmurs, voice husky, intimate, like a secret only for me.

His other fingers sweep across my cheek to dust away a smear of flour. Heat blooms in the trail he leaves behind, my skin tingling, my whole body tuned to him. I should move. I don't. I can't.

The air thickens, humming, pulling us closer. My throat tightens on a swallow, my pulse tripping fast and wild. I want to lean in, to taste the salt and heat of his skin where his thumb lingers at the corner of my mouth.

His eyes lift, locking on mine. Dark. Serious. And then, almost without realizing, he leans closer, the space between us shrinking, smaller, smaller. My breath catches, and I sway toward him, helpless against the pull.

For a heartbeat, it feels inevitable. Like we're seconds from crossing a line we can't uncross.

But then he blinks and his hand falls. The moment snaps, leaving the air buzzing, charged with everything we didn't do.

I sit frozen, skin still sparking where his fingers touched, chest tight from holding in a breath I didn't even realize I'd taken.

And I know it. We're teetering on the edge of something dangerous. Something I might not want to resist.

Before I can speak, he leans in just slightly, his voice low and familiar, sending a shiver right through me. "Remember when we used to play hide and seek in this house?"

The memory rushes back so vividly it makes me ache. The two of us as kids, barefoot and reckless, slipping behind curtains and under tables, darting through the garden when we thought my mom wasn't watching.

"You used to hide under the window seat," I murmur, smiling at the memory.

"And you always hid in the pantry," he says, smirking. "It made you smell like cinnamon."

"You cheated," I remind him. "You *always* found me first."

His grin softens into something tender, nostalgic. "Yeah. I did."

For a moment, it feels like no time has passed at all. Just two kids again, laughing in the kitchen, playing games no one else quite understood.

I clear my throat, trying to dispel the spell that's weaving itself between us like steam from a kettle. "Do you...do you have more bottles?" I ask, teasing now, remembering the messages in a bottle he's been leaving at the bookstore ladder.

His answering grin is slow and mischievous. "Why? Are you finally ready to admit that you like my messages?"

And with that, he turns back to his mixing bowl as though we didn't just share something soft and fragile. But my chest is still tight, breath catching when he shoots me another of those sideways glances that say he remembers everything.

By nightfall, the contest is over (I win, obviously), and the kitchen is a disaster zone of dirty dishes and half-eaten slices of pie, pumpkin bread, and crumble.

We all pitch in and get it right again, then wrap my mom in a group hug before heading out. Tate left a little quicker than the rest of us, and I can't help but wonder why. What did he have planned for the evening?

The thought sneaks in that maybe he has a date. Maybe that's why he was in such a hurry. The idea needles at me, sharp and unwelcome. It shouldn't matter. He's free to see whoever he wants. But the twist in my stomach says otherwise.

I shake it off, forcing a smile as I step into the cool night air. Still, the question lingers, uninvited: who is he rushing to, if not me? It's been one of those days that fills the soul, and yet somehow, the moment I let myself think of him with someone else, I feel unsettled, restless.

I'm walking home alone, scarf pulled up against the evening chill, cheeks still warm from cider and laughter. The windows of Wisteria Books & Brews glow softly, lanterns swaying outside the door as a breeze rustles the mums on the stoop.

I step inside, listening to the buzz of the fridge. But something catches my eye immediately.

At the top of the ladder leading up to my little attic apartment, balanced carefully on the top rung is another bottle. I don't know how or when he got it in here, but he did.

I pause at the bottom step, heart hammering.

The moonlight catches the glass, making it gleam. Inside, there's a slip of paper rolled up tight, just like before.

I don't open it. Not yet.

Behind me, the town is quiet except for the creak of the harbor swings and the soft chime of wind bells from the apothecary next door. Wisteria Cove feels like it's holding its breath, waiting, watching.

I glance up one last time, smiling to myself.

Chapter 10
Tate

I wake up before the sun, but just barely. Wisteria Cove is just beginning to stir. I close my eyes again, but my phone buzzes on the nightstand, vibrating with a stubborn urgency. I groan as I reach for it.

Mom.

I hesitate but swipe to answer, dragging the phone to my ear.

Before I can even say hello, she launches in. "Taters. Good, you're awake," she says briskly, her voice sharp and familiar in the worst way. "I wanted to let you know that I need to sell the house and boat. Randy and I are going to put an offer on that new vacation house, and we're going to use that money."

My gut twists hard and fast. I sit up slowly, rubbing a hand over my face. "Mom..." I say carefully, "I live here. I'm fixing up the boat. I was going to work at the harbor again next season."

There's a pause, but not the kind that suggests she's thinking it over, more like she's waiting for me to catch up. "Yeah, but they are mine, not yours," she says, matter-of-fact. Like she's discussing the weather. "Randy and I can't pass this house up. It's what we want for our family."

What they want for *their* family. As if I'm not part of their family. Which I guess I'm not. I never was. My jaw clenches so tight it aches. It has always amazed me she just up and left after my dad died, like neither of us mattered.

"This was Dad's, too, Mom," I say softly, still trying to process these blows that she's laying, one right after the other, without a thought of how this is landing.

"He's dead, Tate. And if he cared, he would still be here. He wouldn't have left us," she says as if he had a choice in when his ship was going down, in whether he wanted to die or not.

"Mom, are you hearing yourself right now?" I ask, wondering if she's legitimately okay. This makes no sense. I just talked to her last week, and she never mentioned anything about selling anything. Why is she all of a sudden selling?

"Tate, you need to be ready. I'm selling them. They're in my name," she clips, getting frustrated.

"Okay...so where am I supposed to go, Mom?" The words are bitter, raw. My throat feels tight, but I try to keep my voice even, like maybe that'll keep me steady.

"It's not my problem anymore," she says. "It's time you grew up and figured it out."

And just like that, she hangs up. No goodbye, no 'I love you'...she just hangs up.

For a moment, I sit there, staring at the phone in my hand, listening to the soft creak of this old house that doesn't even feel like mine anymore. My breath shudders as I exhale, pushing back the sting behind my eyes.

Time to grow up and figure it out. As if I haven't spent the past five years doing that without my parents. One by choice and one by death. And that she insinuated my dad had a choice in that is just bullshit. I've always known my mother was selfish, but this takes the cake.

I've maintained the house and boat for the past five years

since she left. I've paid for it all. She has paid nothing. And now she's going to take the two things that I have left of my dad.

By the time I'm out the door, the town is bathed in that early-morning glow. Wisteria Cove is beautiful right now, with boats bobbing and swaying gently in the harbor, gulls screaming overhead, the scent of salt, leaves, and morning fog hanging in the air. The water's soft hush should feel calming. But right now, after talking to my mom, it only makes me feel more lost. Like I'm losing it all and Wisteria Cove, too.

Without thinking, my feet take me toward the one place that's always felt like a safe space. Lilith Maren's place.

Her garden is waking up, too, golden light glinting off dew-soaked wisteria vines, petals spilling over the trellises and winding through the gazebo where she sits as if she knew I was coming. A steaming mug that looks like tea rests between her hands, and her piercing gaze finds mine before I even reach the gate.

"Well, here you are, Mr. Tate Holloway," she calls, smiling gently but knowingly. "Come sit."

I don't hesitate. My chest is tight, and my legs are heavy, but I walk straight to the gazebo, sinking into the chair across from her. I don't even bother with pleasantries. "I need to talk."

Lilith nods, setting her mug aside. Her silver hair glints in the light, and there's a kindness in her eyes that undoes me a little. "Then talk, Tate."

And so I do.

I tell her about the phone call. About my mother's selfishness, about how she didn't even hesitate to tell me to "figure it out" like this whole life I'm trying to build back here means nothing.

Lilith listens the way she always has, quietly, patiently, with no judgment, just presence and intuition.

When I finish, my shoulders sag with relief, and I feel better just being able to share it with someone.

Lilith leans forward. "Grief and healing change people, Tate," she says gently. "Sometimes it twists them up so tight they forget how to be who they used to be. Sometimes...they're never the same."

I swallow hard, staring at my hands. They look rough, calloused from fishing. I wonder if I'll have to go back out fishing and not stay now. I think about what Willa said about never being with a fisherman.

"I feel like I should know what to do with my life. But right now? I don't," I admit.

Lilith reaches out and folds her hand over mine, her touch warm and steady. "You've been carrying a lot alone, sweetheart."

That word, a word my mother's never used for me, nearly undoes me. She never called me anything other than Taters. And now I just hate hearing that. She used to call me that when I meant something to her. And now I don't. So it all feels like a lie. Because she doesn't care, and it now makes sense that she never did.

She lets the silence stretch before she asks softly, "What do you want, Tate? Do you really want to fish?"

I stare out at the harbor in the distance. My dad's boat sits tied up out there in the harbor, waiting for me to finish the repairs I'd already started. The thought of spending every day out on that water like I used to...it should feel right. Familiar. But all I feel is a dull ache. The tug that used to pull me out to sea...it feels more like an anchor now. Maybe that's not me anymore and not what I'm supposed to do.

"I don't know," I say honestly, my voice rough. "I thought I did. But maybe...maybe I don't."

Lilith nods slowly, like that's an acceptable answer. Like not knowing is perfectly fine.

"Do you actually like living in the house?" she asks next, tilting her head. "Are you happy there?"

That catches me off guard. I shake my head before I even think about it. "No." The word feels like a confession. "It's not home."

Lilith smiles gently, her eyes soft, wise, and understanding. "Then you have things to think about," she says. "You have so many options, Tate. You're a strong and amazing man."

The way she says it, like it's a fact, not a platitude, makes my throat tighten again.

"You can choose anything, honey. You don't have to stay tied to a past that doesn't fit anymore. Not for anyone."

I let her words sink in as we sit together beneath the gazebo with the wisteria cradling us. The breeze stirs the vines, and the wind chimes clink softly in the distance. I look down the street and see familiar faces beginning their days.

Wisteria Cove is full of memories, yes. But it's also full of possibility. The townspeople nod and wave as they pass by, their dogs on leashes and arms full of flowers or coffee cups. Even now, when my whole life feels like it's slipping out from under me, there's comfort here. This place has always been a safe space for me.

Lilith gives my hand one last squeeze before pulling away, but she doesn't leave me hanging. "You're welcome here anytime, Tate. You know that. I love you as a son. I'm sorry your mom doesn't appreciate the joy that she has."

"Thank you," I murmur. And I mean it.

The warmth in her gaze feels like a balm I didn't even know I needed. I sit a little straighter, breathe a little easier.

Maybe I don't have all the answers yet. Maybe I don't know what's next.

But for the first time in a long time, I don't feel completely lost.

*   *   *

The sun's setting when I pull up outside the Bennett house, but the place is glowing. String lights twinkle from the porch railings, soft amber against the night, and laughter drifts through the windows, warm and welcoming.

This house feels like the beating heart of Wisteria Cove tonight. I can already smell the sharp tang of tomato sauce, something cheesy and herby in the air, and a hint of fresh-baked dough.

Inside, the chaos is pure joy. Remy Bennett is at the kitchen island tossing dough in the air with exaggerated flair while his youngest brother, Finn, heckles him from the other side of the kitchen island. And smack in the middle of it all is Junie, perched on a stool, legs swinging, her hair full of messy curls, bright eyes wide as she holds a tiny paintbrush in one hand and a bottle of glittery polish in the other.

"Tate's here!" Junie announces excitedly, like this is the best news of the night, which, honestly, makes my chest ache in the best way.

"Finally!" Finn grins, clapping me on the back as I step inside. "Thought you were gonna bail on pizza night. That's sacrilegious, man."

"Wouldn't dream of it," I say, setting a six-pack of bottled root beer on the counter for our floats later. I hand Finn the bag of vanilla ice cream and he tucks it in the freezer behind him.

"You're just in time to witness culinary greatness," Remy declares, tossing the dough again, narrowly missing the ceiling. Junie squeals in delight while Finn groans and reaches to stop the disaster-in-progress.

"Pizza night is very special, Captain Tate," Junie says solemnly, her tiny feet swinging, polish brush waving. "That's what Daddy says. And you should never miss it."

"Is that so?" I grin, ruffling her curls as I pass.

"Absolutely," Remy confirms. "And tonight's movie was Junie's pick, so...prepare yourself."

I glance at the TV, already queued up. *Pirates of the Caribbean*. I can't help but laugh. "Good choice, kiddo."

"Captain Jack Sparrow is a legend," Junie says with a dramatic flourish. "I'm going to marry him someday. And guess what? I'm making a sparkle pirate map."

Finn laughs. "You're five!"

"Almost six," she corrects without missing a beat. "And I've been drinking coffee with my Nana since I was three. I am grown."

I laugh. This kid is hilarious.

The night unfolds easily and with warmth. Remy's house feels like a home. Something I've dreamed of having someday. A place to make memories and to make other people feel welcome and safe. Remy's pizza is really good. He's come a long way from the bachelor I used to know him as before he became a husband and a dad. Golden crispy crust with generous heaps of cheese and pepperoni. We lounge around, root beer floats in hand, plates balancing on our laps, and the glow of the TV casting soft shadows across the room.

Junie wedges herself between her dad and me, chattering nonstop through the first half of the movie, sharing fun facts about pirates, asking questions about sword fighting, and offering commentary on costumes and scenery. She's endlessly curious and funny.

I find myself relaxing in a way I haven't in a long time. Here, in this house where laughter comes easy, where family feels natural and welcoming, everything else seems to slip away. The ache from this morning's call with my mom is still there, but it's dulled.

Halfway through the movie, Junie snuggles into her dad and lays her head on his arm.

"Want me to help you find your treasure on your boat?" she asks sweetly.

"Sure, we could do that sometime if your dad says it's okay," I say.

Remy catches my eye with a soft smile. "She's a relentless negotiator," he says quietly.

By the time Jack Sparrow is making his final escape, Junie's fighting sleep, her head drooping. She blinks slowly, eyelashes fluttering, before finally curling into him completely.

Remy brushes a stray curl off her forehead, tenderness in every motion. "Movie night champion couldn't hang," he whispers, standing carefully and scooping her up with ease.

"Be right back," he says, carrying her upstairs, her small arms slipping around his neck in sleepy trust. I haven't been around many little kids. But this one makes me wonder if I could have a kid myself someday. I wonder what it would be like to have a family. I didn't have any brothers or sisters, but I had plenty of friends.

The house quiets when he disappears down the hallway. Finn gathers plates, shooting me a grin. "Thanks for coming tonight, Tate. It's good to have you back."

"Yeah," I say quietly, and I mean it. "Thanks."

When Remy comes back, he drops onto the couch beside me, rubbing the back of his neck. "You okay, Tate?" he asks gently, leaning forward to grab what's left of his float.

I hesitate, then shrug. "Rough day," I admit. "My mom called this morning. She's selling the house and the boat."

Remy's smile fades, replaced by something quieter. He nods, thoughtful. "I'm sorry, man. That's shitty."

"Yeah," I say softly. "Feels like everything I'm trying to build just keeps slipping away, you know?"

"I know," Remy says, leaning back, elbows on his knees. "But you've got options, even if it doesn't feel like it yet."

He's quiet for a beat before glancing at me. "You know...I've actually been looking to hire a manager at the tree farm," he says, almost casually. "Would that be something you'd even consider?"

I blink. "The tree farm?"

"Yeah," Remy says with a small smile. "It's a lot of outdoor hard work, which you're no stranger to. I think you'd like it. And honestly? I wouldn't mind having someone I trust running things with me."

That word: trust. It catches in my chest.

People trusting me...excited that I'm staying here. That's something I didn't realize I was starving for until this moment.

"Really?" I ask, almost afraid to hope.

"Really," he says firmly. "You're solid, Tate. Always have been. And if you need somewhere to stay, you know you could take one of the cabins on the back property. They're small but cozy. No pressure, but the offer's there."

I stare at him for a second, overwhelmed but grateful. This is the lifeline I didn't expect tonight.

"You don't have to figure everything out all at once," Remy adds, softer now. "But I'd be glad to have you at the nursery. You're good with your hands, and patient. You'd fit right in."

Something loosens in my chest, something tight and tired. For the first time in days, I allowed myself to believe that maybe there's a future for me here that isn't tied to my dad's old boat or a house my mom doesn't care about.

"Thanks, Remy," I say sincerely. "That means more than you know."

"You're family, Tate," Remy says. "Always have been."

When I finally leave, it's late and cool and still. The wind carries the scent of pine and wood smoke, and Main Street is quiet but bathed in a warm glow from the old-fashioned streetlamps.

I walk slowly, letting my boots scuff the worn sidewalks and looking into the darkened windows of the little shops I've known my whole life as I go. Wisteria Books & Brews. The harbor just at the edge of town, with boats rocking gently under the moonlight.

But tonight, for the first time, I don't feel entirely shut out. Maybe I'm not meant to follow in my father's footsteps after all. And maybe this town still has a place for me. And it doesn't have to be who he is. It's who I am.

That thought warms me all the way home.

Chapter 11
Willa

Every morning, like clockwork, I've been looking forward to unlocking the front shop door and flipping the open sign. Not for the first hot coffee or even the routine comfort of the place. But because I know what will wait just beside the flower box, tucked away. Another message in a bottle.

I try to tell myself I don't care. But my fingers always tremble when I pull the cork, my breath hitching as I unroll the scroll inside.

Today's message? "*Someone once told me forgiveness isn't*

earned, it's given. But if it can be earned, I'll spend every day showing you."

The words hit me right in the chest. Infuriating, tender and perfect. And far more effective than I'm willing to admit to myself. Damn it. He knows I love romantic gestures. He's playing right to my heart. And I'm falling for it, hook, line, and sinker.

I tuck the bottle behind the counter with the others, a whole little collection now, lined up like glass soldiers guarding memories I swore I wouldn't linger on. I take a deep breath, willing my heart to slow down.

Then the bell jingles, and he's here. Right on cue. Tate Holloway, in all his broody fisherman glory. His presence stirs the air, draws gazes, quickens my pulse. He's different now, quieter, softer somehow. The grief of losing his father still clings to him, tucked in the corners of his smile, heavy in the way his shoulders set when he thinks no one's watching. But I don't miss it. It's impossible not to feel it. I know how hard it is to carry the grief of losing a parent. It's not a club you want to be a part of. I wouldn't wish that on anyone.

Donna pauses her knitting. Lilith lifts her mug in silent commentary, a familiar, knowing smirk spreading across her face. Donna opens the notebook that she carries and scribbles a few things in it. Probably fodder for a future book. The bookstore practically hums with excited whispers whenever he's here. Everyone is watching and enjoying this. Conversations slow, and customers pause and glance over.

"Morning, Willa," he says, his voice that warm, rough-edged tone that slides under my skin no matter how I try to harden myself against it. His eyes catch mine for just a second, a flicker of vulnerability in their depths, a glimpse of something real and raw, and I feel my defenses let down just a little more. This is happening more and more every time he sends another message and comes around.

He leans on the counter, easy, familiar, the edge of his mouth curving into that damn dimpled smile I've sworn I'm immune to. "Usual?"

"Obviously," I mutter, already wrapping his sandwich and pouring his black coffee, my hands moving on autopilot while my heart beats far too fast.

Every day, he shows up, and he smiles that patient smile. Every day, he leaves another bottle. And he's been doing this so often that he's even become a regular around here.

Today, though, something changes. It feels different.

Just as I hand over Tate's order, setting his plate down in front of him, his eyes catch mine for the briefest second. My chest tightens, but I force myself to keep moving, collecting empty mugs and plates from the next table. It's busy enough that I can lose myself in the rhythm of the work, let my pulse settle.

I balance the stack carefully in my hands and make my way back toward the counter. Halfway across the room, though, I'm cut off by a man in a light blue polo and cargo pants who swivels in his chair, blocking my path. He flashes me a grin that makes my skin prickle. "Hey, darlin'," he drawls, southern accent thick enough to drip. "Got a number to go with that smile?"

I shift the plates in my hands, keeping my tone polite but firm. "I'm flattered, but no. I've got a shop to run."

He leans closer, undeterred. "Come on now. It's just dinner." His eyes flick down, lingering far too long before crawling back up to meet mine.

My shoulders stiffen. "I'm not available. But the diner is—"

"Not interested in restaurants," he cuts me off, smirking. "I'd rather spend my evening with you."

I try to sidestep him, my arms are still full, but he shifts with me, too close, invading my space. "You locals always this hard to crack? Bet you're sweeter once you loosen up."

I force a smile that doesn't reach my eyes. "Sir, I really need to get back to work."

And then, just as I shift my weight to move past, he reaches out, hand lifting toward my hair. My stomach twists. My hands are full. I can't even brush him away—

But I don't have to.

Tate is there in an instant. Silent, sudden, like he's been watching the whole time. His fingers close around the man's wrist before it can reach me, grip unyielding.

"Don't," Tate says, his voice low and steady. "You don't put your hands on people without their consent."

The whole shop seems to still. The man startles, blinking up at Tate, who towers over him with a calm so sharp it feels dangerous. Tate doesn't raise his voice. He doesn't need to. The quiet authority in it vibrates straight through the air, leaving no room for argument.

I suck in a breath, my heart hammering. Relief, gratitude, something else I can't name, all of it knots in my chest as I watch the tourist yank his hand back, muttering something under his breath before sinking into his chair.

Tate doesn't look at him again. His gaze finds me, checking me over like he's making sure I'm intact.

And damn him, it's hot. Way hotter than it has any right to be.

Donna's smirk widens as she sips her coffee, eyes twinkling with delight. I give it about fifteen minutes before the entire town knows about this incident. In fact, Donna and Lilith are practically narrating this incident unfolding like Samuel L. Jackson.

"Everything okay here?" he asks, his voice gentler but still thick with protectiveness.

My heart hammers so loudly I'm surprised no one can hear it. "It's fine," I whisper, though my breathless voice betrays just how not fine I am. He's still got his arm on mine.

The tourist gets up and retreats quickly, mumbling an apology as he goes. As soon as the door closes behind him, the tension breaks like a snapped fishing line.

Donna lets out a bark of laughter from the pastry case. "Looks like Captain Broody Pants has staked his claim!"

Lilith claps, practically glowing. "I love a man who defends his woman!"

I shoot them a look that's supposed to be a glare but lacks any real heat. They're loving this, eating it up, and honestly... maybe part of me is, too.

But I'm also frustrated. I'm independent, and I don't need someone interfering with my life. I don't need a protector, and I don't need him.

When Tate steps just a little closer, the scent of salt air and cedar envelops me, grounding and dizzying all at once. His dimple flashes again as his gaze lingers on mine, warm and intimate, like it's just the two of us in this room full of prying eyes.

And for a moment, it feels good. Too good. And I forget that I'm supposed to be mad at him.

I want to roll my eyes at him, shove him away, pretend I'm unmoved, but I'm not. My heart twists, my breath catches, and somewhere deep down, I know exactly what this means. I still care. I hate that I care. Hate that I like the way he stepped in front of me. Hate how he brushes his fingers lightly across mine as he picks up his sandwich, a featherlight touch that lingers far longer than it should.

But I do like it. I think I more than like it. I want it.

I watch him as he returns to his usual seat at the counter, sunlight sliding over his hair. He doesn't look away. He meets my gaze across the bookstore, his smile soft but steady, full of quiet determination.

Outside, a pair of tourists peek in the window, curiosity written all over their faces. Wisteria Cove's favorite soap opera continues, and the audience is absolutely captivated.

I pretend to return to work, but my gaze drifts back to him, over and over, my thoughts spinning. Every bottle, every message, every quiet, broody smile, it's working. It's chipping away at the walls I thought I'd built strong enough to keep him out.

And when I finally let my lips curl into the smallest smile, his answering grin is devastating.

My heart stutters and swells all at once, and all I can think is: I am in trouble.

God help me, so much trouble.

* * *

A few days later, the community center is utter chaos, which, honestly, feels exactly right for Wisteria Cove's Annual Pie Baking Contest. The aroma of every type of pie you can imagine fills the air. Kids dart between tables, playing games and having fun. Wisteria Cove takes this event very seriously and people work hard all year to perfect the best pie to share and win the contest. Donna's already barking orders at volunteers with a wooden spoon in hand like it's a microphone. And somehow, despite my very vocal protests, Tate and I have been roped into this as well.

Because of course we have. Donna and my mom said it's part of our committee duties. Whatever. I don't remember my mom ever having to do this when she was in charge. They're just setting us up again, and I've come to expect it now. They're all relentless.

The whole town seems thrilled about it, naturally. I'm pretty sure they consider the main event to be not the pies, but the spectacle of me sitting next to Tate Holloway at a table for two solid hours.

"Perfect pairing!" Donna declares with a wink that makes me stare at her skeptically.

"Donna, what book are you working on right now?"

She grins even bigger. "Oh, just a small town second chance romance about a broody fisherman and a smitten bookstore owner."

I sigh. Donna has written over a hundred romance novels over the past thirty years, and many of them have featured real-life people and stories in our small town. She brings in a lot of tourists every year. But the funny part is that she never does social media or interviews, so no one actually knows what she looks like or who she actually is when people ask. So when tourists flock here and see an old lady knitting on a park bench, they would never think that it's her. I've even watched her speak to tourists about her books before, and they do not know that they're speaking to the author. And no one in our town would dare tell on her, either. She's been great at keeping our town thriving. And while this town will gossip relentlessly about each other, they won't share important details with tourists.

Tate settles into the chair beside me, close enough that our knees brush beneath the table. That familiar scent, salt air, cedar, and something distinctly Tate, wraps around me before I can steel myself. I sneak a glance at him. He looks so at ease, leaning back in his chair like he hasn't noticed.

Or maybe he has and is enjoying the effect.

I try to ignore how my pulse jumps when he leans forward to whisper, "Ready to eat pie with me, Willa?"

"Yes," I mutter, though a smile tugs at my lips despite myself. "I'm always available for pie."

"Just pie?" he teases and nudges me with his shoulder.

The warmth of his shoulder brushing mine is completely casual, completely innocent...and yet it sends a ripple straight through me, settling somewhere low and achy. I shouldn't let it. I shouldn't read into every little thing he says, every smile, every touch. And the way he's looking at me right now, playful, sure, but with that familiar glint in his eyes like he's testing the line between us, makes my heart stutter.

The first pie arrives, and we set about our very serious judging duties. I keep my head down, determined to remain professional, until Tate cuts a perfect bite of cherry pie, lifts his fork, and holds it toward me.

The entire room goes silent.

A chorus of delighted gasps follows Donna's gleeful shout: "Feed her, Tate! Feed her!"

I shoot him a warning look. "Don't you dare."

His grin is infuriating. "Part of the judging process," he says smoothly, his eyes twinkling with mischief.

And because my pride has apparently gone out the window along with my common sense, I lean forward and take the bite. His eyes never leave mine as I close my lips around the fork. The pie is good, tart and sweet, but it's nothing compared to the taste of Tate's attention lingering on my skin.

Not even able to stand it, I let out a moan and cover my mouth. "That is divine."

Donna hoots from the sidelines. "If that's not chemistry, I don't know what is!"

My mother takes all of this in as if she isn't surprised in the least.

The people around us erupt with laughter over something that Donna and Lilith say, and more people glance over. I feel my cheeks flush deeper. But I can't help it; a laugh bubbles up from my throat, genuine and warm. The town is eating this up. And I have to admit: so am I.

Tate leans close, his voice a low rumble meant just for me. "You gonna share that pie, or keep making me jealous?"

I blink, startled, fork halfway to my mouth. "You want a bite?"

"Mm." His gaze locks on mine, unreadable. "I want *your* bite."

Heat floods my cheeks. My fingers tighten around the fork, but before I can move, his hand comes up warm, steady, wrapping lightly around my wrist. He guides the fork the rest of the way, his eyes never leaving mine, and I can do nothing but watch as he leans in and closes his lips around the piece I'd just lifted.

My breath stutters. My heart thumps so loudly I'm sure the whole room can hear it.

He lingers just a moment, pulling back slowly, and then drags the edge of his tongue along the fork where my mouth had been seconds before. My throat goes dry. My pulse races.

For half a second, I think he's doing it for show, hamming it up for the table, playing into the town's relentless matchmaking. But when I glance around, no one's watching. Everyone's busy chatting, waiting for the next pie to be judged.

It's just us.

And the heat sparking low in my belly tells me he knows it.

More pies arrive, and the banter continues. He critiques crusts like he's auditioning for a baking show, and I pretend not to notice how he keeps leaning in, his shoulder brushing mine more often than seems necessary. I notice he only offers high praise and makes all the contestants blush.

I'm about to toss back a witty reply when it hits me.

This exact table.

A flash of memory, sharp and uninvited. I'm small again,

maybe six or seven, sitting cross-legged on a bench, watching my parents at this very table. Mom leaning into Dad, both of them laughing as they taste pies, fingers brushing as they passed each plate between them. Their peaceful rhythm, their banter, the way they made it feel like love wasn't just safe but possible.

And it sears through me, hot and sudden, because for a second, I can almost hear their laughter again. Almost see the way my dad used to wink at me across the table as he stole another bite from my mom's plate. And I feel him in this moment, as if he is still here, although I know he isn't.

But he's gone. And when I glance over at my mom, she's watching me with a small, sad smile on her face like maybe she is remembering, too.

And suddenly I'm back in my skin, heart thudding too hard, breath catching in my throat.

Yeah...*this* is why I can't do this. Especially not with Tate.

Because what if I let myself sink into this, into him, into us, and then one day he's gone, too? They don't always come home.

What if one day I'm sitting at this same table, and there's no one beside me, no laughter, just silence and empty chairs and a hollow ache that never quite heals? And I'm standing there where my mother is now with a sad smile on my face. No. I won't let that happen to me.

He's a fisherman. He leaves. That's what they do. They leave the harbor, and sometimes they don't come back.

I can't go through that again. I won't go through that again.

The laughter and clinking plates around me sound distant now, like they belong to another world, one I can't touch, one that's moving on while I sit here frozen, jarred by the weight of it all.

Tate says something next to me, light and teasing still, but I can't process it.

I just nod, smile, and hope he doesn't see the way my hands tremble when I reach for the next slice of pie.

"Everything all right, Willa?" he asks, voice softer now but still roughened by the edge of protectiveness that makes my stomach twist and flutter all at once.

My heart is pounding so loud I swear the whole town can hear it. "Fine," I say, though I can't quite keep the breathlessness out of my voice.

The crowd releases their collective breath as he finally sits, smirking just a little as he leans back in his chair, thoroughly pleased with himself.

I bury my face in my hands for a moment before peeking through my fingers at Tate. He just raises his fork again, cutting another perfect bite of pie.

"Don't even think about feeding me again," I warn.

"Oh, I'm thinking about it," he says, his voice low, teasing, and just this side of sinful.

And just like that, I feel it again, that awful, wonderful truth tightening in my chest: I still love him.

Despite everything, I still do. I can't turn it off, no matter how hard I try.

The contest continues, the chaos resumes, and the town watches like we're their favorite show, which, let's be honest, we probably are. But all I can feel is the warmth of Tate's shoulder brushing mine, the heat of his gaze every time I laugh, and the way my defenses crumble a little more every time he so much as smiles at me.

Damn him. Damn this town. And damn how much I secretly love every second of it.

Chapter 12
Tate

The salty harbor air slaps me in the face the second I step off the dock, full of sharp salt, cold wind, and a chill that cuts straight through your clothes and into your bones. The old boat groans beneath my boots as I step on deck, wood creaking like it remembers me. Like it knows this might be one of the last times I touch it. I crouch low, fingers moving to the dock lines out of muscle memory. Dad drilled it into me: tight knots, strong grip, no slack. You take care of what you love, and it'll take care of you. Dad was meticulous about safety and keeping things right. That's why losing him made no sense. He and Mr. Maren did everything by the book. Whatever happened out there had to have been bad. They didn't take chances.

This boat was his pride and joy. His escape and his kingdom. Now it's just another thing my mother's trying to sell off, like it doesn't mean a thing. Another ghost she wants to bury while pretending none of it ever mattered.

I pull the line tighter. Not because it needs it. I do it because just the thought of someone else's hands on this deck, someone else's name on the papers, someone else driving her out into the sea while I'm stuck watching from the shore burns deep down in my chest in a way I'm not ready for. It's not just a boat for me. It's the last piece of him I have left. And I'm not ready to let it go.

I look at the supplies stacked, ready for the remodels and repairs. I'm still going to do them. Because someone is going to get this boat and appreciate it. And somehow it will live on for my dad—just with someone else. And I'll admit that it makes me sad.

Finn hops down beside me, brushing sawdust off his sweat-shirt. "She's holding up all right for an old girl," he says, running a hand along the weathered wood.

"Yeah, what do you think about rebuilding that rotted wall?" I nod to the side.

"Not a problem, I can help you," he offers. Finn is a great carpenter and a magician with building things.

Junie's already climbed into the wheelhouse, pretending to steer, her curls wild in the breeze. "Aye aye, Captain Holloway!" she shouts.

I manage a smile and tell her as I step past, "Careful, Captain Junie, keep her off the rocks."

Finn chuckles and then glances at me again, probably taking in the sadness I'm trying my damndest to conceal. "You all right?"

I shrug, settling onto the bench at the stern. The water laps against the hull, slow and rhythmic, like it's trying to rock me into admitting something I'm not ready to say. "Yeah, just thinking about what I'm going to do when this gets sold."

Finn leans back on the railing, arms crossed. "Have you given any more thought to Remy's offer of the job at the tree farm?"

"Yeah," I mutter. "It was nice of him to offer it."

Finn raises an eyebrow. "Nice? He's running himself

ragged. You'd be doing *him* a favor taking that job. He's burning the candle at both ends. He needs a manager and a nanny. But he is not good at hiring help. He's too proud. But if he's asked you, trust me...he meant it."

I scrub a hand over my jaw. "I don't know if I'd be any good. All I know is fishing. My whole life, it's been fishing. What happens if I take the job and let Remy down?"

Finn shrugs easily. "You could always take it until you figure out what you want to do. At least you know Remy. You know he'd be good to work for."

Junie drags a piece of cloth behind her like a pirate flag and tells me, "You won't mess up, Captain Tate."

I look down at her, her face full of absolute certainty.

"Everyone loves trees," she adds wisely. "Even pirates."

Finn snorts out a laugh, and I can't help but grin. "Even pirates, huh?"

She nods, all seriousness. "Daddy said so."

I lean forward, elbows resting on my knees, watching the gulls wheel overhead. "It's more than just the job. My mom...she's selling the boat."

"The pirate ship?" Junie gasps, wide-eyed.

I nod slowly. "Yeah, kiddo."

Junie's face crumples a little as she looks at me. "Why?"

I sigh, unsure how to answer that in a way that makes sense to a five-year-old, or even myself. "I guess she doesn't see much point in keeping it around."

Junie puts her tiny hand on mine, her expression soft and earnest. "That makes you sad. I can tell."

Her words catch me off guard. She's right, of course.

"Yeah," I admit quietly. "Yeah, it does."

"Are you coming tonight?" Junie asks suddenly, swinging her legs as she looks up at me. Her tone brightens, like she's decided that a change of subject is exactly what's needed. "Daddy has all the pumpkins ready. And a big bonfire, too."

"Pumpkin carving?" I ask.

It's been a town tradition for decades. Pumpkin carving at the Bennett Tree Farm. Remy's working today, so Finn's got Junie, and I invited them out on the boat. We're not sure how many more rides we'll get, so we're taking advantage of this one.

She nods enthusiastically. "You have to come. It's tradition."

I glance at Finn, who gives me a knowing look. "Come on, man. You know you want to. Wisteria Cove bonfires are practically a requirement."

I laugh under my breath, but there's this tightness in my chest that won't let go. The kind that feels like hope trying to claw its way back in.

"Okay," I tell Junie finally, nudging her shoulder gently. "I'll come carve pumpkins tonight."

Her face lights up as if I just promised her buried treasure. "Good! And you can sit next to me!"

Finn grins. "Better be ready. Junie's competitive. You're going down, Holloway."

I glance out over the water, watching the gulls swoop and the sunlight shimmer across the waves. This cove has always felt like both a home and a prison at times. Every creak of the boards, every rope and knot, every salt-slicked memory—it's all wrapped up in the person I thought I'd be.

But tonight...pumpkin carving. Bonfire. Warm cider. Laughter. Maybe a little bit of Wisteria Cove magic to remind me that home can be more than salt, wood, and ghosts.

Junie's hand tugs at my sleeve, small and insistent. "And we'll save a seat for Willa too. She has to come."

That catches me off guard, but in the best way.

I smile at her. "Yeah. Willa, too."

* * *

When I wind down the road later that evening to the Bennett Tree Farm, it glows like a damn postcard. Strings of fairy lights crisscross between the tall pines, flickering gently in the cool breeze. The smell of wood smoke drifts from the giant fire pit in the center of the clearing, where a makeshift s'mores station is already set up. Picnic tables stretch out under the trees, each one covered in pumpkins of all shapes and sizes, carving kits, and paper towels.

Thermoses of cider sit ready on every table, steam curling into the chilly night air. It's a fall wonderland, Wisteria Cove at its most charming, and honestly, it's exactly what I need.

"About time you showed up," Remy calls from near the fire pit, grinning as he drops another log onto the flames.

I lift a hand in a lazy wave and spot Junie immediately. She's perched on top of one of the picnic tables, swinging her legs as she surveys the pumpkins like a general about to declare war. She sees me and beams, waving so hard I swear she's going to fall right off the table.

But it's not Junie who steals my breath. It's Willa.

She's standing off to the side near the cider table, bundled in a deep maroon sweater tucked into the front of her jeans, her worn brown boots making her taller than she is, her hair falling loose around her shoulders. She's laughing at something Ivy says, head tilted just so, and when she turns and sees me...

Yeah. There it is. That familiar flicker. The one that's been humming between us since the day I rolled back into this town like a storm front.

I raise a brow in greeting, and she rolls her eyes, but she doesn't look away. That's progress, right?

Junie barrels into me a second later, grabbing my hand and

tugging me toward the pumpkins. "Come on, Tate! I saved us a spot!"

"Us?" I ask, letting her drag me along.

She nods, completely serious. "Me, you, and Willa. You have to sit next to her."

Oh, subtle, Junie. Real subtle.

I glance over and catch Willa's eye again. Her lips quirk like she's fighting a smile as she walks over, carving tools in hand. "Looks like we've been assigned specific seating."

"I guess we have to go where we're told," I say, dropping onto the bench beside her.

The second I sit, it hits me, a memory sharp and unbidden.

I used to sit right here at this very table, years ago. I remember carving pumpkins with Willa when we were kids, laughing and teasing each other because mine always ended up looking like a disaster. Her dad would tease us gently from across the table, carving with an expert's hand while her mom handed out cider and called us "the pumpkin pirates."

Those nights felt easy and safe. But that was before it all went wrong. Man, I'd give anything to go back to that time just for a little bit. I miss those times.

Willa's voice pulls me back. "You're staring into space," she teases, a hint of warmth in her tone.

"Just a memory passing through," I reply, picking up a carving knife and spinning it idly between my fingers. "Remember when I used to carve way better pumpkins than you?"

She smirks. "Yeah, right. I've had years of practice since you left."

That last word hangs in the air for a beat too long, but she doesn't seem angry tonight. Just...teasing. Comfortable.

I can work with that.

I lean in a little, lowering my voice so only she can hear.

"Careful. You keep looking at me like that, and people are going to start talking."

Her eyes flash, but she doesn't back down. "People are already talking, Tate."

God, she's good at this. At banter, at keeping me just slightly off-balance, at making it feel like we're right back where we left off, and yet somehow on brand-new ground.

Junie plops a pumpkin in front of me, nearly knocking over a thermos of cider. "Here! This one is for you, Tate. I picked it special."

I grin and move it closer, "What makes this one special?"

"It's big and bumpy like a pirate's face," she says proudly.

Willa lets out a snort beside me that's sharp, unexpected, completely unfiltered and it hits me like a damn sucker punch. That laugh. I swear, it does more damage to my heartbeat than a storm on the open water.

She leans in, close enough that her shoulder brushes mine, her voice low and warm against my ear.

"She's adorable," she whispers.

And just like that, I'm wrecked. The scent of her wraps around me with the familiar cinnamon and vanilla, soft and sweet, like home if home ever felt safe. It fills the small space between us, and I breathe it in for a second, just to stay in the moment.

God help me, I don't think she even knows what she does to me. Luckily, Junie fills the table with laughter and jokes, and we get to work, the three of us squeezed together on the bench, pumpkin guts flying, tools clattering, cider steaming. The clearing fills with chatter and laughter, with the occasional burst of applause as someone finishes an impressive jack-o'-lantern.

Junie insists that I carve "the scariest face ever" on mine, but I'm hopeless, as usual. Willa leans over at one point, eyebrow raised. "You call that scary? Junie, you should have just given him a Sharpie. He probably could have handled that better."

Her shoulder brushes mine, warm and solid, and suddenly the air feels different. Charged.

I smirk. "Want to help me out, expert?"

She leans in, fingers guiding mine as I carve. She's so close I could tilt my head just slightly and brush my lips against her temple.

Dangerous. But I don't pull away.

"I think you secretly like being terrible at this," she murmurs, smiling.

"Maybe I just needed an excuse to have you this close," I murmur back, watching the flush creep into her cheeks.

Before she can answer, Junie yells, "Piggyback ride! Captain Tate! Please!" tugging on my sleeve, her face alight with excitement. "Please? Please-please-please?"

I glance at Willa, who's watching me with amusement, arms folded as if she's trying not to look too pleased. "Guess I have duties to attend to," I say, rising and swinging Junie onto my shoulders.

She squeals in delight, and I jog a quick lap around the fire pit while she waves dramatically at all the other kids like she's queen of the world.

When I circle back to our table, Willa is watching me with a soft and thoughtful look that nearly undoes me. Her eyes trace every move like she's seeing me for the first time.

I set Junie down gently and meet Willa's gaze.

"What?" I ask, teasing.

She shakes her head, but that smile lingers, tugging at the corners of her mouth in a way that feels dangerous and promising all at once.

"Nothing," she says lightly. "Just...didn't expect you to be so good at this."

"At what?" I prompt.

"At...this." She gestures vaguely to the whole scene, pumpkins, cider, firelight, me with Junie on my shoulders. "At fitting in again."

Her words hit me harder than I expect. Because I don't just want to fit in. I want to stay. And it's starting to feel a lot more like home than it ever did.

Even if part of me still feels like a mess of guilt and grief... here, at this table, with Willa's knee brushing mine and Junie laughing and the entire town glowing with fairy lights, I almost feel whole.

"Maybe this is where I was made to be," I say, voice softer now.

Her eyes meet mine, and for a second, it feels like the entire world narrows to this one perfect moment. The fire crackles, and Junie hums as she adds triangle eyes to her pumpkin.

And Willa smiles, and I swear I'd carve a thousand crooked pumpkins to keep that look on her face.

Chapter 13
Willa

The rain starts just after I lock the front door and step inside. My mom took a trip up to New Hampshire for the night with Donna and asked me to house-sit for her. One moment, the wind is tugging at the porch mums, and the next, it's like the sky splits open and sheets of water come down in silvery waves, battering the windows and drumming against the roof of the old house. Lightning flashes, illuminating the living room in ghost-light, and then thunder cracks, low and rolling.

The power flickers but holds. Barely. I wrap the knit throw tighter around my shoulders and light the last of the pillar candles on the mantle. My mom's house is already warm and cozy in that cluttered, witchy way only she can pull off. Bundles of dried herbs hang near the windows. The wood stove clicks as it warms, and there's a faint scent of orange peel and cloves simmering from the tea I made, which is still a little too hot to drink.

It should feel peaceful and safe. But instead, I feel unsettled and restless. I blame Tate Holloway.

Because ever since pumpkin carving night, when he made me laugh more than I have in months, and then sat beside me like he belonged there, with Junie on his shoulders and firelight in his eyes, I can't stop thinking about him. And the possibility of there being an us.

And now, while I'm curled up in my mom's living room in the middle of a rainstorm, the thought of him out there somewhere makes my chest ache in a way I didn't expect.

I jump a little when there's a knock on the door. Three short raps, then one pause, then another. Like a code.

I pad across the wood floors, heart hammering for reasons I absolutely refuse to unpack right now, and open the door a few cautious inches.

Tate stands there, soaked to the bone, rain dripping from his hair and jacket. For a heartbeat, his expression flickers, surprise lighting his eyes when he spots me standing there. But then the corners of his mouth curve, soft and unguarded, like he can't help himself. He's smiling at me, even through the storm.

"I need your help," he says, and slowly opens his coat to reveal a small, wriggling bundle of black fur, clinging to his flannel chest.

My jaw drops. "Who is this?"

"A stowaway," he says. "Found her down by the docks. She was shivering so badly I couldn't ignore her, and I wanted to bring her to Lilith."

I open the door wider. "Get in here before you get sick."

He steps inside, gently cradling the kitten against him as I shut the door. The house smells like cloves, cedar, and rain now, earthy and warm, and a little like Tate. I don't know when his presence became that familiar, but it hits me full force as he kneels in front of the fire, gently unwrapping the kitten.

She's tiny. Soaked and shaking, with matted fur and wide green eyes that blink up at us like we're the strangest thing she's ever seen.

"Oh, sweetheart," I whisper, grabbing a dry towel and crouching beside him. "You poor baby."

Tate hands her to me with so much care it makes my throat catch. "She's freezing," he murmurs. "I had her wrapped up inside my shirt. Took me a while to catch her, but I couldn't leave her out there."

"Of course not," I say softly, glancing up at him as I carefully pat the kitten dry. "I'm so glad you brought her here."

His eyes meet mine, and something warm and wordless passes between us.

That's when I notice how he looks. Really notice. Tate is drenched, water dripping from his hair, plastering the dark strands back from his forehead. His jacket clings to him, heavy with rain, and his shirt is soaked straight through, molding to every hard line of muscle underneath.

"God, you're going to catch your death," I say, grabbing another towel and rising to my feet. My voice comes out a little breathless. "Take that off."

He blinks, startled. "What?"

"Your shirt." I thrust the towel at him, heat blooming under my skin even as I force my tone to stay brisk. "You're soaked through. Get it off before you freeze. I'll grab one of the throws for you, and you can dry your jeans by the fire."

For a moment he just watches me, rain still dripping from his lashes, a flicker of something unreadable in his eyes. Then he obeys, peeling the shirt over his head in one slow, fluid motion.

And I nearly forget how to breathe.

His chest is broad, defined by years of hauling nets and ropes, every line of muscle cut and honed by hard work. A light dusting of hair spreads across his chest and narrows into a trail that disappears beneath his waistband, a path that makes my mouth go dry. My pulse hammers in my throat, traitorous and loud.

I toss him the throw blanket a little too quickly, trying to mask the way my hands shake. "Here. Warm up."

He smirks faintly, like he knows exactly what he's doing to me, then drapes the blanket loosely around his shoulders. The firelight glances across his damp skin, gilding him in a way that feels unfair, like the universe is conspiring against me.

I look down at the kitten in my arms, clinging to the excuse of fussing over her so I don't give in to the wild thought beating in my head because if I look up again, I might not be able to look away.

We sit there for a while, side by side on the rug in front of the fire, taking turns drying her off, whispering quiet encouragements like she's a baby bird and we're trying not to spook her. I warm some milk in a shallow dish, and Tate digs out an old box from the pantry and lines it with one of Lilith's worn old towels.

We don't speak much, but it's not uncomfortable. It's easy, actually.

Eventually, when the kitten is dry and curled up near the fire, her tiny body rising and falling with each breath, I sit back against the couch, exhaling for what feels like the first time all night.

Tate stretches out beside me, legs long and damp jeans drying by the fire.

"So," he says softly, watching the kitten. "What would you name her?"

I glance at him, already smiling. "Cobweb."

He blinks. "Cobweb?"

"Yeah." I shrug. "It's witchy and perfect."

He grins. "It fits."

"I mean, look at her." I point at the scruffy little creature, now snoring softly with her paws tucked under her chin. "She's basically one of Lilith's spells come to life."

Tate laughs, full and deep, the kind of sound that burrows into your chest and makes a home there. "Cobweb," he repeats. "Okay. I can get behind that."

"She could live at the bookstore," I say before I even think about it. "I've always wanted a bookstore cat. Maybe she's a familiar and has witch energy, too."

The second the words are out, I feel something shift in the air, like I said too much. Like I gave something away. But Tate doesn't tease me.

He just looks at me with that steady, thoughtful expression of his, and says, "I think she'd love it there."

The fire crackles. Cobweb sighs in her sleep and burrows against me even closer.

And suddenly, I feel it in my bones, that sense that maybe this isn't just a one-night rescue mission. Maybe it's something else entirely.

"Do you think you'll really stay here this time?" I bite my lip nervously as the words tumble out of me before I can chicken out.

"Yeah. I wasn't ready before. But I want this. I want all of this," he says as he looks around and smiles.

"I used to think I didn't want any of this anymore, either," I admit quietly. "The town or the bookstore. When you left, all I saw were memories, and they weren't good. Maybe they can be good now."

Tate doesn't interrupt me; he just waits for me to finish. Like he always has, hanging on every word like he likes what I have to say. And that is one of the things I've always loved about him. He is my person. He always wanted to hear what I had to say.

I swallow. "I don't know. Sometimes it feels like maybe I didn't let myself want it because I was afraid of losing more than what I already had. Like my dad or...you. Again."

"Yeah," he says, voice low. "I get that."

I glance at him. "You do?"

He nods. "More than you know."

The storm picks up again, wind howling against the windows. But inside, it's warm, safe, and steady.

I tuck my legs beneath me and rest my head against the couch cushions. "I'm glad you're back."

He doesn't move for a long moment. Then he leans back beside me, his shoulder brushing mine. "Me too."

And I believe him and the quiet possibility that maybe he's not going anywhere this time.

We sit there until the fire burns low, the storm slowly giving way to silence.

And in the soft glow of candlelight, with Cobweb curled between us and the world tucked outside, I let myself believe at least for tonight at least that I don't have to protect myself from this.

That maybe this is the beginning of something new and real this time.

The fire crackles, low and golden, and the wind howls against the windows like some old ghost is trying to get in.

For a long time, neither of us speaks. Not because there's

nothing to say, but because the quiet feels like its own kind of truth.

Then, finally, he exhales, slow and heavy. "She's selling everything," he says, his voice low and rough.

I glance over. "Your mom?"

He nods, staring into the fire like it might offer some kind of answer he hasn't been able to find on his own. "The house. The boat. All of it."

"Oh." My chest tightens. "Tate, I'm so—"

"She told me over the phone like she was giving me a weather report." He rubs a hand over the back of his neck, fingers dragging through his hair, jaw tight. "She didn't even ask if I wanted it. Just said she was calling the realtor."

There's a long beat where the only sound is the storm and Cobweb's soft purring.

I reach out instinctively, resting a hand on his forearm. His eyes flick to mine, surprised, but he doesn't pull away.

"I'm sorry," I whisper, and I mean it in more ways than one.

He lets out a quiet, bitter laugh. "It's not like I wanted to live there again. Not really. But still..."

"That was your home."

"Yeah." His voice goes quiet. "And despite all the pain of losing my dad, there were still some good memories. My mom used to hang lights on the porch in the fall, even if she didn't feel like celebrating. She hated most holidays. I carved my first pumpkin on those steps. So many memories happened there. Good and bad, I guess."

"I just thought..." he continues, the smile fading again, "maybe someday I'd go back and fix it up. Make it mine. Maybe eventually use the boat again, not for fishing, but something different. Tours. Harbor trips. I don't know." He shakes his head. "But I guess that was just some stupid idea I had in my back pocket."

"It's not stupid," I say gently. "She just took it all away without finding out what you wanted. Typical April."

He doesn't respond for a moment. Then, quietly says, "I feel like I'm standing on the shore watching every last piece of the life I thought I had drift away. And I don't know if I should chase after it or just...let it go."

The rawness in his voice punches something soft in my chest.

"You don't have to have it all figured out right now," I say. "You've been carrying so much."

"Feels like I've been carrying it forever."

"You don't have to do that anymore," I murmur.

We fall quiet again. Outside, thunder rumbles low. The rain's still steady but softer now, like even the sky's calming down to listen.

I shift a little closer and tug the throw tighter around my shoulders. "Do you want to know what I think?"

He nods slowly, eyes still locked on the fire.

"I think your mom doesn't get to decide what stays with you. You do."

He looks at me, really looks at me. "What do you mean?"

I nod. "You carry those memories. The good ones. The ones that matter. You carry the porch memories and the dream of harbor tours. She can sell the house and the boat. But she can't take away everything."

He blinks, and I see the way his jaw works, like he's thinking about something.

"Besides," I say softly, "what if that dream isn't in your back pocket anymore because it's already here?"

He frowns. "What do you mean?"

"I mean," I say, my voice trembling just slightly, "maybe it's not something you fall back on. Maybe it's something you start building now. With what you have. With who you are. You have a lot of experience. People trust you here."

Tate doesn't move. He just watches me with a gaze so steady I feel like I'm coming apart at the seams.

"You make this town feel like home again, Tate. Maybe this was how it was always supposed to be, and how it was supposed to turn out."

For a second, I think I've said too much. Opened the door too wide. But then he shifts closer, hand brushing mine as he speaks.

"I was never any good at talking about stuff."

"I've noticed," I say with a faint smile.

He chuckles under his breath, eyes crinkling. "But I want to be better. With you."

My heart does a full-body somersault.

"I don't want to be some drifter fisherman who shows up and disappears again. I don't want to lose everything and call it starting over."

I look up at him. "Then don't."

His hand finds mine, this time fully, fingers twining around mine like it's the easiest thing in the world. Like he's meant to. He exhales, like he's finally breathing for the first time in a long time.

Cobweb shifts in her sleep, curling tighter against my chest. The candlelight flickers. The rain outside slows to a quiet hush, more lullaby than storm now. Tate sits close beside me on the sofa, his arm stretched along the back, blanket draped over both our shoulders.

For a while, neither of us says anything. We don't need to. The silence isn't awkward, it's heavy with warmth, with something I can't quite name. His thigh brushes mine every time he shifts, and each touch sends a spark skittering through me.

I should tell him to stay in the spare room. I should stand up and move, create space. Instead, I just sink further into the cushion, letting the weight of him anchor me.

My eyelids grow heavy, the fire crackling low and steady. Tate's hand, resting against the back of the sofa, drifts down, not on purpose, I don't think, until it brushes lightly against my shoulder. He doesn't move it away. And I don't ask him to.

The last thing I'm aware of is the steady rhythm of his breathing, the comforting heat of his body beside mine, and the kitten's tiny purr rumbling against my chest.

I wake to the sound of my mother's voice. "Well, well, well," Lilith singsongs, bracelets jingling as she sweeps into the room. "What have we here?"

My eyes fly open. The morning light spills across the room, gilding everything in soft gold, and I realize with a jolt that I'm not alone. Tate is still here. Still on the sofa. And at some point in the night, I must have shifted, because I'm curled against him now, my head tucked under his chin, his arm snug around me like it's the most natural thing in the world.

Cobweb is sprawled on his chest, purring contentedly, as if she's claimed him, too.

Heat floods my cheeks. I try to sit up, but Tate's arm tightens instinctively, pulling me back for a second before he blinks awake, groggy and confused. Then his eyes focus on me, and the slow, sleepy smile that spreads across his face makes my stomach flip.

Lilith gasps dramatically, clutching her chest like a scandalized Victorian aunt. "Oh my stars! Is this what happens when I leave you children alone for one night?"

"Mom," I groan, burying my face in my hands.

Tate chuckles low in his throat, rubbing a hand over his face, his voice rough with sleep. "Morning, Lilith."

"Morning, indeed," she says, grinning like the cat who caught the canary. "Looks like someone had a very cozy night."

I want to disappear into the floor. Tate just shakes his head, amused, as if he's not remotely fazed. Which, of course, only makes my pulse race harder.

And as Lilith bustles off toward the kitchen, humming smugly, Tate's gaze lingers on me, warm and unreadable. We don't speak, but something passes between us again. Something wordless. Something that feels like it's just beginning.

Chapter 14
Tate

The sound of tires crunching on the drive makes me glance out the kitchen window. Junie's already out of the truck before Finn can call to her to wait, bounding toward the front steps like a sparkle hurricane.

"Tate! We brought pizza and garlic balls!" she sing-songs, proudly hoisting a grease-stained bag with napkins falling out of it like a trophy.

Finn climbs out slowly, holding a stack of Marco's pizza boxes with a bag swinging from each arm, and he corrects Junie. "We got garlic *knots,* too. Marco threw them in. Said he wanted us to taste-test the new seasoning blend."

"Marco is a saint," I mutter, stepping back to let them in and helping Finn with the pizzas.

Junie makes a beeline for the back porch. "I'm gonna look for the mermaids!"

"What mermaids—" I stop myself. No use arguing with magic.

"She's fully committed to the idea that one lives under the dock," Finn says, setting the bags down on the kitchen counter. "Apparently, it has a glitter tail and a bad attitude."

I laugh and open up the bag of garlic knots, and taste one.

"She's also convinced she saw one off the dock last week." Finn grins as he watches her peer over the railing toward the harbor. "I told her it was a seal. She told me seals don't wear sparkly bras."

"Fair point," I mutter, chewing. "These are good. Thanks."

He points a garlic knot at me. "If only we could live in a magical world like Junie."

I snort. "Like half this town," I reply, popping open the pizza box. Steam rises. Pepperoni and sausage, thick crust, bubbling cheese. My stomach growls loudly enough to echo throughout the kitchen.

Finn slides a plate toward me. "Eat up. You know Marco's is a local legend."

He's not wrong. We lean against the counter, chewing in silence for a few minutes like men who have truly earned this moment.

"This house still giving you hell?" Finn asks, gesturing around with a knot.

I glance at the cracked molding near the ceiling and the old cabinets that creak. "Yeah. But I'm not doing much to it. Just cleaning it up. I'm going to take Remy up on that job offer. Maybe see if he's got one of those cabins still open."

Finn swipes his mouth with a napkin. "Seriously?"

"Yeah."

"I've always loved this house," he says as he looks around at all of the old woodwork.

The house was built in the early 1900s. My parents kept it maintained but did little updating through the years.

I shrug and take another bite. "House's gonna be someone else's problem soon."

He's quiet for a minute, just studying the ceiling beams like he's seeing potential no one else has.

"There's so much cool stuff you could do to this place," he finally says. "The beams? The wainscoting in the front room? This place has character. Old soul kind of stuff."

I pick at the garlic crust. "I care more about the boat than the house. That's what I'd keep if I could."

Junie comes back in through the screen door, her hair wind-tangled and wild-eyed. "Okay. I need to change."

I blink. "Why?"

"Because we're going to the bookstore, duh." She spins dramatically. "Story time. And Nana's book is out. Big event. You can't wear dock clothes to a party."

Finn chuckles. "She's been talking about this all week."

"Thought it didn't start until six?"

"It doesn't," Finn says, grabbing another slice. "But Willa said we could come early, help set up a little, maybe sneak in some cider before the crowd shows. Plus, we still have a ton of food. You know she won't turn down Marco's."

I'll take any excuse to see Willa, so I pack up the pizza to take over.

Junie's already halfway towards the bathroom, shouting, "I FORGOT MY WITCH HAT!"

By the time we make it to Wisteria Books & Brews, Finn and I are both laughing at the way Junie insisted we walk and 'arrive fashionably early.'

"Where does she learn this stuff?" I grin.

Willa's outside arranging pumpkins and sweeping fallen leaves from the stoop. She looks up when she hears us, and her smile hits me like it always does, right in the chest.

"You guys are early," she says, brushing a strand of hair behind her ear. It's pulled up in a loose twist, messy and perfect. She's wearing a forest green dress, sleeves pushed up, and tall boots. She looks beautiful.

"Junie insisted," I say. "And we brought Marco's."

"She said you had cider," Finn adds, like that explains everything.

Willa laughs. "Well, she's not wrong. Come on in. I sold out of everything earlier today, and I'm starving, so Marco's sounds amazing."

Inside, the store smells like apples, cinnamon, and book pages. The lights are dimmed, candles flickering on side tables inside glass lanterns. The front window display is glowing with string lights and stacks of Donna's latest hardcover: *The Wishing Well Witches.*

"You all eat?" Willa asks as we step into the shop.

I hold up a plate I made for Junie, who was apparently too excited to eat while she was on Mermaid duty, "The rest is all yours," I say, as I hold out the bags of the remaining food we brought over to share.

"Yeah, I'm basically eighty percent pizza now," Finn mutters.

Junie runs to the children's corner and immediately begins organizing the beanbags like a little librarian general. Willa watches her with a fond expression, then glances back at Finn. "Have you been reading to her?"

"Yeah. *Mermaid Mayhem.* There was a glitter battle. It got intense."

Her mouth curves. "She loves everything mermaids and pirates right now."

Finn leans against a shelf and points to the book display. "So. Expecting a big crowd?"

"Oh, yeah. All of those are signed by Donna and prepaid for the event," she says.

"Who did she feature in this one?" I ask, knowing that our locals make cameos in her books.

Willa shakes her head. "Donna never tells. But everyone will pore over them and speculate."

I raise an eyebrow. "Are you in a book yet?"

Willa smirks. "No, and don't encourage her."

Finn snorts. "My mom will probably drop little hints at her reading."

A sudden tension shifts in the room as Ivy enters from the back. Her lips are tight. Rowan trails behind her, holding two paper cups and looking concerned.

"He's not coming," Ivy says flatly. "He said he's got other plans."

Rowan glares and shakes her head. "Ivy's boyfriend. AKA Miranda. Because everything Ivy says can and will be used against her."

Willa crosses her arms. "Let me guess, he also said he couldn't pay you back for the money he borrowed last week?"

Ivy flinches. "It's not like that."

"It is exactly like that," Rowan mutters.

"He promised he'd come this time," Ivy whispers. Her voice is fragile around the edges, like a page worn too thin.

"He's been constantly breaking promises and letting you down," Willa says. "You deserve better."

Finn leans into me and whispers, "This guy is a piece of work. Uses her and never shows up when she needs him."

Willa nods in agreement.

Then I speak before thinking. "Where's this guy at?"

Everyone looks at me.

I step forward, arms crossed. "Because it's not right. That's taking advantage."

Finn fake coughs into his fist. "Tate for mayor."

Ivy blinks at me, stunned.

"I mean it," I say. "You deserve better."

Ivy forces a laugh. "Guess I need to figure out what I'm going to do."

"Nothing wrong with coming home," I say, the laugh catching in my throat. "Sometimes it's the only thing that makes sense…even if it takes you a while to admit it."

This does get a small laugh from Ivy, "Yeah, you're right. I just wish I hadn't wasted so many years on Derek."

Lilith walks in just then, her arms full of stickers and bookmarks for Donna's new book. She catches the last line and sets everything down with a huff.

Lilith lays them out on the counter with the books. "He is going to get the karma that he deserves."

"Mom," Ivy groans. "Promise me you won't do anything. He still thinks you're the reason his hair is falling out."

"What? It's a full moon, and I'm feeling feisty." She grins, not denying the accusation.

The front bell jingles.

Junie gasps, scandalized. "Your mom put a spell on him!"

Remy steps through the door in a windbreaker, his usual backwards ball cap tucked under one arm. He pauses, just in time to catch the tail end of the chaos. "Hey, Pumpkin," he says to Junie without missing a beat. "Who put a spell on who?"

The whole room cracks up.

"Oh, nothing," Lilith breezes, pulling Remy in for a hug.

"Well, hey, brother," Finn grins, raising his cider.

Even Ivy's smiling now, cheeks flushed, and Rowan's grip on her cup has finally loosened. Junie's giggling under a beanbag fort with her pizza next to her, finally eating her dinner.

Willa looks at me from behind the counter, a soft, amused little smile playing on her lips. Her eyes catch mine, and for a beat, everything else fades out.

And in that moment, with a full belly, full heart, in a bookstore lit with string lights and apple-scented candles, I feel something settle and click into place.

Remy catches my eye and gives me a nod. I tilt my head toward the side reading room. "Got a sec?"

I follow him into the quieter nook off the bookstore side, where a cozy circle arranges the chairs and they dim half the lights for later. He glances out the window, then looks back at me.

"If that offer still stands..." I start, rubbing my hands on my jeans. "The job and cabin. I think I'm ready to take you up on it."

Remy doesn't say anything at first. Just nods slowly, thoughtful. "You sure?"

"I am."

His mouth curves into a small, relieved smile. "Good. I meant what I said. I could use someone steady. Someone I can trust. I'm about to go into the busiest season of the year, and I already feel like I'm drowning under the weight of everything. I need you."

We shake on it. His grip's solid. Familiar.

"You know," he says, tapping his knuckles on the side of a bookshelf, "this town has a way of keeping the right people. Even the ones who try to run from it."

I glance back out toward the main room, where Willa's laughing at something Finn said, and Junie's showing Ivy her glittery witch hat.

"Yeah," I say. "I'm starting to figure that out."

*** * ***

It's late now. The moon hangs low and sleepy through the windowpanes, and the streets of Wisteria Cove are empty except for the glow of porch lights and streetlamps and the rustle of the leaves.

The bookstore is quiet, and the crowd's long gone, and I'm sweeping up confetti stars from a toddler's sparkly disaster while Willa straightens books behind the counter. Her cardigan's hanging off one shoulder now, and she's humming some soft melody that I don't recognize.

I don't want to leave. So, I just help her clean up.

She glances up. "You don't have to do that, you know."

"I'd rather be here than anywhere else tonight." I keep sweeping.

She laughs, low and tired and real. It lands in the center of my chest. She's finally letting me in.

I carry the bag of trash out back, where the air bites cooler than before. When I return, she's wiping down the tables, hair falling into her face. She pushes it back with her wrist, not realizing there's whipped cream on her sleeve.

"You've got—" I gesture. "Frosting? Cream? Something sticky and mysterious?"

She groans, inspecting her arm. "Fantastic. The hazard of the job."

"It's a good look on you," I say before I can stop myself.

Her eyes flick up to mine. She doesn't look away.

There's something different in her now, some invisible wall lowered an inch. Still guarded, but softer around the edges.

"I think the window by the front door is loose," she murmurs, walking past me toward the entrance.

"Which one?"

"That one," she points, "It rattles when it's windy. I think the latch is off."

I follow her to the front, where the old glass pane shivers faintly in its frame as the wind whispers down Main Street.

I kneel beside it and inspect the hardware. One screw has come loose. Easy fix, if I had my drill.

She disappears behind the counter and returns with one. Of course, she has tools. She's running this place and running it well. I'm impressed with how organized and methodical she is with this place and with everything she does.

When I crouch to fix it, she leans down beside me to watch. Close. Too close.

Her shoulder brushes mine, and my breath gets shallow. The scent of cinnamon and old paper clings to her sweater. Her hand lands lightly on the edge of the frame, fingers just inches from mine.

"How do you always know how to fix things?" she asks quietly.

I tighten the screw, heart pounding. "I don't. I just try."

She's watching me. Like she's trying to figure me out.

"I remember when your dad would always take the time to show you how to fix things," she says softly. "Once he even had me help. I was maybe ten? He let me hold the flashlight and told me I had steady hands."

I look up. She's smiling at the memory, but her eyes are wet around the corners.

"I miss them both," she admits, voice raw. "I miss knowing someone always had the answers."

"I know," I say, my throat catching as I swallow. "I miss them too."

She doesn't say anything for a moment. Then, so quietly I almost miss it. "It hurt so much, watching my mom try to stay strong after he was gone. Like...she was folding in on herself. Grieving and smiling at the same time. Like she didn't want us to see her fall apart."

I straighten up. We're still too close. Her shoulder touches my chest now. She doesn't move.

"Sometimes I think that's why I love fiction books so much," she says. "They're safe pain. You feel it, but you know it's not real. You know the ending's coming. You know someone wrote it, and it's not real pain, not usually, anyway."

"But real life?" I say.

She nods. "That hurts in a way that doesn't always get wrapped up."

God, I want to kiss her. I've missed her so much. And she's finally letting me see her. All of her. Not the careful shop owner or the stubborn Maren sister, but the woman underneath who's been carrying grief like a backpack full of bricks and still shows up every day with a book in hand and hope on her face. Still pours her heart out to this community and is the one who includes and loves everyone.

"I wish I could take all the pain away, Willa."

She looks at me then. Fully. And it's not guarded this time.

"I used to think you were the storm," she whispers. "But maybe instead, you're the anchor."

"What do you mean?" I ask softly, equally intrigued and afraid of her answer.

"You hurt me by leaving. But maybe you were always meant to come back."

My throat tightens. "You want the truth?"

She nods.

"I couldn't stay away if I tried," I say. "Not just because I grew up here. Not just because the docks are familiar or because fishing is all I really know. But because of you. Because every time I try to walk away from this town, it pulls me back with your voice, or your laugh, or the way you belong. I want to belong."

Her breath catches. "Tate..."

We're so close I can feel her heartbeat through her sweater. I could lean forward, just a few inches, and finally know what her lips taste like when she's not guarding them behind a wall of stubbornness.

She doesn't move. I don't either. But the tension is electric, thick, dizzying.

"You know," Lilith calls from the back room, "I think you both forgot I was still here."

We both whip around.

She stands in the doorway and grins from ear to ear as she shrugs on her jacket.

Willa groans and hides her face in my chest for half a second. I catch her waist instinctively, and her body fits mine like it's always meant to be there. "Mom, seriously?"

Lilith shrugs. "Just letting you know I was here before you all start kissing or whatever. I'll see myself out. So, I'm just going to head home. Love you! Night!"

She disappears out the front door with a small wave.

Willa looks up at me, cheeks flushed, eyes bright.

"Sorry," she murmurs. "She thinks she's the town's own fairy godmother the way she's playing this matchmaker game hard."

I grin. "She really is."

We finish cleaning in silence, but it's not awkward. It feels right.

She flicks off the last light except the fairy lights in the front window, and I carry the last trash bag out back while she finishes up.

When I come back in, she's curled up in one of the reading chairs with a blanket around her shoulders, a book open on her lap.

"Sit," she says softly, patting the chair next to her.

I do.

And for a long while, we just sit there, legs stretched out, the hum of late-night stillness pressing in.

"I'm scared," she finally says.

"Of what?"

She glances at me. "Of trying again. Of trusting."

I reach over, brush her pinky with mine. "This time I promise it's going to be okay."

And she nods. Not because she fully believes it yet. But because maybe...she wants to.

Chapter 15
Willa

When I left, I told myself you were better off
without me.
But that was a lie.
Because I'm not better off without you, Willa.
I'm nothing without you.
-Tate

The light hurts. Even with the curtains drawn and my quilt tucked up to my chin, the sliver of morning sun slicing through the curtains over the window feels like a blade straight to my skull. Cobweb's curled up beside me, purring like she's perfectly pleased with the world while my head is spinning. I try to shift, but the motion sends a fresh wave of nausea and pain crashing over me.

Damn it. Not today. There's too much to do. Book inventory, new display tables to set up, Rowan is working in her garden today, and Ivy's busy with her first day as an assistant to her real estate agent, so it's just me.

I force my eyes open. Then I hear the front door open downstairs. A pause. A long beat of silence. Then footsteps. Heavy and familiar. Tate. The creak of the floorboards as he crosses the shop. A faint click of the light switch.

Then his voice, low and steady, floating up. "Willa?"

I wince and try to sit up. "Up here," I manage, though it barely comes out above a whisper.

I hear him come up the ladder slowly. It groans under his weight, and when he reaches the top, his eyes land on me instantly. No teasing, or smirking. Just concern. "You're still in bed," he says softly, moving to the side of the room. "Lilith gave me the key and asked me to check on you. Someone called her and told her you weren't open yet."

I try to brush it off. "Just a migraine. I get them sometimes. It'll pass."

"Doesn't look like it's passing." He crouches beside the bed, eyes scanning my face like he's cataloging the damage. "You look like someone hit you with a freight train."

"Thanks," I croak.

He smiles, just barely. "Beautiful freight train."

His hand comes up, rough and cool against my overheated skin, his thumb brushing lightly along my cheekbone. The touch is soft, careful, like he's afraid I might break apart under his fingers. The coolness soothes some of the pounding heat in my head, easing the edge of the nausea.

I lean into it before I can stop myself, the simple comfort undoing me in ways I don't have the strength to fight.

I try to sit up straighter, but the effort sends another jolt of pain ripping through my skull, and I suck in a sharp breath. His hand steadies me instantly, thumb stroking once more, steady and grounding.

Tate frowns, the crease between his brows deepening. "That's it. Stay in bed."

"I'm fine. I just need—"

But before I can finish, he's already on his feet, moving with quiet efficiency. He crosses the room, grabs the orange prescription bottle from my nightstand, and shakes two pills into his palm after a brief study of the label. Then he pours a glass of water from the carafe by the bed and sets it gently in my hands.

"Here," he says, his tone leaving no room for argument. "Take these."

I swallow them obediently, the cool water soothing my raw throat. When I hand the glass back, his fingers brush mine, steady, grounding, unshakably calm in contrast to the storm pounding in my skull.

He eases me back against the pillows, tugging the blanket up over my shoulders with a tenderness that steals my breath. "Now sleep," he murmurs, his voice low and sure. "I'll be right here."

"But the store—"

"Will survive one day without you." He lowers his voice. "Willa...I've never seen you take a break. Not once since I've been back."

"I can do this by myself," I whisper, defensive even as my voice trembles.

His eyes soften. "But that doesn't mean you have to."

I look away, throat tight. "It's just easier when I do it."

He crouches down again. "Then let me be the one helping you handle it. Just today."

I don't say yes. But I don't argue again, either.

He squeezes my hand gently, then brushes a thumb along my wrist before standing. "Sleep. I've got it."

And somehow, I believe him, and I drift off again.

Time passes in strange little stretches...ten minutes here,

half an hour there, never long enough for a full dream, but just long enough to forget where I am and drift off.

The next time I surface, Cobweb is snuggled under my chin, and the faint smell of coffee drifts up.

There's laughter. Tate's voice. Deep and smooth, saying something about soup and how ridiculous any book is with a title longer than ten words.

Rowan laughs. "You're ridiculous. And that's not how alphabetizing works."

"Oh? Then why does *The Mysterious Midwife's Magical Moonlight Misadventures* belong under 'M'?"

More laughter. Mugs clinking. Footsteps, chatter, movement.

I can picture them downstairs, Tate behind the counter, probably making a mess of the coffee station. Rowan reorganizing the entire store like she always does. Ivy popped in, fresh-faced and anxious from her first day as a real estate agent's assistant for her lunch break.

"I wore heels," she says through a mouthful of what sounds like a sandwich. "They said business casual but didn't warn me about three flights of stairs and a listing with a rooster that apparently comes with the house and lives in the kitchen."

"Oh my god." Rowan cackles. "A *real* rooster?"

"Yeah, apparently his name is Harvey." She adds, "And he's a really rude rooster."

"Did it wear a little hat?" Tate asks.

I smile, eyes still closed, and let the sounds wash over me. They're holding it down for me. And I'm not panicking about it.

* * *

I wake again to the soft creak of the door. Tate slips in, quieter this time, a tray in his hands. He's carrying tea, soup, and toast.

He sets it down on my nightstand and crouches again. "Still alive?"

"Barely."

"You look better."

"Liar."

He grins. "Well, Cobweb looks rested and well-fed, so at least one of you's thriving."

I glance down at the kitten now sprawled across the blankets like she owns the bed. She blinks at me, yawn-purring.

"What time is it?" I ask.

"Little after one. Ivy is having her big real estate assistant debut. Rowan's rearranging the tea shelf. I made dozens of sales, and it was to tourists who said to tell you they will be back to get an autograph."

I laugh, "That's weird."

"Nope. You're an icon around here."

Despite everything, I laugh. It hurts, but it's worth it.

He watches me, expression soft. "You worried me this morning."

"I'm fine," I insist.

"You don't have to be," he says and then adds. "Not all the time."

I look at him, this man who showed up before I asked, stayed when I tried to push him away, and somehow knew exactly what I needed.

"You're kind of relentless," I whisper.

He shrugs. "Only with you."

That should scare me. But right now? It just...doesn't. It feels good. It feels like maybe I don't have to be so lonely anymore.

* * *

I'm curled up in the big armchair by the front window, blanket over my lap, hair still damp from my shower. I probably look tired, because I am, but I'm taking it slow. I wanted to get up and move around, maybe shelve some books, but Tate wouldn't stop hovering. He tried to get me to stay in bed. Like that was going to happen. Rowan finally convinced me to at least stay put in the chair.

Tate's behind the counter unpacking a delivery box, sorting books into neat stacks like it's some kind of delicate surgery. He thinks I don't notice, but his eyes keep flicking toward me every few minutes. And each time he looks, there's this...softness. Like I'm a page he's memorizing.

The bell over the door jingles, and in breezes Donna like the store is her stage and she's the main act. "I'm here to sign more books," she announces, brandishing a wrapped copy like it's a trophy. She leans toward Tate and stage-whispers, "And yes, before you ask, it's the best thing I've ever written. Again."

I smile, amused despite myself. "Used the good pen?"

"Obviously." She drops into the chair across from me like she's settling in for a show.

Then she swivels toward Tate, her eyes sparkling like she's about to light a match. "And how's the boat, Tate?"

Here we go.

"Still getting sold," he says.

"And the house?"

"Same."

She narrows her eyes, all mock-detective. "I heard you're going to work for my son at the tree farm."

The words hit me sideways. I blink, turning sharply toward Tate. "Wait—you are?"

He shifts a little under the weight of my stare, but he doesn't deny it.

For a moment, I can't find my voice. The thought barrels

through me that he's not leaving. Not disappearing out to sea for months at a time. No more vanishing into storms and silence. He'll be here in Wisteria Cove. Close enough that I could see him every day if I wanted to.

My stomach twists. Relief, sharp and sweet, rushes in first. Then something deeper, warmer, that I shove down before it can take root.

"You didn't think to mention this?" I manage, my voice lighter than I feel, though my heart is thudding wildly.

His eyes meet mine, steady, unreadable, and for a long beat I just...look at him. At the man who's haunted my memories for years, now tethering himself to this town.

"What are you going to do about the boat and house?" she asks, too casually. "You gonna fight it? Buy it?"

I snort into my tea, because this is what Donna does, interrogates people with a smile and somehow gets away with it.

Before he can answer, the front door swings open again. And the whole air in the store changes. I don't have to look at Tate to know he feels it too; his posture tightens like a rope pulled taut.

April Holloway—or whatever her new last name is. Tate's mother. And she's not alone. Randy is right behind her, along with two kids I've never seen before.

They all bring in the cold with them.

"Surprise," April singsongs. "Thought we'd come check the house and boat before everything is sold."

"Why didn't you call, Mom?" Tate asks, voice even.

"It's fine," she says with a shrug. "We're going to stay at the house for a bit. Used the spare key."

My spine stiffens. Used his spare key? Without asking? My hand tightens around my mug.

"It's your house," he says flatly.

"Oh, don't be dramatic," she waves him off. "It's just for a few days. We're already unpacked."

Randy chimes in, cheerful in that fake way that makes my skin crawl. "We even stocked the fridge. Real homey now. You don't have to live like a bachelor anymore."

Tate's jaw works, but his hands stay hidden behind the counter. I can tell he's holding himself together with every ounce of willpower.

"This place is quaint," Randy adds, scanning the room.

"It's Willa's," Tate says, steady as stone.

April's lip curls. "Willa? As in Willa Maren?"

The way she says my name makes something old and bitter twist in my stomach. I turn toward the window, mouth pressed tight, refusing to give her the satisfaction of a reaction.

"It's a great place," he says, looking straight at them. "It's a cornerstone of this town. And yes, it's Willa's. She built it herself. Every single customer who walks in here walks out better because of her."

The air freezes. I don't move. Can't. But heat blooms across my cheeks, not from embarrassment. From pride. From the way he says it like it's gospel.

Donna clears her throat, breaking the tension. "Well. I'll leave you to your little family ambush." And just like that, she's gone, probably plotting her next book with this exact scene.

April, Randy, and the kids linger a minute before finally drifting back out into the street. The bell jingles, and the store feels lighter again.

* * *

That night, Tate doesn't go home. He doesn't have to tell me why. The kids took his room. His mother took his space. And

149

the pieces of his father he has left, what little there are, are probably next.

He stretches out on the bookstore couch, Cobweb curled up on his chest like she's appointed herself guard dog. I bring him a blanket, draping it over his legs. He looks at me like I've just handed him something more than fabric.

"You didn't have to defend me," I say quietly. "But thank you. I'm sorry about your mom. She doesn't treat you right, Tate."

"I know. Is it okay if I crash here tonight?"

"Of course," I say. Then, before I can lose my nerve: "And Tate?"

"Yeah?"

"Thank you for all your help today. It means a lot."

His voice is low, sure. "Anytime."

* * *

Eventually, I climb down the ladder with two steaming mugs in my hands. Tate's still awake, stretched out on the rug, staring at the ceiling like he's waiting for the stars to rearrange themselves.

I set one mug down beside him and flop cross-legged onto the rug. My hoodie sleeves dangle over my hands. "Couldn't sleep either?"

He takes the mug, nodding. "Too quiet. Weird."

"Weird?" I laugh. "After months on a boat, you can't handle my bookstore silence?"

"Exactly." He sips. "Where's the seagulls? The diesel engines? The drunk guy singing sea shanties off-key?"

I grin. "If you want, I can hum *My Heart Will Go On* while you fall asleep."

He groans. "Please don't. I still haven't forgiven you for your *Titanic* phase."

I gasp. "Excuse me, every girl our age had a *Titanic* phase."

He smirks. "You cried for a week when you found out Leo smoked."

"Shut up," I mutter into my mug, cheeks heating. "At least I didn't go through a puka-shell necklace phase."

His jaw drops. "Hey. Those were cool."

"They were so not cool," I shoot back.

"That was one summer!" he protests, laughing now.

I grin, victorious. "One summer too many."

We fall into easy banter like that, trading old humiliations and laughing until Cobweb stirs, glaring at us from her spot on the blanket. Tate leans back on his elbows, watching me with a lopsided smile that makes my chest warm.

"You haven't changed," he says. "Still bossy. Still ruthless."

"Someone has to keep you humble," I fire back, though my lips curve against my will.

For a while, we just sip our tea, not heavy, not complicated. Just us. Laughing, remembering, catching up. The night folds in around us, easy and light, and for the first time in a long time, it feels like nothing's missing.

Chapter 16
Tate

The dock creaks beneath my boots as I settle on the edge, elbows resting on my knees, gaze fixed on the still, silvery reflection of the moon on the harbor.

It's early, just past six. The sun's barely thinking about rising, fog curling low around the boats like it's trying to keep them tucked in a little longer.

I need the quiet. It's been a few days since my mom and her family crashed the house, and I have nowhere to stay, so I've been staying at the bookstore. Not ideal, but better than being where I'm not wanted.

Need to breathe before I walk back into the house and deal with the circus inside. Randy, my mom, and the two kids think screaming is a valid form of communication, and their grandmother, who flew in last night, thinks microwaving fish is fine at any hour. She said, "When in Rome," as if eating fish sticks was something that had something to do with the east coast. I didn't bother explaining to her that frozen fish is eaten everywhere. If she wanted a fresh fish experience, the frozen fish sticks aren't it.

But whatever. She thought I was the maintenance man until one of Randy's kids told her I was April's brother. I politely explained that I was April's son, and she looked like she didn't believe me.

The water, at least, is calming and peaceful.

From the next dock over, I hear a grunt and the clatter of rope hitting deck.

Old Pete stands on the deck of his rusted-out trawler, squinting at me like I'm part of the landscape that doesn't quite belong.

"If you're gonna sit there all broody like some romance cover model," he calls out, "you might as well come give me a hand, Fabio."

I huff a laugh, standing. "I didn't realize helping you was mandatory."

"You're within thirty feet of my boat. That's consent."

I jump down and make my way to his side. The deck's still slick with dew, but Pete moves across it like a man twenty years younger.

"The lines are tangled," he grumbles. "Damn fool college kid who helped me last week knew nothing. Nearly tied the boat to itself like a goddamn pretzel."

Together we get to work. I fall into the rhythm without thinking, checking the pulleys, re-coiling the lines, tightening a few bolts. Pete watches without hovering, only offering a grunt or the occasional snarky mutter when I do something he likes.

"You always did know your way around a boat," he says after a bit. "Even when you were a scrawny thing with a mop of hair and no idea how to keep your damn shoes tied."

"Still have trouble with the laces," I joke.

He smirks. "That checks out."

We work in companionable silence for a while. It's easy with Pete and always has been. He says exactly what he means, then shuts up about it. No games, passive aggression, or bullshit. I appreciate a straight shooter.

When we finish, he claps me on the back. "Now, I'd say that's worth a coffee, wouldn't you?"

I nod, following him down the dock. "As long as you're buying."

He snorts. "You wish."

The Driftwood Diner is already buzzing when we get there, the usual blue-checkered curtains pulled open, the scent of bacon and fried blueberry muffins thick in the air. We don't stay, just grab two coffees to go and a couple of breakfast sandwiches that may or may not still be warm depending on how fast Old Pete walks back to his bench by the wharf. And yes, it's literally his bench. Has his name on it and everything. This town doesn't mess around when it comes to taking care of its own. The town respects Old Pete, who has been the harbor master for a long time. He looks out for people, and he cares.

We sit, the wood damp beneath us, the harbor stretching out in front of us like a postcard.

He takes a sip, sighs. "You know...I'm proud of the man you've become."

My grip on the coffee tightens slightly. I nod, but I say nothing.

"And I know your dad would be too," Pete continues. "I know she's your mom, but April wasn't even nice to your pops when he was alive. It's kinda hard for a zebra to change its stripes, son. I mean that in the most loving way. Sometimes we get dealt a hard hand."

I stare straight ahead.

"You were young," he says gently. "Probably don't remember it all, but your dad put up with a lot from her. She hated he went out fishing. Hated that he did that for a living. Thought he should've worked someplace else and played it safe. But he loved the water more than anything. And she hated that most of all. Sometimes it didn't seem like she even liked him much or wanted him to be happy."

The words hit somewhere deep, somewhere I've locked up and left dusty for years. I remember the fights. Not the words, but the tones. The volume. The way dishes would clatter in the sink, and doors would slam, and I'd sit at the table pretending to read a cereal box like I didn't hear a damn thing.

I thought that was just life, and that everyone lived like that. Walking as if on eggshells, knowing silence wasn't peace, just a pause between storms.

Thinking it was normal. And now I realize it's not.

I don't answer Pete right away, except to nod in agreement. I know he's right.

Instead, I take a sip of coffee, watch the sun finally break through the fog, and think about the Maren house and how it wasn't like that there.

It wasn't quiet like someone was holding their breath. It was warm, cluttered, full of half-finished projects and the smell of whatever Lilith was cooking in the oven and laughter coming from the next room. Even when Willa and her sisters bickered, it never felt like the world was cracking apart. It felt like...life. Normal. Messy, but good.

Sitting at their kitchen table while Willa scribbled in a notebook and Rowan braided her own hair and Ivy sang off-key in the other room...I just breathed easier there. I remember their dad inviting me out to the garage with him while he worked on their cars. He'd sneak me ice cream cups from the freezer out there before dinner and say in his thick New England accent, "Don't tell your mother."

"Guess I thought that was normal," I say finally, voice low. "The yelling and tension. Thought that's just what family looked like."

Pete shakes his head slowly. "Kid, that wasn't normal."

He's right. It was survival. And I think I was living in survival mode for so long that I didn't even recognize it for what it was. I just knew I didn't want to live like that.

He lets it settle and doesn't push. That's the thing about Pete. He'll call you out, sure, but he won't push it.

"You ever think about what you want now?" he asks after a beat.

I glance over.

He's not talking about boats. Or work. He's talking about *life*. About home. I think about Willa. About the way she sat in that armchair yesterday, blanket over her lap, hair a little damp, eyes soft as she watched the shop come alive with me and her sisters helping her. The way she smiled when she thought no one was looking.

I think about the bookstore. And how it already feels more like home than the place I grew up in ever did.

"Yeah," I say. "I'm starting to."

Pete grunts. "Good. 'Bout time."

We sit there a while longer, sipping coffee, watching the boats rock gently in their slips.

The fog burns off and everything turns slow and golden. Somewhere down the wharf, I hear someone playing a harmonica out of tune.

The town's waking up. And for once, I'm not just watching it like an outsider. I'm part of it.

* * *

The bell over the bookstore door jingles, soft and familiar. Feels a little like walking into a dream I didn't know I wanted until I was living it. I'm avoiding going back to the house as much as possible. My mom has been sitting at the kitchen table over there poring over lists and things to sell. It looks like she's selling anything not nailed down. She even asked me if I wanted to keep my bed or not.

Willa's at the front table, sorting through a box of new books, hair pulled back, face a little flushed, but brighter. Healthier. There's color in her cheeks again. Her eyes lift the second the door closes behind me and she grins. "There you are. I was thinking about putting your face on a milk carton."

I hold up the paper bag. "Brought you a breakfast sandwich. Pete made me stop at Driftwood. Pretty sure I'm part of the official old man morning coffee crew now."

She walks toward me, arms still wrapped around herself, until she's close enough to reach, and then she wraps her arms around my waist and presses her cheek to my chest like it's the most natural thing in the world.

I blink and pull her in close, breathing in her shampoo or soap scent that smells really good.

"Thanks," she murmurs. "For yesterday and...everything."

"Of course," I say into her hair. "Always."

She pulls back but doesn't go far. Just enough to meet my eyes. "You sleep okay?" she asks.

"Better than I would've at the house. Thanks for letting me crash here."

Her brow furrows. "How's it going with...them?"

I shrug. "As good as it's gonna get."

There's a pause, heavy with unspoken things.

"Can I crash here again tonight?" I ask.

Her answer's immediate. "Of course. Stay as long as you need to stay. Cobweb doesn't mind."

And I don't miss it, how her eyes brighten at the idea. How her voice softens. How her hands fidget like she's trying to tuck her excitement into the folds of her cardigan and pretend it's not there.

"Just Cobweb won't mind?" I tease.

"I don't mind, either," she says softly.

"Want help with those?" I nod to the open box beside her.

She nods, and just like that, we fall into step.

We unpack the books together, shoulder to shoulder, dust jackets brushing our knuckles every few minutes. She reads off titles, sorts them by genre, and passes me stacks to shelve.

It's quiet work, but I like it. Cobweb naps on a windowsill. Somewhere outside, the wind knocks a few dried leaves against the glass.

"This really is the heartbeat of Wisteria Cove," I murmur.

Willa glances over. "You think so?"

"I know so."

She blushes, but she doesn't argue.

We keep working.

"Ivy's been around more," Willa says after a bit, her voice dropping into something gentler. "She's a realtor's assistant now. She has to help them prep the house to sell."

I slide a novel into its spot and pause. "Well, someone has to do it."

"She hates it," Willa admits. "Says she wishes she could just walk dogs for a living."

I smirk. "Honestly? Same. What happened to the doggy daycare job she had?" I ask.

"They cut her hours, and she wanted to take the real estate job. Her stupid boyfriend made fun of the doggy daycare gig. He's a piece of work," she mutters.

I don't like this guy. I've heard enough to know he's a jerk.

"She's good with animals, though. But real estate would be good for her, Ivy could charm the bark off a tree if she had to. She just feels bad that she's selling *your* house."

"Well...hopefully someone buys it who wants to make it an actual home," I say quietly.

She softens, gives me a smile like it's just for me. "She won't say it, but she's doing it for us," Willa says. "We're trying to get the building next door. She wants to maybe get her real estate license, but you know how she is. She's had a lot of jobs."

"The one right next door?" I ask, pointing to the left of the building.

She nods. "If we can buy it, Rowan will turn it into Salt & Root. We'd finally have enough space for an herbal workshop, a yoga studio on the top floor, and an apothecary shop. And maybe a little tea bar."

I glance at the wall between the shops, trying to picture it. "That would be great."

"I hope so," she says, and there's a flicker of hope in her voice. Fragile but determined.

I nod. "It will. The three of you make magic. Everyone in this town knows it."

She looks at me, really looks at me, and for a second I feel like I'm the only man in the world.

"You always say the exact right thing," she says.

I laugh. "I've said plenty of wrong ones."

"Not to me. It only hurts me when you don't say what you want to say and just leave."

Later, Ivy shows up, hair in a ponytail, wearing a blazer that's two sizes too big and sneakers with laces that don't match. She drops her bag and slumps into the reading nook like a woman who has just finished hiking up a mountain.

"I swear to God," she groans. "If I hear the words 'charming curb appeal' one more time, I will personally set the curb on fire."

Willa laughs and slides her a cup of tea. "Rough day?"

"Someone made me explain what a water heater is. Another person asked if the ghosts were *included* with the house." She lifts her head, sees me. "Hi, Tate. I see you're still pretending not to live here."

"I'm working my way up to full-time squatter," I say.

She lifts the tea in salute. "Solid plan."

"Any buyers seriously interested?"

Ivy sighs and nods. "Yup. Lucky me."

"You're good at it, Ivy," Willa says. "You really are."

"I want to be walking a golden retriever named Pretzel right now," Ivy mutters.

"Still time," I say, glancing at my watch.

She snorts. "That's the dream."

We chat for a bit, light stuff. Ivy rants about real estate. Willa teases her. I stay quiet and soak in the laughter, the teasing, the rhythm of this strange little trio of women who've seen more than their share of heartbreak and still show up, anyway.

Eventually, Ivy heads out, grumbling about back-to-back showings tomorrow. The shop is quiet again.

Willa slides another book into place, then looks at me. "Thanks for helping."

I shrug. "I like it here."

Her smile is slow, steady. "I do, too."

"Do you think Ivy will ever find what makes her happy?" I ask.

She nods. "Yes, I do. She's been stuck with bozo Derek, who has led her on, used her, and it's been hard to watch. Everyone saw it but her."

We stay after closing, sorting the last of the books in the quiet. At one point, she sits on the floor, and I sit beside her. Neither of us moves.

"It's weird," she says softly. "Letting someone in like this. Not just in the store. In the quiet moments. In the places I don't usually share."

I don't speak. I just reach over, slide my hand into hers.

She lets me. And that's all the answer I need.

Chapter 17
Willa

The truth is, I still talk about you like you're mine.
I catch myself...
and then I realize I need you to be mine again.
—Tate

I t's so peaceful in the shop that it makes you want to stay forever. The bell above the door jingles softly each time the fall wind nudges it, and the scent of cinnamon and old books drifts in lazy waves from the candles I lit an hour ago. Rowan's behind the apothecary display shelf, restocking bath soaks and humming to herself.

I'm restocking the front table with fall favorites, witchy reads, and cozy small-town romances when the door opens again.

And just like that, the atmosphere shifts. Randy and April and their two kids barrel in like a hurricane. The kids scatter immediately, one darting toward the puzzle shelf, one climbing onto the reading nook bench with muddy boots, the littlest grabbing for the stack of free bookmarks near the register like they're party favors.

My jaw tightens. "Hey there," I say, forcing a smile as I come around the table. "Let me know if you need help finding anything."

April doesn't acknowledge me. She strolls around like she owns the place, oversized sunglasses pushed up on her head, pumpkin spice latte in hand bearing a logo from a chain coffee shop on the edge of town. Randy's trailing behind, already swiping on his phone like he's doing something important. He mutters, "Kids, don't break anything," but never looks up.

The oldest child, probably nine or ten, immediately starts unzipping every single pencil pouch on the novelty shelf. The youngest, who looks around seven or eight, is now aggressively spinning the book carousel. I glance at Rowan, who meets my gaze with a quiet *oh hell no* expression and slowly steps around to shut it down with a scary look and hands on her hips.

April walks over to the counter, not to buy anything, of course, but to lean against it and scroll through her phone while sipping her drink.

I clear my throat and step over to the table her youngest just knocked half a display off of. I crouch to gather up the scattered books.

"So," April finally says flatly, not looking up from her phone. "Didn't know you and your family were still around."

I smile with my teeth but not my eyes. "Yep. Still here."

"Hmm." Her tone makes it sound like a personal failure.

The eldest kid walks by, drops one of our shop pencils on the floor without noticing, then grabs a free water cup from the dispenser we keep near the door and *spills half of it* on the doormat. He walks away. Doesn't even blink.

I grab a towel from behind the counter and mop it up, one hand clenched around the fabric like it might keep me from screaming.

April still does nothing.

Randy's wandered to the back now, flipping through a thriller novel he's definitely not going to buy. He turns a page loudly and sighs.

Rowan walks over to the fall display and steps into view beside me, eyebrows raised in solidarity. She's got her hands clasped in front of her like she's actively resisting the urge to hex someone.

The smallest kid now has a bookmark in her mouth and attempts to put it back on the shelf. Gross.

I bite my lip.

April finally glances up at the kids. "Randy," she calls, her voice sharp and flat. "We're leaving soon."

No one responds. No one stops. Fifteen more minutes of pure chaos. Fifteen minutes of grabbing bookmarks off the floor, putting tea tins back on shelves, trying to gently stop a kid from climbing onto a display table without sounding like a villain in my *own bookstore*.

Fifteen minutes of April pretending not to notice the havoc, of Randy muttering to himself and putting creases in book spines. If I had my way he'd go straight to hell for that one. What kind of animal does that?

When she finally decides it's time to go, April rests her sunglasses back onto her nose, spins on a heel, and says, "Let's go."

Randy groans and shuffles forward. The kids follow, one of them kicking over the basket of rolled-up reading maps on the way out.

I don't say a word.

I just bend down and start picking them up, one by one.

April pauses at the door and looks back at me. The glare is subtle, but there's something in it. Like she wants me to know she saw the mess and doesn't care. Like the whole thing amused her.

They leave without buying a single thing. Didn't even say thank you for the free water. Just left the half-empty cups everywhere.

The bell jingles as the door swings shut.

Silence again.

Rowan exhales dramatically and flops against the counter like she just survived a battle.

"What just happened," she says flatly, "was a crime."

I laugh, but it's hollow. "You think the ghost of Wisteria Cove could haunt them a little?"

"Oh, she's already brewing something," Rowan mutters, grabbing the broom. "You good?"

"Yeah." I sweep a handful of bookmarks back into their basket, picking up the soggy one and putting it in the trash. "Just tired."

"You're too nice, you know that?"

"I didn't *do* anything."

"Exactly."

I give her a look.

She sighs. "You shouldn't have to put up with that in your own shop."

I don't say anything, because if I do, I might say something I'll regret. Like how I saw April watching me while I cleaned up after her kids. Or how I swear there was a flicker of satisfaction in her eyes. I know that kind of silent cruelty too well. I saw her do that to Tate for years. And it got worse after our dads went missing.

I just keep working. Because that's what I do.

Rowan steps over and rests a hand on my arm. "You want me to ward the doorway with salt, rosemary, and lavender?"

I crack a real smile this time. "Tempting."

She grins. "One day, people are gonna understand this place isn't just some cozy Instagram backdrop. This shop means something. And you? You're the reason it runs. You make it magic."

I glance around at the soft lamplight glowing over shelves, the candle still flickering at the register, the little jar of fresh mums by the scone samples.

Yeah. This place *does* mean something. Even if people like April don't see it. Even if they never will.

"Thanks, Row," I whisper.

She nods, stepping back and grabbing the now slightly soggy "Autumn Staff Picks" sign. "Let's make this look cute again."

I grab the cinnamon broom hanging on the wall and sweep up the muddy bootprints with one long exhale.

Tomorrow will be better. It always is.

* * *

The weather's perfect in that golden, early-fall way when the sun is warm on my shoulders, the air crisp with just a whisper of cinnamon in the breeze. Wisteria Cove glows in September and October. Main Street is all pumpkins and dried cornstalks, little scarecrows guarding doorways, tables draped in plaid tablecloths. It should feel peaceful.

But I'm fuming. Not at my mom, who's currently chatting with the florist about eucalyptus bundles for her to dry. Not at Ivy, who offered to cover the shop this morning so I could spend time with my mom.

But at *them.*

I spot them from halfway down the street. Randy in that

green fleece pullover, hands shoved in his pockets like he owns the sidewalk, walking two steps ahead like the world should keep pace. April's behind him, phone in one hand, gesturing like she's recapping some dramatic episode of her life for an audience. And their kids trail behind, looking bored, loud, and wild as ever, chewing gum and swatting at each other like no one's watching.

They remind me of the Wormwoods from *Matilda*.

They pass right by Tate, who's standing near Remy's truck, talking to Finn and unloading wooden items that Finn makes to sell. He pauses, glances up when they pass, and for just a second, I see it.

The flicker in his expression and the way his posture shifts. I don't miss the way he tries not to show it hurts. But I see it. Hell, I can even feel it for him from over here.

April barely even glances at him and doesn't acknowledge him. Randy glances at him and then off again as if he doesn't even know him. Nothing more. And that? *That's it.* Something inside me snaps. Because he's right there. Solid and good and quietly trying his best. And they don't see it. Or worse, they *do,* and they ignore him anyway.

No. Absolutely not.

"Mom," I say, setting down the eucalyptus bundle. "I'll be right back."

Lilith doesn't even ask. Just watches me go with that slow, knowing nod of hers.

I stride across the sidewalk, fast and sure, because I've been waiting to do this for years.

"April," I call out, sharp enough that her heels pause on the sidewalk.

She turns, one eyebrow already lifted, her mouth curling around a condescending smirk like she *expected* me to break. "Willa."

Randy glances at me, then away. Of course.

"I've been quiet," I say, loud enough for the town square to catch a little stillness. "I've been polite. But today? I'm done with polite."

April lowers her sunglasses. "Excuse me?"

"You heard me."

Remy shifts beside Tate and mutters something under his breath. Finn lets out a long whistle, low and drawn out. A few folks at the café table turn their heads.

"You come into my shop and let your kids tear it up," I say, my voice steady and loud, "and you don't say a word. You treat Tate like he's a stranger, as if he's *nothing*. Like he didn't lose the same person you lost."

Her face flattens. "Shut your mouth. What I do is none of your business, Willa Maren."

"It is when you drag it through this town and when you *hurt* him. And it is *definitely* my business when you treat someone like they don't matter."

April's nostrils flare, but before she can speak again, she looks past me. Her gaze locks on something, and her lips twist in a cruel snarl.

I don't even have to turn to know what she sees. Tate. Standing behind me now. Watching. Shoulders rigid, eyes unreadable.

"We're not friends with *them*," April practically spits, venom coating every syllable. "This is exactly why, Tate. *This*. This is why we can't have a relationship. Because you're friends with *them*. With *her*."

She jabs a finger toward me like I'm the reason the world turned sideways.

And that's when Tate speaks, his voice a warning. "Mom..."

But she's not done.

"This is why I can't trust you," she snaps. "You *always*

choose everyone else over your mother. You run off, and you still practically worship *him*."

He stares at her, lips parted as if he's about to speak, but no words come.

She shakes her head. "You don't get to be the victim here. You're the one who walked away."

Tate looks stricken. Like she reached in and twisted the one place still sore.

But before I can say a word, a second voice cuts through the air, calm, clear, and lethal.

"You know what, April?" my mom says and steps up beside me, sunlight glowing in the white streaks of her hair, arms crossed over her chest. "I understand grief," she says, voice low but firm. "I do, and I know what it's like to lose someone and want to build a wall around yourself so nothing else can ever hurt again."

April flinches but doesn't speak.

"What I *don't* understand," Lilith continues, "is how you took that grief and twisted it into something cruel. How you threw away the people who loved you most. How you looked at Tate, this good, kind, *loyal* kid, and decided *he* was the villain in your story."

The silence is thick now. Even the kids fall still.

"Tate *matters*," Lilith says, taking a step forward. "He matters to *us*. To Wisteria Cove. To me. So if you can't see that, if all you're here to do is pick at old wounds and cash out what you think you're owed, then do us all a favor."

She tilts her head slightly. "Go back to Florida."

April's face goes pale.

Lilith's voice softens, not gentle, but final. "You sell your house, get your money, and then you leave. But if you're not going to treat him right, or put in any effort, then leave him *alone*. He deserves better."

April doesn't say a word. She pivots on her heel and walks away, calling for her kids. Randy follows, face unreadable.

And just like that, the storm moves on.

My mom lays a hand on Tate's arm and goes back to her table, giving him a minute.

I turn toward Tate. His eyes are locked on the sidewalk, jaw tight. He looks like he's holding it all in by sheer will.

I touch his hand, gentle. "Hey." He lifts his gaze to mine. And I see it there. The grief and hurt. But also, gratitude. Relief. The kind of relief when someone finally sees you.

"I didn't need you guys to do that," he murmurs.

"I know," I whisper. "But we did it anyway. It's what we do for the people that we care about."

He lets out a slow breath.

Then he smiles. Just a little.

And somehow, it feels like everything is going to be all right.

Chapter 18
Tate

I pull into the gravel lot just before eight, tires crunching slowly as the fog lifts over the Bennett Tree Farm. The air smells like pine needles and damp earth. I'm nervous but excited to be here. Fishing, I know, but I know nothing about trees. I do love working outside, though, and I love that feeling when you put in a long day and feel exhausted. Looks like I can get that working here.

Remy's place sits fifteen minutes outside of town and looks like a damn postcard. Not the cheesy kind, but the kind you keep in a drawer even after the holidays are long over. Like the Hallmark movies that people love this time of year. This place could double as a filming location.

Acres of perfectly spaced evergreens stretch across the land like an army of green, their branches dusted with early frost. Wreaths hang from old wooden posts, waiting to be bought and either shipped or brought home and fluffed. What looks like a freshly painted red and white barn stands proudly at the end of the parking lot, its roof lined with string lights that haven't been plugged in yet but still manage to shimmer in the early morning sun.

This is it. This is where Christmas lives. I can see why Remy stays so busy. This place is magical. It's also a huge operation, so it makes sense that he needs more help.

I spot him halfway down one aisle of firs, already deep in work, gloves on, saw over one shoulder, and a scowl like the trees offended him. He's all business. Grumpy and stoic like he would rather eat nails than ask for help.

So I get why asking me was a big deal; he must mean it. And I'd never let Remy down. He and Finn have always been like brothers to me. We've been friends since elementary school.

He straightens when he sees me, brushing pine needles off his flannel and offering a tired but genuine smile that says *Thank God you showed up,* even if he doesn't put it into so many words.

"Tate," he says, exhaling like he's relieved to see me. "Man, I'm so damn glad you're here."

I grin. "You sound surprised."

"I thought you might change your mind and run for the seas," he says, clapping me on the shoulder. "But you didn't. And I seriously owe you one. Or ten."

"Don't get sappy on me yet," I tease, falling into step beside him. "We haven't even made it past the first day. You might give me the boot when you realize I know nothing about trees."

He laughs, the sound low and honest.

"You weren't kidding when you said this place was big," I add, glancing over the rows of evergreens stretching toward the horizon.

He nods, eyes scanning the land like it's both a blessing and a burden. "Yeah. It's beautiful. And totally kicking my ass."

"Well," I say, rolling up my sleeves. "Let's get our asses kicked together. Tell me about it."

"We sit on about thirty acres. Fifteen in trees, ten in nursery stock. The rest are barns, prep sheds, and loading zones. Cabins are up that way." He juts his chin toward the lane. "Got a little farm stand shop we have year-round. Donna's idea. People like their snacks while they wander. It's becoming a family tradition to come here. Some people come up here every weekend just to get a couple of dozen cider donuts."

I raise an eyebrow. "That sounds good."

Remy scowls again. "It's annoying, is what it is. We sell more cider donuts than trees some weekends. Then we move onto hot cocoa and other treats, if I can hire some more help for that."

We pass by rows of baby pines, each one no taller than Junie, and I notice little hand-painted signs tucked into the earth.

Junie's Grove – DO NOT TOUCH – unless you're me or Dad.

I smile. "She has her own grove?"

"Of course she does. Kid's the boss around here. I just work here." He laughs.

He's not wrong. Even at five, Junie runs the place as if she owns it. But this morning, she looks less CEO and more stir-crazy. She's still on the porch swing, dragging her unicorn slipper in the gravel, watching us like she's waiting for something to happen, and not in a good way.

Remy notices, too. His shoulders drop just a little.

"She's been struggling without her mom," he mutters, tugging on a pair of worn leather gloves. "The upcoming holidays make it worse."

"She misses her mom?" I ask carefully.

He shrugs, but his jaw tightens. "This time of year is hard. Every year, she promises to visit, but she never shows up. A lot of empty promises."

I shake my head, and we work in silence for a while, trimming some of the lower branches off trees marked for early harvest, hauling piles of cuttings to the discard pile. The cold works its way through my flannel, but it's not unpleasant. Not when the sun peeks through the trees and the whole place lights up gold and green.

The trees stretch on for what feels like forever. Remy explains them all to me, and I know I won't remember everything, but I've got most of it. Fraser firs, blue spruces, and white pines, each with their own tags, are carefully logged and cataloged. The nursery section is tucked behind a weathered picket fence, full of pots and planters of winter berry, holly, and rosemary. Wind chimes made of copper and pinecones sway from the beams of the prep shed. Everything is organized chaos, a blend of workhorse and wonderland.

I can see why Remy fights to keep it running. It's not just a business. It's a legacy for him and Junie.

"Wasn't this your uncle's?" I ask, pausing beside one of the larger trees.

"Yeah. Uncle Carl. He ran it for decades until cancer got him suddenly four years ago." Remy's voice is quieter now. "He was here one day, gone a few months later. Didn't have kids. Left it to me and Finn. Finn didn't want it, so I bought him out. I didn't know the first thing about running a tree farm, but..."

"But you're doing a great job," I finish. "I mean...look at this place. It's incredible, man."

He shrugs. "When I took it on, Junie's mom had just left. I needed something solid. This was it. She wanted nothing to do with the tree farm or us."

We work a while longer, and even though we don't say much, I feel the weight of it, the pride, the grief, the fierce love that got built into the dirt of this place. Every nail in the barn, every plank on the farmhouse porch, Junie's fingerprint on every part of it—it's all part of Remy's fight to build something lasting for him and her. I love that for him. This place is special.

Just as I'm about to ask if he wants help organizing the wreath station, a familiar voice calls out from the driveway.

"Well, if it isn't my two favorite lumberjacks," Donna says, stepping out of her car with a big tote bag slung over her shoulder and lipstick already perfectly applied. Tucked behind her ear is a pencil, which I've noticed she usually has.

Junie bolts up from the swing like her little butt was spring-loaded. "Nana!"

She runs to meet her, unicorn slippers flapping wildly, and I swear Remy's whole face softens at the sound of her laugh.

Donna scoops Junie into her arms and twirls her in a little circle. "You ready for our girls' day, sugarplum? I brought the glitter glue and the Christmas cookie sprinkles. And guess what I rented?"

"*Frozen!*"

"No, something better. *Practical Magic*. I think it's time."

Remy groans. "She's five, Mom."

Donna waves him off. "Emotionally, she's thirty."

"Whose fault is that?" He grumps. "You let her do whatever she wants."

Junie wiggles in her arms. "Are we gonna make mermaid cookies again?"

"You bet your frosted sugar cookie we are, Juniebug."

Remy meets his mom's eyes with the kind of expression that says *Do not encourage her*, but I just grin and lean on the rake I'm holding.

"Sounds like you need a night off, son. Go have some fun." Donna says to Remy.

"Please, I have so much to do here," Remy mutters, handing over Junie's overnight bag.

Donna plants a kiss on his cheek. "You boys don't forget to have fun."

And just like that, they're gone, driving off toward the edge of town in Donna's Subaru, Junie talking animatedly to her.

Remy exhales as if he has just survived a natural disaster. "I don't know how she did it, having two of us."

"Magic," I say. "Clearly runs in the family."

He huffs a laugh, surprising both of us.

For a minute, we stand there, watching the wind blow through the trees and listening to the distant sound of a bell chime from the barn. The tree farm is quiet again. Peaceful.

"I'm glad I'm here," I say finally, voice low.

Remy looks at me. "Yeah?"

I nod. "You're building something real here. That's rare. You need the help. And I needed the reminder."

"Of what?"

"That there's still good stuff left," I say. "Even after all the shit. Especially after."

He doesn't say anything right away. Just nods once, then jerks his head toward the prep shed. "Come on. Let's fire up the baler. Got a shipment of wreaths going out tomorrow."

And just like that, we're back to work. But something's shifted.

Out here, among the trees and the frost and the scent of cedar, it feels like I've walked into a new chapter. One where the past isn't the only thing that defines me. One where maybe, just maybe, I can build something of my own.

* * *

By the time I leave the tree farm, my shoulders ache in a way that feels earned. My flannel's damp with sweat, and my hands smell like sap and sawdust, the scent working its way into my skin like it wants to stay, and I want it to.

It's quieter out here in Wisteria Cove than I remembered.

The road curves like old memories, and part of me wants to keep driving past the harbor, then the bookstore and past the weight of everything waiting for me.

But I promised myself I'd stop running. So I turn toward home. Or...what used to be home.

The house sits as it always has, on Main Street and back a bit, half-hidden behind overgrown hedges and a rusted iron fence that leans a little more each year. The house is a grand old thing if you squint. Victorian bones with peeling paint and too many windows that creak in the wind.

It was home for a long time. Until she showed back up with new kids, a new husband, and a real estate agent on speed dial. I park on the street and sit in the truck for a beat too long, letting the engine tick and cool while my hands stay on the wheel. My jaw's tight. My stomach's tighter. I don't want to go in there. I haven't talked to her since she yelled at me in the town square. I was shocked when Lilith and Willa stood up for me. But I wasn't surprised. With my mom, there's nothing I can ever seem to do to make things right with her.

The porch light's already on even though the sun hasn't finished setting, casting long shadows across the cracked steps. I told myself I'd just crash at the bookstore until I figure things out. One night. Maybe two. But stepping through the door is like stepping back into a version of my life I never want to remember.

The house smells like potpourri and lemon polish, like someone's trying too hard to erase the ghosts. There are open suitcases spilling out by the hall table, shoes scattered like land-mines, and voices upstairs, high-pitched and loud.

I head for the back staircase with a plan to avoid the noise and *them.*

My old room is at the top, small, tucked under the eaves, still painted that god-awful navy blue I picked out in middle school when I thought I was cool. The walls are bare now, but the closet still holds the same busted door, and the window still overlooks the backyard where Willa used to throw pinecones at me when she wanted to get my attention to go do something fun.

I open the closet, searching for the flannel-lined sleeping bag I think I left behind years ago. And that's when I see it. A shoebox on the top shelf. I pull it down without thinking; the cardboard is soft with age, its edges frayed. Inside: photographs. Notes. Ticket stubs from the county fair. A dried daisy tied with string. And near the bottom is a picture of us.

Me, Willa, Ivy, and Rowan, crammed together on the beach during one of those rare perfect fall days. I was sixteen, maybe seventeen. Willa's nose is sunburned. My arm's around her shoulders, and she's holding my hand like it's nothing. But it was *everything*. My throat tightens. This is what I'm fighting for. Not the house. Not the boat. *Her*. I want to make her proud of me.

Before I can spiral any further, I hear footsteps on the stairs.

And then...her voice. "Really, Tate, what are you doing here?"

I exhale slowly and close the box. "Hi, Mom. Didn't realize I couldn't come home or be in my own room."

She breezes in wearing a cream blouse and navy slacks with way too much perfume that enters the room even before she does. She's holding a clipboard as if it's practically a weapon.

"I made a list," she says, handing it to me. "The realtor said the siding needs pressure washing. The front stairs should probably be repaired...again. And the faucet in the downstairs bathroom is still dripping. Honestly, I don't know what you've been doing all these years."

My jaw flexes. I take the paper, glance at it, then set it down on the desk. "Yeah, I'm not doing any of that."

Her brows shoot up. "Excuse me?"

"I'm not your handyman, Mom. I'm your son. And I've paid to maintain this house for five years. Taxes, insurance, the plumber, the HVAC guy. Every damn thing. And now you're selling it. With barely any notice, and certainly no reward or even a thank you. So...yeah. I'm not doing that just so you can take everything away from me that Dad worked hard for."

She blinks as if she's shocked at my response. Like she expected the quiet kid who always did what she told him to do, not the man who's finally done playing polite.

"You knew this day would come," she says coolly. "It's not like this house was ever going to be yours."

I turn and she follows me down the stairs and out onto the porch. I want to just leave and never come back, but I can't.

"No, you're right. I did know," I say, standing, voice steady. "But I took care of it for you. But you didn't care. You just come here with your new family and treat me like the guest."

She opens her mouth to argue, but something behind me catches her attention.

I turn and look at the street.

Lilith Maren is walking by the front hedge, carrying a paper bag. She sees us and slows just a little, gaze landing on my mother like she's surprised she's still here.

Lilith's wearing a long cardigan the color of burned sugar and boots with a heel sharp enough to kill a man. Her hair's pinned up, messy and perfect, and when she sees the look on my mother's face—part confusion, part disdain—she smiles.

Not a kind smile. A *beautifully terrifying* one. "Well," Lilith says lightly, stopping by the gate, staring up. "Good to see you, too, April."

My mother narrows her eyes.

"You're glowing," Lilith adds sweetly. "Stress must suit you."

I nearly choke.

Lilith tips her head toward me. "Tate, darling. I'm making pumpkin bread with sea salt caramel glaze. Come by if you need a snack or a place to hide."

"Thanks," I say, voice rough. "I might take you up on that."

She nods once, then continues down the sidewalk, the scent of her passing, something warm and woodsy, lingering in the air like smoke after a spell.

My mother exhales sharply. "She's always been so conniving."

"She's kind," I correct.

April turns back to me, clipboard forgotten. "You always did like that family more."

"I always enjoyed feeling *seen and wanted*," I shoot back.

It lands like a slap. She says nothing.

I tuck the box under my arm. I don't need the house. I have a fresh start here.

Chapter 19
Willa

Every time I think I've got you figured out, you surprise me. And I love that more than I can explain.

-Tate

I don't *mean* to hover by the window, wiping the same spot on the counter for at least four minutes now. My eyes dart up every few seconds like a total obsessed weirdo. Ivy would say I'm manifesting. Rowan would say I need to get laid.

But I know what this is. It's stupid, traitorous, aching hope. And then there he finally is, Tate Holloway. He's standing out front in a navy Henley that's tight across his shoulders and clings a little to the sweat at his collar. He's crouched in front of the old wooden bench just outside the bookstore, tool belt slung low on his hips, forehead creased in concentration as he works on the cracked leg.

I didn't ask him to fix that. But there he is. Doing it,

anyway. I push the door open, and the little bell tinkles above me like it's announcing something far more dramatic than my entrance.

"You know," I say, trying for light, teasing, not-too-invested, "most people knock before performing unsolicited repairs."

Tate glances up, squints against the sunlight. There's sawdust on his beard, and a line of sweat at his temple. His hand pauses on the screwdriver, but he doesn't stop. "Figured you'd want it done right," he says.

That's it. Just like that. Like it doesn't send a whole thing rolling through me. I don't say anything right away, because I *do* want it done right. And I hate that he's not just talking about the bench. He's talking about us.

"You want a cider?" I offer instead. "It's apple-ginger. From Rowan's weird organic box."

He nods once. Doesn't say no. So, I duck inside and grab two bottles, palms sweating more than they should be. I tell myself it's the humidity. I tell myself it's *not* the way he looked at me like I mattered for a second.

I hand him the bottle. Our fingers graze and linger. God, he looks good. He's built like a freaking unit in that Henley. A warm spark shoots straight up my core, and I swear the air between us dips into slow motion. He doesn't pull away, and neither do I.

I clear my throat and look down. "I made muffins. Your favorite cinnamon ones that you like. At least I think you like them. You used to." I glance up at him from under my lashes.

"But if you're not hungry..."

His expression doesn't change. But something in his shoulder's shift, the air around us thickening as his voice dips lower. "Muffins, huh?" he says finally, the corner of his mouth tugging. Then, softer, almost a growl, "Oh, I'm definitely hungry."

The words land low in my stomach, heat rushing through

me so fast it's dizzying. My thighs press together instinctively under the table, and I'm suddenly, achingly aware of every inch of space between us...or maybe the lack of it.

I force a shaky laugh, trying for lightness, but my pulse betrays me, hammering in my throat.

His gaze lingers, dark and steady, making it very clear he's not talking about muffins.

Tate follows me inside, and for a few moments, all I can hear is the scuff of his boots on the old hardwood floor. I hand him a muffin on one of the mismatched bakery plates and watch as he peels back the wrapper without a word.

And that's when I finally realize it. Something's bothering him. He's quiet, and it's not his usual silence, the kind that's sometimes filled with stubborn brooding. No, this one feels *heavier*. Like he's carrying something too big and too bitter to put into words. "You, okay?" I ask, trying to keep it casual.

He doesn't look up.

I smile. "Rough day on the tree farm? Did a pinecone insult you?"

Still nothing.

He finally lifts his head, and the look in his eyes nearly steals the air out of my lungs. Something's wrong. Really wrong. The corner of his mouth twitches like he's about to speak, but nothing comes. He swallows instead and shakes his head just barely.

That's when it hits me with how badly I need to fix it. Whatever it is. I hate that he's hurting. I'd do anything right now for him not to be hurting.

Which was so *not* the plan when he first came back. Tate Holloway hurt me. Left me. Made me rebuild walls I didn't even know I had the blueprints for. But right now, all I can think about is how hollow his silence feels. Like someone carved out part of him and didn't bother putting it back.

I watch him quietly, the way his jaw ticks, his fingers tapping absently against the side of his cider bottle like he's trying not to *feel* something.

He hasn't said much in the last few minutes, just those sad smiles and half-hearted jokes. And for once, the silence between us isn't easy. It's thick. Raw.

So I ask softly, "Is it April?"

Tate doesn't look at me right away. He just stares at the far bookshelf like it's safer than my face.

Then, finally, he nods. Once. "I think..." His voice is hoarse. "I think I've been hoping that she'd come around. That maybe she was just angry or confused or...something."

He swallows, and my heart clenches as I wait, not pushing, just *being there*.

"But that's not going to happen," he says, his eyes dropping to his hands. "Watching her walk through town with her new family like I don't exist...I realized I've already lost her."

His breath catches. "I mean, I probably never *really* had her, not in the way a kid should have their mother. But I thought that if I worked hard enough, stayed out of trouble, showed up for her... maybe she'd see me. Maybe she'd love me."

He laughs bitterly, blinking fast. "But she doesn't."

I want to reach out, touch him, hold him, but I can feel how close he is to unraveling, and I don't want to make him feel like he can't talk to me right now. I can feel that he needs this.

"It's like..." he continues with a whisper, "I'm mourning a mom who's still alive."

And just like that, I feel the depth of it and the grief he's carried around for years with first his father, and now her. It's an ache that doesn't show up in loud sobs but in empty glances and tired shoulders and words he's never said out loud.

And I hate she did this. She's still alive, and she's making her kid grieve her like she's dead. I hate her for that.

"I'm sorry," I say, because it's the only thing I can think to say without bursting into tears myself.

He finally looks at me, and there's something so raw and real in his gaze, I almost can't breathe.

"Don't be," he says. "You and your family are the only people who never made me feel like I had to earn love."

And just like that, I know I'm done for.

Because Tate Holloway may be broken in places, but he's not empty. He's not disposable. He's *everything*.

And tonight? I think he finally sees it, too.

His eyes meet mine. Something flickers behind them again, softer this time.

"You don't have to do that," he murmurs.

"Do what?"

"Make me feel better."

"Maybe I *want* to make you feel better," I snap.

He blinks.

And suddenly the air between us is thick with something else entirely.

He sets down his muffin, steps a little closer. Just enough to make the hair on my arms stand up.

"You do?"

I swallow. I *should* tell him I don't care and that I was just being polite. That I made the muffins for Remy, and that I didn't watch the way his shirt stuck to the muscles in his back while he fixed the bench. That my hand didn't tingle where it brushed his.

But I don't lie. Instead, I say, "Of course I do." And it's the truest thing I've said all day.

For a heartbeat, neither of us moves. Tate steps in, closing the space between us until the air feels charged, humming. His hand lifts slowly, hesitantly, like he's about to tuck a strand of hair behind my ear... or cup my cheek, thumb grazing the corner of my mouth. My breath catches, my chest tight, waiting.

But just as his fingers hover close enough that I can feel their heat, the bell above the door jingles. We both startle, the sound sharp in the quiet. Tate's hand falls back immediately, curling into a fist at his side, like he's caught himself too close to a line he wasn't ready to cross.

I watch him step back, putting space between us again, though the charged air lingers. My skin still tingles with the ghost of the touch that never came.

"I swear to the moon and stars, if one more person tells me to smile more..." Ivy bursts through the door, her braid unraveling in frizz, cheeks flushed with the brisk air. She drops her oversized bag with a dramatic sigh that rattles the bell above the door.

"Uh oh," I say, leaning over a stack of new romance releases. "Let me guess, rough day?"

"I need coffee. Buckets of it. Maybe a vat of it I can swim in." She kicks off one shoe, then the other, glaring at them like they personally offended her. "And definitely not in these ridiculous heels ever again. Whose idea was this? Certainly not mine."

I chuckle. "The shoes or the smile?"

"Both," she groans, flopping onto the stool behind the counter. "Honestly, I think I'm meant to go barefoot through life and just talk to goats."

Tate glances up from where he's still nursing his cider and what's left of his muffin. "That bad?"

Ivy rounds on both of us like we're part of the problem.

"Do you want to *know* what your mother did?" she says with a look of relief mixed with disappointment.

"What?" I ask, afraid of the answer.

"She made my life miserable for days," she says with defeat.

Tate shifts on the stool beside the counter, expression unreadable again. A flicker of anger passes through his eyes, but he smothers it and focuses on what Ivy's saying.

"And then," Ivy adds, pointing dramatically at herself like a prosecutor before the jury, "guess who got *fired* this morning?"

I blink with disbelief. "What?"

"Yep. Fired. After dealing with the rudest client, overpriced houses, and coordinating someone's freaking Botox appointment. Apparently, April told the agent that she couldn't trust a Maren."

"Oh *hell* no," I snap, straightening up. "She *what?*"

Tate flinches a little, like my tone caught him off guard.

"She said I was 'unstable' and 'too close to the situation,'" Ivy says, using air quotes so violently she nearly knocks over the tip jar shaped like a cauldron. "I was *literally* doing everything they asked. I didn't even *speak*. But apparently, just existing in the same space as their family is enough to get me blacklisted."

The words hit something deep in my chest. A heavy, molten wave of protectiveness unfurls inside me, hot and immediate.

This isn't just petty drama anymore; it's personal. April's messed with someone's job and livelihood. My hand grips the counter harder than I mean to.

Ivy sighs. "It's okay," she says, voice full of defeat. "It's not like it was my dream job anyway."

Tate narrows his eyes. "No. Don't do that. Don't minimize it."

She shrugs one shoulder like she's trying to make herself smaller. "I'm just saying. Who even knows what a dream job is?"

"Something that doesn't end with you getting kicked out because of your last name," Tate mutters.

Ivy gives him a quiet smile. Not bitter, not angry. Just tired.

But I'm not tired. I'm *done*.

"She doesn't get to do this," I say, loud enough to make them both turn toward me. "Not to you. Not to us. Not in *our* town."

Tate blinks. "Willa—"

His eyes lock on mine, and the room suddenly feels *too quiet*. Too still.

"You don't have to fight this battle," he says, voice barely above a whisper.

My throat tightens. "Maybe I want to."

Ivy's watching us now like we're the main characters in a soap opera she didn't mean to audition for but is *definitely* not leaving.

"Okay," she says, sniffling, "I'm still mad, but that was kind of hot."

Tate huffs a soft laugh, but there's something watery about it. He runs a hand through his hair and looks at me like he's seeing something he forgot existed.

"I mean it," I say, stepping a little closer. "You're allowed to be angry. You're allowed to want better. And you're allowed to have people in your corner."

There's a long silence. Then, slowly, Tate nods. "Okay."

Just that. But it lands like an earthquake under my skin.

"Also," Ivy cuts in, sniffing dramatically and yanking a tissue from her bag, "I just want to say this is peak sister behavior. I'm proud. I will now accept muffins and your strongest tea blend for my emotional damage I went through today."

"I made cinnamon apple," I say, already walking toward the back to grab more.

Tate calls after me. "Those were *for me*, huh?"

I pause in the doorway, looking back at him over my shoulder. "Yeah," I say, smirking. "You."

His smile is small. But real.

And I think for the first time in a long time, he's happy.

* * *

By the time we finish organizing the last batch of flyers for the festival, and sorting through the chaos that is the sign-up sheet for the festival activities, the bookstore feels like it's humming with life. The glow from the string of lights above the counter is casting a honey-like haze over the room.

Tate leans back in the chair next to me, stretching one arm behind his head and groaning like an old man. "I think I'm never doing this again."

I laugh, full and unguarded. "That's what you get for not speaking up when Donna and my mom manipulate us."

He gives me a tired grin, and I realize for the hundredth time today how ridiculously handsome he is. Hair mussed, sleeves pushed up. A smudge of ink on the side of his hand.

"I gotta say," I murmur, curling my fingers around the last of my cider, "this isn't how I thought this was all going to go."

He tilts his head. "The festival?"

"Everything. Us. You helping and being here."

His lips twitch into a slow, knowing smirk that makes my toes curl in my boots. "You did, didn't you?"

I raise an eyebrow. "Did what?"

"You hoped," he says, voice dropping to something lower. Warmer. "You hoped it'd get better."

I blink. "You think *I* hoped?"

He leans in, eyes never leaving mine. "I know I did."

My heart squeezes. "And has it?"

Tate nods, his smile soft now, a little shy. "Yeah. It has."

And just like that, everything in me goes quiet.

I don't realize I've moved until my leg brushes his under the table, and neither of us pulls away. Outside, the wind kicks up, rattling the front door just enough to remind us the season is shifting. Inside, though? Inside, it's warm. Electric.

We fall into an easy silence, the kind that hums with things unsaid but *understood.*

Then Tate clears his throat. "So...this town ghost tour thing. Please tell me you're dressing up."

"Oh, *absolutely.* I've got a velvet cape, dramatic eye makeup, the works."

He laughs, head tipping back slightly. "Of course you do."

"What about you?"

He shrugs. "Old Pete says if I don't dress up, I'm banned from the harbor. So, yeah. I'm going full pirate mode for Junie."

"Please tell me you're going to have a sexy eye patch."

"You *know* I am."

I giggle, and it breaks something in the air between us. The tension that's been simmering all evening boils over.

He's watching me now. "You've got cider on your lip," he says, voice low.

I go to wipe it, but before I can, he leans forward and brushes his thumb across my mouth.

The touch is featherlight, but it steals every coherent thought from my brain.

"Got it," he whispers.

I swallow, hard. "Thanks."

We're close now. Too close to pretend we're just friends or festival co-planners or two people who happened to share a bench-fixing moment a few days ago.

My breath hitches. So does his.

"Willa," he says, like it's the only word he remembers how to say.

And then he kisses me. Soft at first.

The kiss deepens, slow and deliberate, every brush of his mouth sending shivers down my spine. His hand slides to my waist, warm and steady, anchoring me as though he's afraid I might slip away. My fingers find the sharp line of his jaw, rough with stubble, then drift higher, tangling in the damp strands at the nape of his neck.

His tongue brushes mine, tentative and teasing, and everything inside me tightens and coils, hot and sharp. We taste each other in that quiet, searching way, like we're learning a language we once knew but almost forgot. He tastes like cinnamon and salt air, like hope, like every late-night fantasy I've tried and failed to bury.

The kiss grows bolder, hungrier. His palm flattens against the small of my back, urging me closer until my chest presses to his. My own hands curl in his hair, pulling him deeper, refusing to let go. His thumb strokes slow circles into my hip, sending sparks scattering through me.

His body leans into mine, solid, unshakable, yet every movement of his mouth is careful, reverent, like he's memorizing me. I part my lips, give him more, and the sound that rumbles low in his throat sets my skin aflame.

And suddenly, nothing else exists. Just us and this kiss that feels like coming home and burning down all at once.

When we finally break apart, we're both breathing hard, foreheads pressed together, as if neither of us can quite let the moment go.

"Well," I say, smiling so big my cheeks ache. "That's definitely not how I thought tonight would end either."

Tate chuckles, his thumb tracing circles at my hip. "Yeah, well. I told you I hoped it'd get better."

"It has."

Chapter 20
Tate

The Wisteria Cove Quilt Guild is ruthless. They look like sweet little old ladies with beaded sweaters and glasses on chains, but don't be fooled, these women could run a small country, plot anyone's demise, or rob a bank and get away with it. And tonight? They've turned the community center into an all-out fall fantasyland for the annual Autumn Quilt Raffle & Chili Cook-Off. In the past, they prepared for this every year. Always have, and it looks like nothing's changed. Only maybe they got even more hardcore; it's hard to tell.

I'm here for moral support. Or I was until Pearl shoved a raffle ticket into my hand with a wink and muttered something about *"manifesting fate."*

I don't know what that means, but I'm pretty sure I've just been hexed.

"All right, darlings!" comes a voice from the front. Carlene, queen of the Quilt Guild and notorious for once knitting an entire scarf during a town meeting, raises a hand. "This year's prize is our handmade *Pumpkin Patch Memories* quilt, stitched with love and just a touch of gossip."

Everyone claps.

"The Maren sisters inspired this beauty," she adds. "Willa herself picked the fabrics last year."

I blink. *Wait. What?*

Before I can react, Betty Lou calls out the number.

"Ticket 1083!"

I glance at the paper in my hand. *Well, hell.* I hold it up.

A cheer goes up from the crowd, mostly because Ivy yells, "Tate won!"

Across the room, Willa gapes at me and looks down at her ticket number in disbelief. "You did *not* just win *my* quilt."

I lift a brow. "Looks like I did."

"That's the one with the crescent moons and marigold flannel backing," she says, narrowing her eyes like I've stolen an irreplaceable family heirloom.

I smirk. "You gonna thumb wrestle me for it?"

She smirks at me, probably at the same memory that I have of us thumb wrestling for everything with as a kid.

She strides over, arms crossed, lips twitching. "What's a man like you gonna do with a quilt that cozy, hmm?"

I glance at the prize in my hands, then back at her. "Dunno. Might need it to keep me warm at night."

Willa raises a brow. "Is that so?"

"Unless..." I lean in a little, lowering my voice. "You're offering a better option."

She doesn't miss a beat. "If you needed to be kept warm, Holloway, all you had to do was *ask*."

My grin sharpens. "Well then. I'm asking."

Her cheeks flush pink, but she doesn't look away. "Maybe you can share it."

Oh, *she's good.*

Carlene practically sings as she hands me the quilt. "Treat

her right, sweetheart. She's made with love and about a ton of Hallmark movie hours."

"Sounds like just my type," I say, just loud enough that Willa hears and scoffs.

But I swear, she's smiling as she turns and walks off. And I'd follow that smile anywhere.

Later that night, the town square is packed for the outdoor movie night. Blankets are strewn everywhere. Lanterns are strung between trees. Cider steam curls into the crisp air.

I show up with the quilt, and I find her sitting on the grass in a sea of pumpkins, mums, and teenagers in plaid, sipping from a thermos.

"You came," she says, like she's surprised.

"You invited me. Sort of. With a veiled threat and mild bribery."

I unfold the quilt, plop down beside her, and toss half of it over her lap without asking.

"I see you brought *my* quilt," she says.

I grin. "It's our quilt now."

"I'm letting you borrow it. Temporarily."

"Sure, you are."

Her hip presses into mine. I feel her laugh more than I hear it. She's warm, relaxed, golden in the lamplight. And I'm toast.

The movie plays. Kids run around throwing popcorn. Ivy accuses someone of a hate crime for putting marshmallows in chili. Lilith is reading a palm. Rowan's passing out caramel apples at a little table in the back. Someone dressed like Bigfoot is flirting with someone dressed like a colonial ghost, and no one's batting an eye.

Willa leans her head against my shoulder.

I turn slightly, brushing her hair back from her cheek. "So," I whisper, "about that offer to keep me warm..."

She lifts her head, amused. "You're really gonna bring that back up?"

"Uh-huh."

"I was joking."

"I wasn't."

Willa bites her lip. "God, you're impossible."

"Yet here you are."

She says nothing. Just stares at me for a second too long.

Then, softly, she says, "You're trouble."

"You like trouble."

"Maybe."

I tilt my head, brushing my nose against hers. "Then stop pretending you don't."

When she doesn't move away, her lips part, and her breath catches like she's daring me to keep going. My mouth crashes into hers, and every ounce of restraint I've been clinging to shatters. She gasps against me, and I take the opening, kissing her like I've been starving for years and she's the only thing that will ever feed me.

Her hands grip my shirt, sliding up my chest, tangling in my hair. I can't get close enough. I haul her against me, feeling the curve of her body fit into mine like it was made for me. My hand finds her jaw, tilting her up so I can go deeper, claim more.

She's making these soft, desperate sounds in the back of her throat, and it's driving me insane. I kiss her harder, like I can pour every unspoken word, every sleepless night, every damn thing I've ever felt for her straight into this moment.

When we finally break for air, we're both breathing like we just ran a mile, our foreheads pressed together, her lips swollen, my heart punching against my ribs. And I know there's no undoing this. Not now. Not ever.

And I know that this is it. This is the moment the walls have fallen. We're both in.

* * *

The full moon hangs over Wisteria Cove like a spotlight, casting long shadows between flickering jack-o'-lanterns and fog machines that wheeze and sputter outside Main Street storefronts. The sidewalks are packed with townspeople in costumes, half of them tipsy, the other half high on sugar and nostalgia. The ghost tour has been an annual tradition as long as I can remember. It's like trick or treating for adults and one of my favorite Wisteria Cove traditions.

And here I am wearing a pirate costume.

"You look ridiculous," Remy mutters beside me, adjusting Junie's little fairy wings. "And yet somehow, it's working."

"It's the eyeliner," I say, tossing him a wink. "Women love a roguish man with dark secrets and a sword."

Junie, dressed in a sparkly green tutu with a plastic crown sliding down her forehead, tugs my sleeve. "Captain Tate, are you really a pirate?"

"Absolutely. I stole a hundred ships and a thousand hearts." I tell her in my best pirate accent.

"You're certifiable," Remy mutters.

"And yet here you are, participating. Nice lumberjack look, by the way. A big hit with the ladies," I tease.

He glares, "This is just the way I look."

I ignore him and hoist Junie up onto my shoulders so she can see over the crowd. "Where to, Your Highness?"

"The book shop! Willa has cookies!"

That's all the motivation I need.

The bookstore is glowing like something out of a snow globe with a warm light in the windows, paper bats flying overhead, a carved pumpkin with a smirking black cat perched on the steps. Ivy stands out front, handing out cider in a cream-colored wrap dress that makes Remy double-take.

195

Not just a glance. A *look*. A slow one. With heat behind it. Interesting. I nudge him. "You good?"

"What? I'm fine." He clears his throat and drops his gaze, busying himself with Junie's wings. "She always dresses like that."

"She always make your ears turn red, too?"

Remy scowls. I grin.

Ivy's face lights up when she sees Junie. "Oh, my little woodland fairy queen! You're just the cutest sprinkle of magic!"

Junie giggles as Ivy hands her a tiny sugar cookie shaped like a mushroom. "Thank you, Miss Ivy!"

Then the door swings open, and Willa steps out, and sweet *hell*.

She's wearing a black corset, a crushed velvet mini-skirt, and fishnets that are doing things to my brain I shouldn't legally even be thinking about in the presence of a five-year-old. Her lips are painted plum and her dark hair is pinned with glittering stars, like she just fell out of a witchy pin-up calendar.

She sees me. Smiles. And I am officially a goner.

"You lose your ship, Captain?" she asks, arching a brow as she hands out cookies.

"Looking to anchor somewhere warm," I say, stepping close enough to smell her cinnamon perfume. "Any recommendations?"

"If you needed someone to keep you warm," she purrs, "you could've just asked."

Jesus. I nearly drop the damn cookie.

Behind us, Ivy nearly chokes on her cider, muttering, "Y'all wanna dial the heat down to a mild flirt before someone combusts?"

"I vote no," Willa says sweetly, eyes never leaving mine.

Junie eats her cookie and declares. "You two should kiss."

Remy snorts. "Okay, time to keep this tour moving."

We join the stream of costumed chaos down Main Street, stopping at the bait shop where Old Pete hands out gummy worms from a tackle box and tells Junie she looks like a "sparkle bug." At Donna's house, she's wearing a medieval dress and leather jacket and handing out signed copies of her latest novel.

"This one's for you," she says, handing one to Willa with a wink. "It's got a very broody fisherman in it."

"I think I already have one of those," Willa says under her breath and gives me a smirk.

I laugh. Junie slides her hand into mine, and we keep moving.

We hit the diner for hot cider and kettlecorn. The liquor store for tiny bottles of whiskey. The ice cream parlor is giving away maple fudge bites and encouraging people to vote for best costume.

And through it all, Willa and I keep brushing hands. Shoulders. Smiles that last a little too long. She laughs as if I haven't ruined everything. I touch her back like I haven't missed her every damn second.

We reach the old train depot, which Rowan, and Lilith have transformed into a "Mystic Oracle Tent." Inside, the air smells like clove and something fizzy.

"Three cards each," Rowan says, smacking a deck onto the table. "Fates are being revealed tonight."

Willa chooses a card. The Sun.

"I'll take it," she says, grinning.

I choose mine. The Lovers.

Rowan gasps. "Oh my God, it's happening. This is it. This is the moment. Do you two feel it?"

Remy grabs Junie and backs out of the tent. "We're out before they start singing Stevie Nicks."

"I love Stevie Nicks," Junie cries out as they walk away.

We follow, and the group starts to splinter off with families heading to the bonfire, Donna heads to the church to read spooky poetry aloud to everyone, and Ivy's eyes trail Remy like a moth to a torch.

That's when Willa tugs my sleeve and pulls me around the back of the bookstore.

"Shortcut?" I ask, raising a brow.

She doesn't answer.

Just turns to face me in the glow of the bookstore light, the quiet hum of the night pressing in.

"You look good tonight," she says, her voice softer than it's been all evening.

I step closer. "You've been looking at me like you want to climb me like a tree."

"Maybe I do."

Heat coils low in my stomach. "What's stopping you?"

Her fingers graze my chest, light and curious. "I think I'm scared."

"Of me?"

"No." Her voice drops to a whisper. "Of what I'll feel when I let go."

I don't answer. Just cup her jaw and kiss her like I've wanted to since the second she walked back into my life.

She melts into it, hands sliding under my pirate shirt, fingers skating over my skin like she's learning me all over again. The kiss deepens—sweet, then searing, then desperate. Her back hits the brick wall and I cage her in, her body warm against mine, lips parted in a gasp when I trail kisses down her jaw.

"Tate," she whispers.

"I've wanted this since the moment we fell apart," I murmur. "Since the day I left and wished I hadn't."

She pulls me back in like she doesn't care about the past. Only this. Only now.

Behind us, a second-story window creaks.

Lilith's voice calls out, cheerful as ever. "You're still within coven jurisdiction, just so you know!"

Willa groans into my chest. "I hate it here."

And for the first time in a long damn time, I love it here.

Chapter 21
Willa

*I've lost a lot in my life,
but losing you?
That's the one thing I can't accept.
Not now.
Not when you're right here.
—Tate*

The next morning when I come back from a supply run, I see Tate standing in front of the bookstore with a coffee in one hand and a smug look on his face.

The second thing I see is Cobweb. *In his hoodie.* Tate's wearing a dark gray zip-up sweatshirt with one of those built-in pet pockets, the kind you see for women with teacup poodles and no shame. But instead of a yapping dog in rhinestones, he's got a black kitten nestled inside the pouch like a king in a hammock. And Cobweb looks *thrilled.*

"I see you've fully committed to your new identity," I say, biting back a laugh.

Tate sips his coffee. "I am but her vessel."

Cobweb pokes her little head out, blinking at me like *sup, peasant.*

Tate strokes the kitten's ears absently. "She screamed at the window for ten straight minutes. I offered her treats, toys, and cat food. But no. She wanted *outside.* So, I improvised."

"You put her in a cat pouch hoodie."

"Correction." He grins and holds up a finger. "I made a *bonding solution.*"

At the Harvest Moon Festival, where we're finishing the last minute set up, they're instant celebrities. Everyone wants to check out Cobweb. Tate struts through the cider booth area like a man with a mission and a sidekick. Cobweb stays tucked against his chest, peeking out at the world like a judgmental baby kangaroo.

A group of retired ladies from the quilting club *lose their minds.* "Look at that face!"

Junie runs up, wide-eyed. "Can I pet her?!"

"Ask the guardian," Tate says solemnly, gesturing to the cat like she's royalty.

Cobweb makes a little chirp and headbutts Junie's hand like she approves. Ivy wanders over, cider slushie in hand, raises an eyebrow, and deadpans, "I like your emotional support animal."

Tate shrugs. "She keeps me grounded."

"She's wearing your hoodie better than you," she mutters. "Tragic."

People keep coming up. Kids squeal. Grown men nod in silent understanding. Rowan insists Cobweb is "channeling harvest magic." Donna calls her Madam *Meows-a-Lot* and insists she wants joint custody. I'm pretty sure Junie is working hard to try and convince Remy that she needs a cat to keep her company.

I can't stop looking at Tate—soft-eyed, hoodie-wearing, kitten-carrying—and thinking: *I really might be falling in love with the man who wears a cat.*

The entire town feels like it's been dipped in cider and strung with fairy lights. Everywhere I look, something glows. Lanterns hang from tree branches amid wreaths of dried apples and corn husks, and scarecrows wear flannel button-downs stolen from someone's laundry line.

The festival is tomorrow, and the final touches are going up fast. Ivy's directing people as if she's the queen of autumn logistics.

Junie shrugs and drags the pumpkin back into place. Cobweb trails behind her, little tail flicking with purpose, like she's the official festival supervisor.

I tug my orange cardigan covered in black bats tighter and try not to melt into a puddle of emotion. Because here's the truth: *I'm happy.* Buzzing, warm, cinnamon-sugar-coated happy. And if I'm being brutally honest, it scares the hell out of me.

Because when life has taught you that good things don't last, that people leave or die, and things fall apart, joy feels like a countdown. A soft, glowing time bomb. And while I know it's not healthy, I'm preparing my heart for that, and I hate that I do it. Like I can't live in the moment and really enjoy life because I'm afraid it will be taken away.

I push the thought away and turn back to the sign I'm hanging by the bookstore steps. It says *Wisteria Cove Harvest Moon Festival: Kisses, Cider, and Community.*

The "kissing booth" is positioned exactly fifteen feet from my door, and of course, it was Rowan's idea, but Finn built it.

Finn has been a godsend throughout the entire festival planning process.

"We can make a lot of money for Salt & Root," she'd told me, wielding her staple gun like a weapon. "It's all for the cause."

Then she smooched Finn Bennett behind it and looked *surprised* when he kissed her back. I was even more surprised when neither of them moved away after. Now they are both pretending it didn't happen, but every time they're always near each other, I feel like I need popcorn and a front-row seat.

Maybe Tate and I aren't the only new lovebirds in Wisteria Cove this magical season.

"Willa!" someone calls, and I spin around to see Donna waving from a folding chair, thermos in hand, lipstick perfectly applied, pencil behind her ear, like she's ready to reign as queen of Wisteria Cove. "That banner needs more work. You want it to feel like it's screaming *celebration*, not *grocery store clearance event!*"

"On it," I call back, trying not to laugh.

I grab the twine and pull it tighter, standing on tiptoes to reach the lantern string. The bookstore behind me smells like cinnamon sticks from the simmer pot I've had simmering on the stove since dawn. Tate and I have been staying there together, tucked up in the little apartment above the shelves, and I swear it's feeling more like home than anywhere else ever has. Sure, we're cramped, but I feel like it's cozy.

Tate's childhood home is officially on the market. It's had a few showings already, and rumor has it an offer's coming in. Finn Bennett's name has been suspiciously tossed around the real estate grapevine. When I asked him, he just shrugged and acted like he had no idea what I was talking about.

Honestly? I hope it's Finn who buys it. As a contractor, I can only imagine what he would do with the place. He'd honor it the way it should be honored. That place isn't home to Tate, and he's not even sad about it. He seems like he's relieved, to be honest. I just wish his mom hadn't handled it the way she has.

I turn to help Rowan with her table, and I watch Tate mingle with people. My knees and heart practically melt when I see him laughing with Old Pete.

They're by the fire pit now, Pete telling some old story, Tate listening with his full body like it matters. Like the moment deserves all of him.

And that's the thing. He gives all of himself to whatever he does and whoever he's with. He's the best. To me, this town, and to everyone.

And I can't help but feel like...*this is what safe feels like*. Not boring. Not perfect. *Safe.* A flutter of emotion wells up, and I don't know if it's love or fear or both. Because the other shoe always drops, right? It's just a matter of time. I don't want to think this could happen, but if I expect less, I won't get hurt.

Later, it's just the two of us after the last lantern is hung and the finishing touches are on everything, and everything is prepared for tomorrow.

The trees are still lit. The bookstore glows behind us.

And I'm on the top step, arms full of tangled twinkle lights, when Tate says, "Let me."

He takes them from me, easily untangling them like it's nothing. We string them across the trees just outside the bookstore, the light catching on the last yellow leaves, the wind soft and chilly.

I don't realize I'm swaying a little until he catches my hand.

"Dance with me," he says.

"But there's no music."

"There doesn't need to be."

I slip into his arms like I belong there. He smells like apples, autumn wind, and pine from working at the tree farm the day before. His hands settle on my hips like they've been waiting for me all day.

We sway.

Just the two of us. Lanterns glowing above. The town quiet around us.

"This is my favorite version of you," Tate says softly.

"Messy hair, and cider breath?"

"Exactly. You in your world. Doing what you love. I love seeing you happy."

I look up at him. "You're part of that world now."

His smile falters, just for a heartbeat, but then it's back. "Yeah?"

"Yeah."

We stop dancing. But we're still close.

I look at his mouth.

He looks at mine.

And suddenly, we're not swaying anymore. We're *kissing*. Hard. Hungry. His hand cups the back of my neck, pulling me in, and I thread my fingers into his jacket like I'll never let him go.

We don't make it far. The door to the bookstore opens with a soft creak, and we stumble inside, mouths still tangled, laughter catching between kisses as we kick off boots and shrug off scarves.

The apartment upstairs is warm and dark. Cobweb followed and is already curled on the couch.

I tug my sweater over my head, the soft fabric catching for a second before sliding free. I drop it to the floor and stand there in nothing but jeans and a thin bra, the air cool on my skin, my pulse thundering. I should feel exposed. Instead, I feel powerful and wanted.

I back toward the ladder, gripping the rail, climbing one rung at a time. My breathing quickens with every step, my body tingling with the awareness of him right below me. Tate follows without hesitation, his movements steady, his presence so close it steals the air from my lungs. Each creak of the wood, each scuff of his boot, coils tighter inside me.

At the top I pause, forcing myself to look down. His eyes catch mine from just a few rungs below, and the sight nearly unravels me. His gaze is sharp and unyielding, dark with a hunger that makes my stomach clench and my thighs press together. He looks at me like I'm the only thing that exists.

His hands come up and catch my thighs, big and firm, halting me on the ladder. A gasp slips from my lips. I curl forward instinctively, threading my fingers into his hair, pulling him closer even though there's still space between us. He doesn't move except for his hands, rough palms sliding up over the backs of my legs, over the curve of my hips, every inch of me claimed in his touch.

The rasp of his calluses against my skin sends shivers racing up my spine. His thumbs trace just above my waistband, a possessive press, a reverent caress. His gaze dips lower, slow and deliberate, and when it lands on the swell of my breasts straining against lace, his jaw tightens, his throat works like he's swallowing back a curse.

"God, you're so beautiful," he murmurs, his voice hoarse, almost broken.

The words hit me like a flame to tinder. I tighten my hold in his hair, pulling harder, needing him closer, needing everything. My body is trembling, breath shallow, heat coursing through me. His stare doesn't waver, and in that moment, I know neither of us is stopping this.

I climb another rung, slow and deliberate, and he follows immediately, his body pressing close, his hands sliding higher, claiming more. The loft looms just above us, shadows waiting to swallow us whole, to keep our secrets.

When we reach the top, he says my name like a prayer. Like a promise.

All I can think about is him, and needing him. I pull him towards me, pulling his sweatshirt over his head, unbuckling his belt. He kisses me, then pauses and unbuttons my pants, and then his hands cup my face as he kisses me urgently.

"Tate, I need you..."

He says nothing, just lowers his mouth to my neck. His lips drag over my skin, soft and wet, before his teeth catch, nibbling in a way that makes my breath stutter. A low growl rumbles from him, vibrating against my throat, and fire licks up my spine. It feels like he can't get enough of me, like he's starving, and the thought makes my whole body clench with want.

His fingers slip beneath the straps of my bra, tugging it down until it falls away. The cool air barely has time to kiss my skin before his hands are there, palms hot, covering me. He groans into my mouth as he takes me in his hands, rough and reverent all at once, and I arch into him, desperate for more.

His thumbs stroke over my nipples, slow circles that send a jolt of sensation straight to my core. The calluses on his fingertips scrape against the sensitive peaks, and the contrast of his rough skin against my softness makes me whimper into his kiss. Pleasure coils low in my belly, sharp and insistent, and my thighs squeeze together, rubbing for even a shred of friction. It isn't enough. I need more. I need him.

He kisses me harder, mouth claiming mine, his tongue stroking deep while his hands keep teasing, kneading, pulling moans from my throat. Every flick of his thumbs has me trembling, every scrape makes me ache worse. His lips leave mine just long enough to trail back down my neck, sucking, nipping, marking me with his hunger.

I'm gasping, rubbing my thighs together, rocking helplessly

into his touch while he devours me like I'm the only thing he's ever wanted.

"Wait, wait," I say breathlessly. He stops and looks at me, holding my hips and searching my eyes.

"I don't want to mess this up..."

He nods, breathless. "Okay."

We stare at each other for a beat, an entire non-verbal conversation passing between us.

I lean up and kiss him again, swiping my tongue across his lip, his soft groan filling the room.

"You want this?" he asks.

I nod, and he says, "No, I need you to say it."

"I want this. I want you, and I want us."

He eases me back onto the bed, his weight a steady press that makes me feel caged and claimed. His beard grazes my skin as he trails kisses down my abdomen, each scrape and drag sending little shocks through me. I arch against the mattress, my fingers clutching at the sheets, my breath already breaking apart.

When his lips reach the waistband of my panties, he pauses. His fingertips trace the edge, featherlight, then slide down my thigh. Slowly, reverently, like he's memorizing every curve, every line. The roughness of his skin against the smoothness of mine makes me shiver. He squeezes, his fingers digging into the soft flesh of my hips, and then he hooks the lace and begins to tug.

It's unhurried, torturous, even, as he pulls them down, inch by inch. His gaze never leaves me, hot and searing, and the way he looks at me—like I'm his, like I'm everything—makes me feel beautiful. Desired. Wanted in a way that I've never felt before.

The fabric slides down my thighs, my calves, until it falls away completely. I'm bare beneath him, only for him, and the power of that realization sends a pulse of confidence through me. He lingers, his hands smoothing back up my legs, palms broad and possessive.

His head dips, lips brushing the inside of my thigh. A kiss, then another, then a slow sucking pull that makes me squirm. He trails a path higher, closer, and I can't stay still. My thighs shift restlessly, my hips rolling without permission, chasing his mouth.

And then he's there, settling between my thighs like he belongs. His lips part against me, pressing soft at first, his breath hot, his beard rough against my skin. He opens me with a gentle stroke of his tongue, one slow, devastating lick across my center. The sound that breaks from me is raw and helpless.

I force my eyes open, desperate to see him, and the sight steals whatever air I have left. Tate looks up at me through his lashes, eyes blazing, dark and dangerous. Needy. Possessive. Like the taste of me is already his addiction.

It's wrecking, seeing him there. His broad shoulders framed between my thighs, his body ripped and defined, muscles flexing as he holds me down. All that strength, all that control, bent to the single purpose of ruining me, worshipping me. He's devastating. He's mine.

I grip the sheets and pull myself back and he wraps his hands around my thighs and pulls me to him, taking his time, licking, kissing, and making me feel so amazing.

He feels the way my body arches into him, the way I gasp and tremble, and his grip tightens on my hips. His fingers dig into me, holding me steady, as if he knows I might try to squirm away from the unbearable pleasure. His tongue slides deeper, stroking and circling, teasing and tormenting until every nerve in me is lit like wildfire.

Sensation shoots through me, sharp and sweet, tightening every muscle. My toes curl hard, pressing into the sheets, and I can barely breathe around the cries spilling from my lips. Heat coils low in my belly, building higher and higher, and I don't know how much more I can take. His tongue is wicked, relentless, coaxing me to the edge again and again.

I gasp his name, broken and needy, and then he closes his lips around my clit. A sharp, deliberate nibble, just enough pressure, and I come undone. The explosion rips through me, blinding and unstoppable, shattering every last bit of control. Pleasure floods me in waves, violent and consuming, and my moans fill the night air.

When my vision clears, I find him looking up at me. Tate's mouth is wet from me, his beard glistening, his eyes dark and fierce. Proud. He looks proud of what he just did to me, and so aroused it nearly breaks me open all over again. His chest heaves, his jaw clenched tight, like holding himself back is costing him everything.

But I can't wait another moment. My body aches, desperate for more. Desperate for him. "Tate," I whisper, voice ragged, "I need you inside me. Now."

He rises, dragging his mouth from my skin with a groan, and his hands go to his belt. The clink of the buckle makes my pulse thunder. My eyes drop, following the movement as he pushes his trousers down his thighs, then his boxers.

My breath catches, my body trembling with anticipation. The sight of him, thick and long, flushed dark with arousal, steals every coherent thought from my head. The kind of sight that makes my mouth water, my body ache, my thighs clench with need. Veins rope along his shaft, and his tip is already slick, proof of how much he wants this, wants me.

It's overwhelming, powerful, and somehow intimate, this moment of seeing him bare. He is beautiful in the most devastating, masculine way. And he's mine.

Every inch of me burns with need. I want him. I want to feel him stretch me, fill me, ruin me completely.

I reach blindly for the bedside table, fumbling until my fingers close around the box. My hand is shaking as I tug a condom free and slide it out, passing it to him. Our fingers brush, and the contact is electric, sharp enough to make my breath catch.

He tears the foil carefully with his teeth, his gaze locked on mine the entire time. The small sound of the rip is obscene in the silence, my pulse thundering so loud I can hear it in my ears. He spits the wrapper aside and grips himself, fist wrapping around his thick length.

I can't look away. His arms flex with the movement, every muscle taut and defined, veins standing out along his forearms as he strokes once, then rolls the condom down. The latex stretches over him inch by inch, and I feel my thighs press together helplessly at the sight.

He's so big, so hard, and the image of him covering himself while staring at me like I'm his whole world makes my mouth go dry. His eyes are molten, burning into me, dark with hunger and possession.

He pulls me close, entering me slowly, pushing and filling me until I feel fuller than I've ever been. God, it feels so good.

He presses against me, the broad head of him sliding at my entrance, and my breath catches in my throat. He pushes in slowly, achingly slow, stretching me inch by deliberate inch. My nails dig into his shoulders, my head falling back against the pillow as my body adjusts around the thick, heavy length of him.

The sensation is overwhelming. Full. Deep. Like he's touching places inside me I didn't even know existed. My thighs tremble, every muscle pulled taut, and a strangled moan slips past my lips.

He braces on his forearms, his weight pressing me into the mattress. The smell of him surrounds me with sweat, salt, woodsmoke, and man, and I breathe it in greedily, intoxicated. His jaw is tight, his brow furrowed, every line of his face etched with restraint as he holds himself back. The tension in him is electric, vibrating through me and making me ache even more.

He moves slow at first, rolling his hips, drawing almost all the way out before sliding back in. Teasing. Drawing out every flicker of sensation until I'm writhing beneath him, my legs locking around his waist. "More," I gasp, nails raking down his back. "I need you."

Something in him snaps. His hips drive harder, faster, his body pounding into mine with a rhythm that steals my breath. The bed creaks, my moans filling the air, and still his eyes stay locked on mine. The heat there is scorching, primal, as if he can't get enough of watching me unravel beneath him.

Our fingers tangle together, his hands folding into mine, pinning them above my head. The move makes me gasp, makes me feel completely taken, completely his. Each thrust hits deeper, harder, until sparks explode behind my eyes.

I arch against him, my breasts crushed to his chest, the rough hair of his torso abrading my sensitive skin in the most delicious way. Every inch of him is on me, in me, surrounding me. The rhythm builds, sweat slick between our bodies, breath mingling, his growls vibrating against my throat as he buries his face there, biting, sucking, tasting.

He shifts suddenly, rolling us so I straddle him, his cock still buried deep. My palms flatten on his chest, feeling the hard planes of muscle, the frantic beat of his heart under my hands. His hands grip my hips tight, guiding me as I rock over him, the friction unbearable and perfect.

I ride him, losing myself in the motion, the slide of his length filling me again and again, each thrust dragging me closer to the edge. His eyes burn into mine, dark and feral, watching me take my pleasure, watching me come apart.

Heat coils low in my belly, sharper this time, and I chase it desperately, moving harder, faster, my moans rising higher with every thrust. His thumb presses between my thighs, finding my swollen clit, rubbing tight circles as he drives up into me. The combination destroys me.

The climax tears through me, violent and unstoppable. My body shakes, clamping around him, cries spilling raw and helpless from my throat. I shudder over him, lost, undone, every nerve alight.

Tate groans, the sound ragged, guttural, as he bucks up into me, relentless, as though he needs to drag every last wave from my body before letting go himself. And God, the sight of him beneath me, sweat-slick, muscles straining, eyes blazing with hunger and pride, is almost enough to undo me all over again.

I collapse against him, trembling, breathless, and still pulsing around him, the air heavy with the scent of sweat and sex and him.

This isn't just sex. It's fire. It's frenzy. It's the best I've ever had. And it terrifies me how much I want it again, how much I want *him*.

He comes hard and pulses inside and holds me tight, and I know that this is it. He's it for me. He's always been my anchor.

Later, tangled in flannel sheets and breathless silence, I lie against his chest, the steady thump of his heart grounding me.

The lanterns are still glowing outside.

The bookstore smells like cinnamon and change.

And in this moment, I believe we might actually be okay.

Even if the other shoe *does* drop...I think we'll catch it. Together.

Chapter 22
Tate

Wisteria Cove doesn't just throw a festival; they turn the entire town into pure magic. Lanterns glow like fireflies strung between the buildings, cider and cinnamon spill warmth into the air, and the whole town hums like it's alive. I can't believe all the work it took to make this happen. But the only thing on my mind right now is Willa and how much being back here with her means to me.

Donna and Lilith might've been the masterminds, pulling

strings behind the scenes to get us together with this festival, but their grand plan wasn't about pies or pumpkins. It was about her and me, remembering what we had and what we have now. And damn it, it worked.

Helping with the planning gave me something I didn't even realize I was starving for, a means of belonging. A reason to be here and to stay. To keep building instead of letting things slip away and fall apart around me. But more than that, it gave me time with her. Watching her laugh with her sisters, tuck her hair behind her ear while she argued about string lights, roll her eyes at me, and then soften and come back to me. I will never know what I did to deserve her, but I will be forever grateful.

Somewhere between hammering stakes into the ground and hauling crates of pumpkins with Finn, I stopped feeling like the outsider who came back too late. I started feeling like a man who still had a shot. And it wasn't because of the town, or the festival, or even the sense of belonging. It was her. It's always been her and always will be.

And for the first time in a long damn while, I don't feel like I'm treading water or just surviving. I'm having fun with Willa and our friends. And I'm not ready to let that go.

The air smells like cider, firewood, and something sweet, which makes sense because there are treats everywhere. Kids dressed like scarecrows and woodland creatures chase each other between hay bales. The sound of laughter mixes with live music from local bands drifting from the gazebo stage. Somewhere, Donna's singing along to a song and probably writing future book scenes about all of this.

The bookstore is lit up like a postcard, lanterns glowing from every tree, pumpkin strings hanging from the porch, and Willa floating around in her maroon-colored sweater, her hair pinned back with a gold leaf clip, passing out spiced scones like the Fall Queen of New England. And she truly is. She's the next generation to Wisteria Cove just like her mother, Lilith. She's special to this town and special to me.

She smiles when she catches me watching her. I smile back, but my chest feels...tight. I can't put my finger on it, but I hate that the feeling is there.

I'm helping with the hayride. Kids climb in, giggling, carrying caramel apples bigger than their faces. Junie's riding shotgun with me, holding the reins like she's steering a pirate ship. "You think this wagon could go airborne if we hit a bump hard enough?" She asks, dead serious.

"Kid, if we do that, your father's gonna kill me."

She nods as if that's fair.

The wagon rumbles down the trail through the tree farm, and everything is golden.

After the ride, I help unload the wagon and head toward the cider booth. I pass Remy, looking like a slightly frazzled lumberjack trying to manage an excited five-year-old, and Ivy sweet-talking a group of tourists into donating to the Root & Salt apothecary shop raising money for Rowan.

Willa's up on a stepladder, fixing a crooked banner, and I want to reach out. Say something. Pull her into my arms and just hold her. But I don't. Because I'm feeling like maybe this is too good to be true. For me everything usually is until it isn't. I grab a cup of cider and try to disappear into the crowd.

Lilith Maren doesn't let people disappear, though. She finds me behind the apothecary tea tent, somehow dressed in an all-black Victorian witch outfit with a moon necklace and an armful of popcorn balls. "Ah," she says. "Broody fisherman lurking but not participating. We must be approaching emotional sabotage o'clock."

I lift a brow. "What are you talking about, Lilith?"

"I have three daughters who are all afraid to love. I know the signs when I see them."

I open my mouth to protest, but she cuts me off with a look that could set fire to wet leaves.

"You're doing what she's doing," she says, sipping her tea. "Waiting for the other shoe to drop."

I blink. "I'm not—"

"You are. Watching her out of the corner of your eye like she's gonna bolt. Bracing yourself for impact. Flinching at all the good parts because you're scared of the bad parts."

I look down into my cup. The steam's gone. Damn. Lilith is good. Scary good, how intuitive she is.

Lilith lowers her voice. "She's doing it, too. You know that, right?"

I nod, barely.

"She loves you," she says simply. "But neither of you is letting yourselves just have it."

I exhale, tight and ragged. "It's just...I like it here. With her. At the tree farm. Waking up with the bookstore smell in my nose and the cat sitting on my chest. I like all of it. But part of me keeps thinking...what if I mess it up?"

She steps closer. "Here's a secret no one tells you about love: you will mess it up."

I look up at her. "Then why would I want it in the first place?"

She laughs. "Because believe it or not, it's worth it. And it works out in the end."

"But does it? You lost your husband. My mom lost my dad. That didn't work out," I say bitterly.

She tilts her head and watches me for a moment. Then she says, "What if you keep showing up and put in the work? If you choose her even when you're scared?" She shrugs. "Then you'll both be believing and fixing it, together. And when the two of you are fighting, what could possibly destroy that? You need to be unified."

I want to believe her.

"Just stop holding your breath, Tate," she says, soft now. "This is the good part, and you're in it."

Then she pats my chest and walks away, calling out to Rowan, "Put down the cider slushie and go flirt with that boy you just kissed earlier!"

I watch her and Rowan argue back and forth playfully and shake my head, but her words are heavy in my chest. Deep down I know she's right.

The rest of the festival is a blur of magic. Junie wins the apple bobbing contest by somehow not getting her hair wet. Donna gives a dramatic reading of her newest book under the big oak tree while children eat kettle corn around her like she's a campfire goddess. And her book characters are suspiciously similar to people we really know in this town.

Old Pete's in his usual spot on the hay bale, waving his arms as he tells some godawful scary story about a ghost ship doomed to sail forever. Every sentence gets more ridiculous, more tangled in maritime metaphors. The kids lean in, wide-eyed. The adults laugh into their cider cups.

Cobweb trots past, tail high, not a stitch of costume on her, yet when the "Best Pet Costume" is announced, somehow, she wins the ribbon. The crowd cheers because even the cat has become a town favorite. People have stopped to take selfies with her.

The festival hums with energy. Strings of lanterns glow overhead, casting warm light across the booths and rides. The sky deepens from gold to purple, stars winking faintly in the indigo. Music drifts from the small stage near the cider press, someone strums a guitar, and couples sway close together.

I wander through it all in a daze, caught between watching the crowd and losing myself in it. Kids squeal from the little Ferris wheel, their laughter ringing through the cool air. A group of teenagers is at the ring toss, jeering at each other with every miss, whooping loud when someone finally lands one on the bottle neck.

"Come on, Tate," one of them hollers. "Bet you can't beat us."

I let them talk me into it. I step up, pay a few bucks, and line up the rings. They heckle, of course, and Willa appears at my side just as I toss the first one. It clangs against glass, bouncing off.

She laughs, eyes bright, cheeks flushed pink from the chill. "All brawn, no aim?"

I shoot her a look, toss another. This one lands, neat as anything, sliding over the neck of a bottle. The teenagers groan. Willa claps, biting her lip like she's trying not to grin too wide.

"What do I win?" I ask the guy behind the booth.

He shrugs, hands me a stuffed pumpkin. It's ridiculous. Bright orange with stitched-on eyes. I hold it out to Willa.

Her dark hair spills around her shoulders, loose and wild, and when she takes the pumpkin, her smile softens. "Thanks, Tate."

We wander together toward the midway games. I let her try her hand at the dart balloons. She pops three in a row, and the guy running the booth hands her a tiny plush bat. She beams, clutching it to her chest like she just won a gold medal.

Next we find ourselves at the caramel apple stand. I buy two, and we walk side by side, chewing sticky bites, laughing when hers drips down her fingers. I grab her wrist without thinking, bring her hand to my mouth, and lick the sugar off her knuckle. She goes still, eyes wide, breath catching. For a second, it's just us and the taste of her skin sweet against my tongue. Then someone calls out, breaking the spell, and she pulls her hand back, cheeks burning.

We circle the fairgrounds. Kids bob for apples in a barrel

while their parents cheer. Couples sit wrapped in blankets on hay bales by the firepit, sipping hot cider. Lanterns sway overhead, glowing golden.

By the time the raffle winners are called and the band plays their last song, the night's winding down. I feel like I've lived a hundred moments in these few hours, each one weaving into something bigger.

"You good?" she asks, her voice soft in the fading noise.

I smile, something loosening in my chest. "Better than ever."

The crowd starts to thin as families herd kids toward cars, arms full of prizes and leftover kettle corn. But the Ferris wheel is still running, its lights glowing soft against the indigo sky. Willa glances at it, then at me, her lips quirking.

"What?" I ask.

She shrugs, curls bouncing. "You think we're too old for a ride?"

"Never." I lead her toward it before she can argue.\

The guy running the wheel smirks as he helps her in, and I climb in beside her, the metal seat rocking under our weight. The bar comes down with a clang, and then we're rising, the ground falling away, lantern light shrinking into a patchwork of gold below.

The air up here is sharper, cooler. The whole town glows beneath us, the harbor a black mirror rimmed in silver moonlight. I glance over at her. She's staring out, eyes wide, lips parted.

"Beautiful, huh?" I murmur.

She looks at me instead of the view. "Yeah."

Something twists in my chest.

The ride pauses at the top to let more people on, leaving us suspended and swaying slightly.

She shifts, her thigh brushing mine, and I can feel the heat of her even through our jeans. I reach for her hand without thinking, lacing our fingers together.

She squeezes once, then leans her head against my shoulder. The world goes quiet up here. Just the creak of the wheel, the distant murmur of laughter below, and her breath warm against my neck.

She looks up at the lanterns, her voice soft. "Feels like the kind of night you wish you could bottle up and keep forever."

I lean down, brushing my mouth near her ear. "Bottle it? I'd put our label on it. That way I know it's always ours."

The wheel jolts, starting to move again, but she doesn't lift her head. We circle down, lantern light brightening around us, and when the ride ends, I help her out, keeping her hand in mine.

We wander toward the edge of the festival, where the crowd has thinned. Music drifts faintly from the stage. Someone's still laughing at Old Pete's wild sea tales, but the sound is softer now, muted.

Willa pulls me toward a quiet spot near the firepit, where the lanterns hang low and the shadows deepen. She takes one of the donuts from the bag, tears it in half, and hands me a piece. Sugar dusts her lips as she bites into hers. I can't help it. I lean forward and kiss the sweetness from her mouth.

She gasps softly, eyes fluttering shut, then kisses me back, slow and lingering, like the whole night has been building to this.

When we part, the lantern light glows gold on her face, and I know I'm done for.

"Come with me," she says suddenly, tugging my hand.

We walk behind the bookstore where the trees are strung with lights and the wind is soft and slow. She pulls out her phone, hits a button, and music starts playing, slow, acoustic, folky.

"Oh, now you have music?" I tease as I brush her lips with mine.

We dance. Right there, just us. Hands at the small of her back. Her forehead against me. The smell of leaves and cider and the slight citrus of her perfume. I'm memorizing everything about this moment. This right here is what I never want to forget. Whenever I am afraid of what's to come, this is the memory I'm going to come back to.

"I love you," I breathe into her hair.

She tilts her face up, eyes locking on mine. "I love you, too," she says, and it's not a whisper. It's steady, warm, like she's been carrying it just as long as I have.

My hands cradle her face before I know I'm moving, thumbs brushing the heat of her flushed cheeks. I kiss her, hard, like the air between us might vanish if I wait another second.

Her lips are soft but urgent against mine, tasting faintly of cinnamon and the cocoa we shared earlier. She gasps into my mouth, and I take the sound, deepening the kiss until I'm half-wild with it.

Her fingers dive into my hair, tugging me closer, pulling a low sound from my throat I don't even try to hide. My palms slide down her spine, feeling the shiver that runs through her as I press her fully against me.

The lanterns sway overhead, their glow casting golden light over her skin. I catch flashes of her lashes lowering, the slight part of her lips between kisses, the way she leans into me like she's giving me all of her.

Every sense is lit up. The faint chill of the night air clinging to her jacket. The way her body fits perfectly against mine. The thud of her heartbeat in sync with mine. I kiss her like I'm memorizing the shape of her mouth, like if I stop, the moment will dissolve. And with every brush of her lips, every curl of her fingers into my shirt, I know this—she—is it for me.

By the time we break apart, we're both breathing hard, foreheads resting together. The lantern light halos her, her lips swollen and glistening, her breath mingling with mine.

* * *

The wind's picking up, curling around the edges of Wisteria Cove like it's looking for a way to be shaken up. Leaves blow everywhere, and it's a never ending battle to keep them cleaned up on the side of the street that has maples.

I step away from the front door of the bookstore where I'm repairing one of the awnings that has been flapping in the wind, phone buzzing in my pocket. I know the number as soon as I see the Pacific area code. It's my old boss, Luke. Voice like gravel and sea salt. The man I spent years trying to impress was hard to walk away from. That man gave me a home and a place to work when I needed it. A brother that I needed during that time away.

I answer anyway and put it on speaker phone and set it beside me. "Luke."

"Hey, Holloway," he says, casual. "You still alive?"

"More or less."

He chuckles. "Listen, I'll make this quick. One of my guys bailed last minute. I've got a crew headed north for a six-week haul. It's rough, but it pays out good. Real good. I need you, man. If you say no, I'll double it. Whatever it takes to get you here."

I swallow. My throat's dry. There's no way I can go out again, but I don't want to say no to him outright after all he's done for me, and it's good to hear his voice.

"I thought you were pissed I left," I mutter.

"I was. But I figured you could use some ocean air, so I'm giving you another shot to come back. You know I need you.

You're the best worker I've ever had. And you know I don't tell everyone that."

It hits me like a fist to the ribs. This would be easy. An easy way to work for six weeks.

But, I love it here. I love what Willa and I have now. I love the tree farm and working with Remy.

And yet it's still new. Unfamiliar.

And fishing is familiar.

Some days this still feels like I'm trying on a life I'm not sure fits. But it's a life I love.

"I'd have to think about it."

"You don't have to answer now. You've got two days. I'll call you soon."

"Thanks," I hang up without saying anything else.

I feel like I'm standing in two places at once, here on the chilly evening of Wisteria Cove, watching the trees sway, and back on a boat, boots soaked, face windburned, nothing but water and fish and noise.

"Tate?"

I turn and Willa stands a few feet away, her jacket pulled tight around her, her face unreadable. I know that look. That tightness. That stillness. She heard me.

Her voice is careful, soft and sharp all at once. "Are you leaving?"

"I don't know," I admit, honest and hating it. "It's a lot of money. I could do it real quick and come back."

There's a beat of silence. She blinks once, slow. "Real quick," she echoes, like the words taste bitter. "What about Remy? What about the tree farm? This is his busiest season. He's counting on you."

"I know, I just—"

"And what about me?" Her voice cracks now, high and tight

and wounded. "What about us? You're just going to up and leave?!"

I take a step toward her, but she steps back as if I lit a match. "Willa—"

"No," she says, breathless. "You don't get to do that right now."

I feel like something is sliding out from under me. The ground is tilting. "It's not like that," I say, desperate. "I'm not trying to leave. I just...I don't know, okay? It's good money. It's familiar. I'm good at it."

"You're good at a lot of things," she snaps. "You're good here. With me. But you're afraid. So you're looking for an escape hatch."

I freeze. She's wrong, but now she doesn't trust me. And that makes it worse.

She exhales sharply, and the wind blows her hair across her face. She doesn't move to fix it. "I thought you were choosing us," she whispers. "I thought we were building something. But if you're already looking for ways to walk away..." Her voice fades.

She shakes her head. One hard shake like she's clearing me out. "I guess it didn't mean anything. Then go," she says. Quiet and final. And she turns and walks away. She doesn't look back.

I stand there, useless, the cold sinking into my skin like it belongs there. She's right. I am afraid.

Afraid that if I stay, I'll screw it up. That I'll let her down. That I'll find a way to fail the one thing I want most.

It'd be easier to leave. But God, I don't want to. I just don't know how to trust that staying won't blow up in my face.

And now? Now I might've messed up everything.

Chapter 23
Willa

Do you know what I realized today?
I never really belonged to the sea.
I belong to you.
—Tate

I slam the teakettle onto the counter hard enough to rattle the sugar jar sitting behind it. If I don't slam something then, I might shatter. And I'm not shattering over Tate Holloway again. I swore I wouldn't.

"Why is he doing this?" I snap, voice sharp and wild in the calm of the bookstore. "Why would he even *consider* leaving again?"

The tea sloshes in the cup. Cobweb lifts her head from her patch of sunlight on the front display and blinks at me like *you okay, mother?*

"No, I am *not* okay," I inform the cat, whose ears are back as she watches me with alarm.

Ivy leans her elbows on the front desk, sipping something with lavender and lemon and zero patience. "I mean, let's be honest, he's a deep-sea fisherman. This is what he knows."

Rowan snorts. "He's also a Scorpio. That means he is impulsive, and he likes danger."

I throw my hands up. "Does it *matter*? He's considering getting on a boat and disappearing for six weeks like this life we've built is just optional. And what if something happens and he doesn't come back? Do you know how I felt all those years that he was gone? I felt like he was dead, like dad. And now he's back, and I could lose him again."

Rowan takes a deep breath, "You're bringing our trauma into this. Tate isn't Dad or Phil. He's safe. And he knows what he's doing. And to be fair, you know that he's a fisherman. It's what he's done for years. You know this. You can't make him stop doing what he loves just because you're scared. That's not right, and you know it."

I don't like being called on my shit by my sisters but deep down I know they're right.

Ivy hums. "To be fair...you're kind of at fault here, too."

I whirl on her. "What is *that* supposed to mean?"

She shrugs, totally unfazed. "You didn't exactly put up a fight, Willa. You said 'then go,' not 'stay.' You didn't ask him to choose you. You practically shoved him out the door. How do you think that made him feel? Like he's not even worth fighting for. You were supposed to fight for him."

"I'm not going to beg someone to stay with me," I snap. "If he doesn't want to stay with me, that's fine. He can just go."

"Clearly it is *not* fine," Ivy mumbles.

Rowan, perched on a stool behind the counter, tilts her head. "No one said anything about begging. But have you *ever* told him you want him to stay? That he's your person? That you're *in it*?"

"I thought I was showing him," I say, quieter now. "I thought that was enough."

Ivy arches a brow. "Sometimes people need the words. And you can always jump his bones, too."

I feel the pressure building in my chest. Like every carefully balanced emotion I've been holding in has just shifted. This is dumb. We're not kids anymore. We're freaking grown-ups, and I can tell him what's on my mind. And he can either decide or break my heart again. And that is the part that scares me.

"Okay, you know what?" I hiss, hands flat on the counter now, shaking. "Maybe I didn't say it or spell it out. But why is it always *me* who has to go first? Who has to be brave? I've been building a life here from nothing. I've been trying, *really trying*, to let someone in for the first time since everything with Dad."

Ivy and Rowan just watch me and wait.

"I've let him in more than I ever thought I would," I whisper. "I've made space for him in my home, my work, my everyday life. I watch him tuck my cat into a blanket and laugh with me. And every time he looks at me like I'm the best thing that ever happened to him, I *want* to believe it's real. But then he gets on the phone and talks about leaving like it was nothing."

I blink fast. Too fast. The tears come, anyway. "He's already thinking about going," I say, crumpling into the nearest chair like my bones gave out. "I was stupid to let myself fall for him again. What if I'm the only one who cares this much?"

The words echo in the room.

Rowan gets off the stool and crouches beside me, her hand warm on my arm. "He's lost a lot, too, Will. His boat and his home. His dad, too. And his mom totally sucks. That kind of grief doesn't just disappear. Maybe he's scared of what it'll mean to stay and let things be good again."

Ivy settles on the arm of the chair beside me, sipping from

her cup. "You're both in unchartered territory and have to learn to trust."

I don't answer. Most of all, I'm scared of loving someone who might leave. Someone I could lose this easily.

I'm scared of believing in something and being wrong again. I'm scared of *hope*. "I don't want to lose him," I whisper.

"But you don't want to be the one left standing on the dock, either," Rowan finishes for me.

My throat closes. I nod. And then I cry. Not the quiet kind. The *messy, ugly, snot-wipe-on-your-own-sleeve* kind.

Ivy gently slides me a tissue from her coat pocket. "There, there. Let it out."

"Shut up," I sniffle.

"Love you, too," she says.

The bookstore is quiet for a beat. Just the creak of the old heater and the rustle of leaves outside the front door.

Then we hear it. A throat clears softly. We all turn. Mom stands in the doorway to the back room, arms crossed, eyes knowing. Her presence hums like candlelight in a storm and always has. She looks at me for a long moment.

Then she says, "It's going to be okay."

I blink at her.

She walks in slowly, heels clicking on the wood floor, a half-folded scarf in her hands like she was doing some mundane task and just *heard things*. And she does that sometimes. Her intuition about her daughters is usually spot on.

"You're both waiting for the other shoe to drop," she says. "You're both bracing for impact. Acting like happiness is a trap instead of a choice."

My heart lurches. She's right. Even though I don't want to admit it.

She stops in front of me, gentle but fierce. "And here's the thing. If you keep expecting love to break, you're going to destroy it before you can get to enjoy it. Could you imagine if I had done that with your dad? Not been with him because he would have left too soon? I would have missed out on him, you girls, and the greatest part of my life."

She looks at me so deeply it makes my eyes water again.

"Real love?" she says, soft now. "It's worth anchoring yourself to. Even when you're scared."

I can't speak. Because I know she's right.

She brushes my hair back behind my ear, just once, like she did when I was seven, too tired and fighting sleep.

Then she hands me the scarf and walks away without another word. The shop is quiet again.

I just sit there feeling cracked wide open.

Later, after Ivy makes another pot of tea and Rowan insists we all eat muffins for emotional grounding, I go upstairs to the apartment and curl up in the window seat.

Cobweb jumps into my lap like she knew this was coming. She tucks her little paws under her chest and stares out at the harbor with me like she's keeping watch.

I think about the way Tate looks at me.

The way he kisses me like I'm the only thing tethering him to shore.

The way he pulled away, not because he didn't care, but because he *did*.

And I think...

Maybe we're both just scared of the same thing, and we've both been hurt enough to think happiness is a trick. But maybe it's not. Maybe it's a choice. And if I want to keep him, I might have to be the first one to choose it.

The bell over the door jingles, and I wipe my face quickly with the sleeve of my cardigan, praying it doesn't look like I just had a breakdown in the tea nook. Again.

* * *

It's late afternoon, the sun slipping golden through the front windows. Ivy and Rowan have stepped out to "forage cider and talk shit." The bookstore's quiet now.

"Hi there," the woman says, stepping inside.

She's probably mid-sixties, bundled in a deep burgundy pea coat with mittens still clipped to her sleeves. Her gray curls are frizzy from the wind, and her smile is warm enough to melt chocolate.

"Welcome in," I say softly, trying to reset my face into something not so *wrecked*.

"I'm looking for a book," she says, glancing around. "A romance. But not one of those 'young things fall in lust and figure it out after 250 pages' types."

I blink. "Okay. More slow burn?"

She waves her hand. "No, no. Not slow burn. I want something with *grit*. I want a love story that almost breaks them apart. But they find their way back. They *fight* for it."

I swallow.

"Like...a second chance story?" I ask, throat a little tight.

"Yes!" she says, lighting up. "Second chances. Third ones, too. Real messy love. The kind that leaves bruises, but you still choose it."

Something stirs in my chest. I know that love.

She leans in, eyes searching mine like we're in on some kind of secret. "My husband and I divorced when we were forty-two. Didn't speak for five years. Then one day he showed up at my work with a sandwich and said, 'I'm tired of pretending I don't still love you.'"

I blink hard. "What happened?"

"We got remarried," she says simply. "Twelve years ago this Christmas."

My hand wraps tightly around the edge of the counter. "That's beautiful."

"It was *terrifying*," she says with a laugh. "But the truth is, real love isn't safe. It's a damn gamble every single day. You just have to decide if it's worth going all in."

I nod slowly, fingers tingling.

She walks over to the romance shelf and picks up a book by an author I know always delivers on a good happily ever after.

"I'll take this one," she says. "And maybe one of those scones. This looks like the kind of place that has good scones."

I blink back a tear. "We do. And I'll ring up this book for you."

"Thank you, sweetheart," she says softly. "And if there's someone you love...don't wait too long to tell him."

I nod again, speechless.

Because the truth is, I think I already did.

The bookstore's quiet again by the time the sun dips past the harbor.

I climb the stairs slowly, every step creaking like it wants to warn me of what's waiting. Cobweb brushes against my ankle as I reach the top, her little black tail flicking like she knows I need company tonight.

The apartment still smells like him. Just traces of woodsmoke, aftershave, pine needles.

It feels like home when he's here. Or what was starting to feel like it.

I pour myself a mug of tea and wrap both hands around it, then sink onto the couch. I should be texting Ivy back, folding laundry, or working on this week's book order, or *doing literally anything* to distract myself.

But instead, I reach into my pocket where I've been hiding the messages Tate's left me over the past few weeks.

He left me little glass vessels. Each one with a note curled inside like a secret. Like a pumpkin spice love spell.

I read the first one. I smile, but it doesn't reach my chest.

Tears prick at the corners of my eyes. Because he meant it. I know he did.

And still...when it came down to it, he didn't know if he'd stay.

He *hesitated*.

The door creaks as the wind pushes against it, and for a moment I imagine he'll walk through.

Smiling, tugging off his boots, asking what book I'm reading tonight.

But it's just the wind.

And the sound of my own heartbeat.

I curl deeper into the couch, Cobweb climbing onto my chest, purring like a lullaby I don't deserve.

"I want him to stay," I whisper to the dark. "I want him to choose *this*. Choose me."

The tea's cold. My chest aches. But even now, surrounded by his words, I don't know if it's enough.

Because I've had people choose me before. And leave anyway.

Chapter 24
Tate

They say the ocean keeps its secrets.
But my secret is simple:
I never stopped loving you.
—Tate

The sky over Wisteria Cove can't decide whether or not it wants to storm. I get it, I feel the same. I slept on a couch in the cabin out at the Bennett Tree Farm last night. It's cold, lonely, and I miss Willa. I even miss Cobweb.

The more I think about it, the stupider it all seems. Why did I even consider that trip? I don't blame her for being mad. It's stupid. Just when things are good, I mess it up. And I can't help but hear my mom's voice in my head. *"There you go messing things up, just like your dad always did."*

I know she doesn't want me to go out fishing anymore. She worries, and rightfully so after what happened. But part of me can't help it. It is who I am. But even I'm doubting that now that

I'm settling in here and working alongside Remy. Fishing isn't everything to me, it was just a job.

Willa is everything to me.

Low clouds stack over the harbor like bruises, and wind curls off the water, cutting through coats, sneaking under doors. The weather feels like it's coming for something. I feel it in my chest and in my ribs. A part of me always expects the tide to drag something precious out to sea. Like I'm not supposed to have anything good. And I'm trying to let that go and accept the good. Claim the good, take the good, and not take less than that. I deserve this, and so does Willa.

Rain pounds sideways against the side of the workshop at the tree farm. Inside, I keep my head down. Keep moving. Keep sawing, sanding, stacking, because if I stop, I'm afraid I'll come undone.

Remy called out today. Junie has a cold, and Donna's up against a deadline. So it's just me, trying to keep up with the daily tasks and get ahead on what's coming. I'm using the distraction of work to pretend like I'm not unraveling thread by thread. Because I am.

This morning, Old Pete came and found me out at the Bennett Tree Farm. I was surprised to see him, and it made me worry. Before this, he never came out to the farm. He sat beside me in the small break room, sipping coffee. He looked smaller than usual, like the flannel he had on was wearing *him* instead of the other way around. I was sipping my coffee when he told me. "Doc says I don't have a lot of time left."

My chest went tight, and I felt like the air whoosh out of it.

"Lungs," he said matter-of -factly, like it was a weather report. "Caught up with me after all these years. There's not much more they can do."

I didn't know what to say. So I said nothing, just slid my chair closer and threw my arm around his shoulders, and he leaned into me. He didn't seem to need my words, anyway; he just had things to say. "I know you'll take care of it. Wisteria Cove. The harbor. All of it. Just like I would. You've always been special to this place."

I was speechless. This moment took me back to when he came and told me that my father and Phil Maren were missing, and they had stopped looking and didn't think they were coming home. My mom had screamed and cried. She stayed in bed for a week after that. I will never forget the look on his face when he told me. And now? Now he's telling me that another good man in my life was leaving. And I know it wasn't easy for him. He looked wrecked.

He clapped my shoulder once. Like that was that. "You've always had a better compass than you think, son."

Then he left, like he hadn't just handed me the responsibility of the whole damn town and taken away another piece of my heart.

And now I can't breathe. I put my face in my hands and cry. Old Pete isn't just special to me; he's special to everyone. And this town is going to have a crater in it when he's gone.

There's no way in hell I would ever leave Wisteria Cove, not that I think I ever would have. But now? Now I need to make the most of every day with Pete.

I get up and finish up work for the day and sweep the shop thoroughly. Making sure everything is perfect, I glance around, then shut off the light and lock the door. I swallow and exhale a deep breath at the bomb Old Pete dropped on me today.

I make my way to the new-to-me truck I bought and start the engine, my breath in front of me. It's cold, but I can't even feel it.

My mom's deadline is looming. Her texts are brief: *"Don't forget, end of the month."* Like I could. She wants me out. I just thought maybe I'd have more time. Time to figure it out. But time doesn't wait. Life keeps on moving, and there's never enough time.

And now Pete is dying. And Willa...God, Willa. She hasn't spoken to me since our fight. Since she told me to go. She's going to be devastated about Pete.

She thinks I *want* to leave. But the truth is, I just don't know how to *stay* without breaking something. Without being the one who ruins it all.

I lose everything. My dad. My mom. And now Old Pete. The man who stepped up for me when my dad died. His boat is going to be gone soon, too. The last place I called home. Every time I reach for something good, I lose my grip. It's like there's a hole inside me that nothing can fill.

I sit on the steps of the cabin, boots wet, flannel soaked through, head in my hands. Rain pelts the roof above the porch like it's trying to punch through.

I want to scream. Instead, I sit on the steps and let it all wash over me.

I think about the night my dad died. How we'd argued before he left. How I told him I wanted to go out with him on that trip. I had a feeling that something wasn't right. And part of me blames myself for not telling him that I had a bad feeling and trying to make him stay. But I know that he probably wouldn't have listened. And I know that I probably let him down. He wouldn't have wanted me to run away like I did. My dad never ran from anything. He faced things head-on and took care of his family. And I know he fought for us even when he was going down. I know he did. I feel it. That's the man he was.

That night I watched him and my mom fight. She didn't want him to go out on that trip, either. But she never wanted him to go out on trips. She screamed at him when he left and told him to not even bother coming back.

And I've carried that ever since. I've carried *him*. For a

while I thought maybe she carried guilt for her words. But now, looking back, I don't think she ever did.

Every decision I've made since he went missing has been a half-hearted apology. Some punishment I thought I deserved for living when he didn't. I sometimes wished I'd gone out with him. Even when I joined that Pacific crew with the rough waters and hard runs, I told myself I was just doing what I had to. I never feared being out on the water, because I know what the water is capable of. I know the risks.

But there was always guilt. And now I'm drowning in it again. I shouldn't have left, and if I hadn't, I'd have had those years I was gone with Pete. Now who knows how much time we have with him.

I don't hear the Jeep pull up beside the cabin until Willa steps out into the storm and walks around towards the front of the cabin.

She's soaked in seconds. Wet hair clinging to her cheeks. Her eyes are wild and shining, and she's never looked more like every dream I'm too scared to want.

"What are you *doing*?" she yells over the rain.

I stare at her, blinking water from my eyes. "I could ask you the same thing."

She moves closer. Angry, fragile, and fierce. "Why are you pulling away? Why are you shutting me out?"

"Because I'm losing everything," I snap. "My mom's pushing me out. I've got no savings, no backup, and the only good thing in my life just told me to leave."

I don't tell her about Pete yet, because honestly, I'm not sure he wants me to, and I know it will gut her.

"I told you to leave because you even considered it in the first place!" she shouts, voice cracking. "You won't let yourself be happy! Do you know what that feels like? To want this and wonder if it will work out?"

I look at her, chest heaving. "I don't know how to stay, Willa. I don't know how to believe something good that I have won't vanish like everything else."

Her face crumples. "So you don't believe in us."

"It's not *you*. It's just..." I cut myself off, the words twisting sharp in my throat. "It's everything."

The wind howls around us. Rain pelts the porch.

"I don't want to hurt you," I tell her. "But I *will*. That's what I do. That's what happens."

She steps back as if I slapped her.

"You said you'd build a life with me," she says, voice quiet and shaking. "You left messages in bottles. You kissed me like I was it for you. And I wanted to be your home. I want you. And now you're what, scared of being loved?"

"I'm scared of losing you," I rasp. "And if I stay and mess it up, that's exactly what will happen."

She shakes her head. "You don't get to sabotage things because you're afraid."

I look away. The storm crashes harder.

And then she turns and goes back her Jeep.

I *don't* follow her. Because I don't deserve to.

* * *

My hand trembles slightly as I reach for the empty bottle on the shelf. It's the same kind I've used for weeks now, tiny, curved glass with a cork top.

But it's also the only way I've ever been able to say the things that terrify me and don't know how to speak out loud. Things I couldn't say to her when she was looking at me with those angry and betrayed eyes.

I uncork the top. Slide the bottle closer. Then I take a breath and grab my pen and paper. And start to write.

. . .

Willa,

I told myself I wasn't going to write to you again. Not like this. Not in a way you might never read.

But the truth is, I don't know how to say what I need to your face without breaking apart. So here it is. All of it. The real truth. What I couldn't say out loud.

Because when I look at you, I see a life I never thought I deserved. Laughter in a kitchen. Cobweb stealing my pillow. Coffee on slow Sunday mornings in bed, and your sleepy voice reading to me from a romance novel you claim is "just okay."

And I want it. All of it. But I don't know how to trust that I get to have it.

Everywhere I've ever landed, the ground's eventually crumbled beneath me. My dad. My mom. My home. The ocean, I thought, was where I belonged. And even more things I can't tell you yet. I feel like it's all been washed out to sea.

You were the first person that felt like I could have something real and safe. Maybe I couldn't lose you, because you were the one real thing. The one that mattered.

And then I panicked because I kept thinking, this is too good. This can't be mine.

I reached for the life I knew to survive. Not the one I want. Not the one I'd give anything to keep.

And worse, I know I hurt you to protect myself. I never want to hurt you. I love you so much it hurts.

You didn't deserve any of it. You are the softest thing I've ever known. And yet somehow the strongest.

I just don't know how to believe. But I'm trying.

And if there's even a sliver of you that still wants me, if you ever read this, just know that I would spend a lifetime undoing what I broke. That I would carry your fears with mine, and your grief. I promise I will never stop fighting to get things right.

I love you. And I will always choose you, even if I have to do it quietly, from a distance. Even if I never get to hear you say it back again.

I will never leave again. I am your anchor. And you are my harbor.

Tate

I don't bottle the message. I fold it once, twice, three times until it fits in the pocket of my coat.

And I keep it there. Close to my heart. I'm going to show her everything I was too afraid to say.

Until then, I'll carry it like a compass, pointing me home.

Chapter 25
Willa

The rain comes down like punishment, and it pounds on the windows of the bookstore in rhythmic slaps, as the wind howls through Wisteria Cove. The shop lights flicker once, then again. This storm is a bad one and feels like it will leave a mark.

I'm restocking a display of fall reads near the front window when the door bursts open with a bang. The wind slams it against the wall, and a drenched silhouette stumbles in, frantic and calling out for me.

"Donna?" I run to her, and she's soaked from head to toe, her hair plastered to her cheeks, eyes wild.

"Willa. It's Pete," she struggles to catch her breath, her eyes wild with worry. "Pete didn't come back in. He went out to check traps, and no one can get ahold of him. Something is wrong! I just know it."

My blood freezes. Not again. Not someone else.

"Where's Tate?" I ask, already sprinting around the counter.

"He's heading to the harbor," Donna calls frantically after me. "He said he's going out to look."

I'm gone before she finishes the sentence. The wind nearly knocks me over the second I hit the street. My boots slip on wet cobblestones as I run, cloak whipping behind me like wings.

The harbor is chaos. Rain lashes sideways. Waves slam against the docks. A group of townspeople stand in huddled silence under the bait shop porch, watching with wide, worried eyes.

Pete isn't just one of us; he is us. If he's missing, I know Tate will literally turn this ocean upside down. Neither of us can handle losing someone else we love like that.

Tate is already on the boat in his wet gear, soaked through, checking the engine and about to pull off.

I scramble to get on, slipping, and he whips around in surprise, his mouth open.

"You're going to get Pete?" I shout over the storm.

His face is pale, jaw clenched. Determined. "I have to."

"Then I'm coming with you."

He freezes. "Willa, no."

I look at him stubbornly, unmoving.

He stares at me for a beat too long and then nods once. He knows this is big, because I haven't been on a boat since my dad went missing. That's all it takes.

I don't hesitate and climb in next to him, helping him with the ropes. He's not the only one who grew up on a fishing boat. It comes back to me, surprisingly, and we work side by side. My fingers fumble as I grab a wet slicker from down below that's way too big and slide it on. I've been out with my dad in all types of weather, but this is the worst. Nobody should be out in this.

The boat bucks as we hit the waves, the engine roaring beneath us. Water sprays up over the sides, stinging cold against my cheeks. We move through the storm like a heartbeat, fast, frantic, desperate, and determined.

I scan the churning water, eyes burning from the rain. And then I see it.

A flicker of yellow and a half-submerged figure. Old Pete's hunched figure, clinging to a buoy, soaked and shivering.

"There!" I scream.

Tate angles the boat hard. We pull up beside the wreck, ropes flying. It's frantic, messy, and Tate's hauling Pete in, me grabbing at his soaked coat, sobbing with relief. "Pete! Oh my god!"

Pete coughs violently, barely hanging on. He wouldn't have been able to hang on much longer, and I'm so glad we got here when we did.

I cradle his face. "You old fool," I whisper. "You scared the hell out of us."

Tate drives us back through the storm. I hold Pete the whole way, his head resting against my shoulder as I whisper whatever comfort I can find. My heart is pounding, not from fear anymore, but from something else. We almost lost him.

Back on shore, Tate and I secure the boat in silence. Our hands are shaking, soaked, frozen. Neither of us says anything, because we don't have to. Finding Pete alive restored something that we had lost in both of us. A sliver of hope that we won't lose another man we both love. The dock creaks under our weight as the rain finally starts to ease. We finally face each other, breathless.

He speaks first. "We made it."

I nod, eyes stinging. "We always will."

He takes a shaky breath. "Willa, I—"

"I'm so sorry," I whisper. "I see it now. I see what I didn't before. You're good at this. You're a great fisherman. If you want this, I'll support you. I'll always support you. I shouldn't have been so selfish. I won't keep you from something that you love."

His eyes search mine.

"If you still want to go," I say, voice cracking, "I'll be right here, waiting. Even if I miss you and will always worry about you."

His face falls, and for a second, I think I've misread everything.

But then he shakes his head. "I'm not going."

My heart stops, and I search his face. "What? What do you mean?"

"I need to take care of the people I love. I'll always be here. For you. For Pete. For everyone who matters. Houses and boats don't matter. People matter. You matter most. I love you."

I step into him, pressing my lips to his. "I love you, you idiot."

He kisses me as if the storm never happened. Like we were never lost. Like we were always finding our way back. And it feels right. Like everything was always going to be okay after all.

Later, Tate makes sure Pete is warm and safe at Donna's while I wring out every inch of my soaked clothes and then take a hot shower. I curl into my cozy sweats afterward, and then head back down to the bookstore to grab Tate's flannel jacket that I took with me out of his truck to stay warm when he dropped me off. I still can't get warm, and also I just want to touch something that smells like him.

The bookstore is quiet. Dim. The storm still knocks gently on the windows, but it's calmed to a soft weep and not the angry slaps that it was. I step behind the counter and reach for the damp flannel he left in a heap. It's the one he always wears, navy, worn, lined in soft flannel. Familiar in a way that makes my chest ache.

As I reach into the pockets and pull it tighter around me, something flutters to the floor. It's a folded piece of paper, creased and damp.

I crouch to pick it up, fingers trembling. At first, I think it might be a receipt or a to do list. But then I see my name and my breath catches. The handwriting is unmistakably his.

I glance toward the door, as if someone might walk in. Like someone might stop me. My heart pounds as I unfold the rest of it slowly and carefully.

I read it and my vision blurs with tears. I read it again. And again. Each word hits me over and over like thunder. Every sentence peels away another piece of armor I had carefully constructed around my heart.

I sink to the floor behind the counter, the coat in my lap, the letter clutched in my hands. I can still feel the heat of the storm under my skin, but this? This wrecks me more than the wind or the waves ever could.

A quiet truth he held close, maybe because he thought he didn't know how to say it out loud. Or maybe because he didn't think I'd want to hear it. But I do. God, I do.

Tears roll down my cheeks, warm and unrelenting. I press the letter to my chest, breathing through the ache, through the heartbreak and the healing. For the storm and the rescue. For the boy who never stopped being my best friend, even when I thought he was gone. And for the man he's become, who will throw everything down to save the people he loves. Who loves with all of his big heart, and for the second chance I never dared to hope for, now resting in my trembling hands. This letter is everything. It's his heart. And that heart is mine.

I don't hear the bell chime on the door or hear the door open. But suddenly, he's standing in the doorway, dripping wet, the storm soaking through his coat and hair. He looks like a man who's walked through fire and rain just to get here, and maybe he has. His eyes lock on mine.

They drop to the letter in my hands. I stand slowly, chest tightening, breath trembling.

"You read it," he says, voice raw like the wind outside.

I nod. Tears fall, slow and silent. I don't wipe them away.

He takes a step closer. The rain hits harder behind him like it's pushing him toward me. "I didn't know if I'd ever be brave enough to give it to you."

"You didn't need to," I whisper. "I've already forgiven you, I love you."

He's standing in front of me now. So close I can see the raindrops clinging to his lashes. The way his jaw ticks, barely restrained emotion. He looks at me like I'm the only thing keeping him from falling apart.

"You said you loved me," he says, like he's afraid to believe it. "Even when I screw everything up. You mean it?"

I nod again. "With every part of me."

He exhales, like the weight of the entire ocean just slid off his shoulders.

I reach up slowly and brush his soaked hair back from his forehead. His eyes flutter closed, and he leans into my touch like he's starved for it. Like my fingertips are the only anchor he has left.

"Come upstairs," I breathe, soft and certain.

He doesn't hesitate.

We walk hand in hand through the quiet bookstore, the storm outside muting everything else. Cobweb is curled up in the window and watches us.

My apartment door creaks open. The scent of cedar, tea, and cinnamon wraps around us.

The second the door closes, he turns to me, and I fall into him. He kisses me like he's drowning and I'm the only air he's ever tasted. His hands tremble as they slide to my waist, then up my back, then cradle my face like I'm something breakable he never wants to break again.

I push him back towards the bathroom, kissing him until we stop just outside the shower. I reach up and turn it on the hottest setting.

He pulls back for just a second, breath ragged. "I love you so much, Willa. Even when I mess it up, I'll never stop. I promise I'll never leave you again."

"I love you, too," I whisper. "And I know."

We move fast. I get him out of his wet clothes as quickly as possible and kiss him into the shower until he's under the hot spray, and I feel his body relax.

I step out of my clothes and pull off my top and throw it onto the floor. I kiss him, pulling him into my body heat. He dips his forehead to mine and lets it rest there.

We stay like that, like our bodies are in a silent prayer of thanks for the do-over. The second chance we're both grasping onto and not letting go. Like we're building something we want to last this time.

He presses a kiss to my shoulder and pulls me tighter. His mouth brushes over my collarbone. My jaw. My lips again. Every touch says *I'm sorry. I missed you. I love you. I need you.*

The shower is already steaming, water pouring over us in a steady rush. I run my hands over the planes of his chest, warm and slick beneath my palms, his skin smelling like salt, rain, and the wild outside. He breathes hard when I hold him tighter, like he needs it more than air, and something inside me aches with the need to be that for him. The one he runs to. The one who steadies him. His safe harbor.

He cups my chin, fingers trembling as he tilts my face up. His eyes are darker than the storm outside. "You're so damn beautiful," he murmurs, his voice breaking. "You always have been."

I can't speak. I just press my mouth to his, slow and sure, tasting water and want, kissing him deeper, longer, until I'm dizzy.

He reaches for the soap, working up a lather in his hands before spreading it over me with a washcloth. The fabric whispers over my skin, dragging heat in its wake. He's gentle, thorough, his touch reverent as he glides it over my shoulders, down my arms, over my breasts. His thumb circles my nipples, teasing until I moan into his mouth. The cloth trails lower, over my stomach, in between my thighs. I gasp and clutch at him, my knees trembling at the slick, deliberate stroke of his fingers beneath the fabric.

"Relax," he whispers, lips brushing the shell of my ear. "Let me take care of you."

He turns me, pulling me back against his chest. I lean into him as he squeezes shampoo into his palms, working it into my hair with slow, massaging circles. His fingers dig into my scalp, firm but tender, and a moan slips from my lips before I can stop it. His cock presses hard at the small of my back, thick and insistent, and I push against him, breathless with the heat curling low in my belly.

I can't help myself. I turn, sinking to my knees on the wet tiles, the spray pelting my back as I take him in my hand. His head tips back instantly, his groan echoing against the shower walls. I lick the bead of moisture from his tip before sliding my mouth down over him, taking as much as I can. His taste fills me, musky and raw, and I hollow my cheeks, sucking harder, loving the way his thighs tense beneath my hands.

"Willa," he rasps, his fingers tangling in my wet hair. His hips jerk, shallow thrusts that make me choke and moan around him. The sound drives him wild. "God, you're killing me."

Before he loses control, he drags me up, spinning me so my back hits the cold tile. The shock makes me cry out, my nipples tightening painfully against the chill. Then his mouth is on mine, hot and demanding, his tongue claiming me as his hands grip my thighs, lifting me effortlessly.

I wrap my legs around his waist as he thrusts into me in one smooth, hard stroke. The contrast of cold tile at my back and his burning heat inside me is overwhelming. I gasp, nails digging into his shoulders as he pounds into me, his rhythm relentless, the water cascading over us in pounding sheets.

"More," I beg, rocking against him, my moans filling the small stall. He growls low, shifting me higher in his arms, angling deeper until he hits that spot inside me that makes me shatter. I cry out, clinging to him as my body convulses, the orgasm tearing through me like a storm.

But he doesn't stop. He spins me, pressing my front to the slick tile, his hand fisting in my hair as he thrusts into me from behind. My breasts flatten against the cold wall, my nipples aching with the sensation, every movement dragging a desperate whimper from me. He lifts one of my legs, hooking it higher over his arm to give him better access, and the new angle is devastating.

"God, Tate," I moan, clawing at the tile, my body arching back to take him deeper.

His hands grip my hips tight, bruising, as he slams into me, his groans ragged, lost to the rhythm. My thighs shake, pleasure building again impossibly fast. When I come this time, it's louder, harder, every nerve ending sparking as he drives me straight into oblivion.

He follows me over the edge, his roar muffled against my shoulder as he buries himself deep, holding me against him like he'll never let go.

When the water finally runs cold, we stumble out, bodies slick, hearts pounding. We collapse into the bed in a tangle of limbs, clinging to each other like it's the only place we've ever belonged.

And when he takes me again, it's slower, softer, like he's mapping me inch by inch, memorizing a place he never wants to lose again.

Our bodies fit together in a perfect, aching way. His hands on my hips. His lips on my throat. My fingers in his hair. It's not rushed. It's not desperate. It's *home*.

We move together like we've done this a hundred times, but never quite got it right until now.

And when I wrap my arms around him and pull him closer, he buries his face in my neck and exhales a shaky breath that sounds like relief.

After, he gathers me into his arms and pulls the quilt over both of us.

Our skin touches from shoulder to toe. His fingers trace lazy circles into my back. My head rests on his chest, his heartbeat slow and steady.

We don't talk. We don't need to tonight. Outside, the storm quiets, but inside, we're finally still.

"I love you," he murmurs into my hair. "I'm sorry I left before. I won't do it again."

"I love you, too," I whisper. "And if you ever leave, just take me with you."

He pulls me tighter. "Deal."

And I believe him. It's a new beginning for us.

Chapter 26
Tate

For the first time in what feels like days, Wisteria Cove is quiet, and the wind's not trying to tear everything apart. The storm passed before dawn, but I barely noticed, because I had my arms wrapped around her, and almost everything is right with my world. Almost. I hate that Pete is sick, and I hate that we almost lost him last night. He scared the hell out of me. Thank God Donna and Pete are close, and she knew something was off. She saved his life, letting us all know that he had done something foolish going out like that. I will be talking to him about that.

I'm awake before Willa, tucked under our quilt that smells like cedar and cinnamon, the soft purr of Cobweb vibrating against my thigh. The little kitten has made herself at home in my lap like this is normal. Like *I'm* her normal. And god, I love it.

The bookstore is still and dark.

I shift slowly, careful not to wake Willa, who's curled beside me in nothing but one of my flannels. Her dark hair's a mess. Her bare legs are tangled in the quilt. Her hand's on my chest like she never wants to let go. I don't want her to, either. I press a kiss to her forehead and let my eyes close again.

Ten minutes later, she's gone from my side and humming in the small kitchen of the loft. Her voice is soft, almost subconscious. She doesn't know she's doing it, but I do. She hums when she feels good. Safe. And I haven't heard that hum in a long time.

I sit up and reach for the mug she set beside the bed. Coffee. Strong and hot. She knows how I take it.

Cobweb stretches and hops off me like she's done her job and now demands breakfast. I sip slow. Let it all sink in. The storm is over. She's here. I didn't lose her. Life feels...good.

I stand, stretch, and wander into the kitchen. She's at the stove, flipping eggs in a cast-iron skillet, her back to me. The flannel rides up just high enough to make my brain short-circuit.

I lean in the doorway, sipping my coffee, smiling like a damn fool. "You're humming," I say, voice still sleep-rough.

She glances over her shoulder and smirks. "And you're watching me like a weirdo."

I shrug, stepping closer. "I like what I see."

She rolls her eyes, but I catch the way her cheeks flush. She plates the eggs and adds buttered toast, handing one plate to me. "Sit. Eat. You earned it."

"How did I earn it? Was it after we rescued Old Pete or what I did to you in that shower and bed?" I grin as I drop into the chair like it's the best seat in the house. Probably because it is. It's across from her.

She laughs and says, "Both."

We eat in silence for a moment, only the sounds of forks and the occasional pop from the fire in the wood stove.

She sips her coffee and raises a brow. "You're quiet."

I smile into my toast. "Just taking it all in."

"Taking what in?"

"This," I say, motioning around the room. "You. Me. Cobweb sleeping over there like she pays rent."

The cat flicks her tail at me, unimpressed.

Willa's eyes soften. "It's not perfect, but I think we can build a good life here together."

I lean across the table. "I know we will. We already are."

She sets down her fork. "Good, but we need to look for a place. Rowan needs the loft up here while she's building next door. Her cottage doesn't have heat right now. It makes sense for her to be here when she's doing renovations."

The second she says it, my fork stills halfway to my mouth. *We need to look for a place.*

The words echo in my head, rattling around my chest like they're too big to fit all at once. She's not just talking about a roof over our heads. She's talking about *us*. About choosing somewhere together. About building something permanent.

For a man who's spent years drifting, convincing himself he wasn't built for roots, it hits me hard. Like the ground has shifted under my boots. My pulse kicks, equal parts shock and wonder, and I can't stop staring at her.

She says it so casually, like it's the most natural thing in the world. And maybe that's what floors me the most. To her, this isn't a question. It isn't a risk. It's just *us*. The two of us, carving out space together in this town, in this life.

My chest tightens, something raw and fierce swelling there. It feels like hope. It feels like belonging. Like finally coming home after being lost at sea.

Her hand drifts across the table, and I take it. Our fingers lace easily, naturally. Like we've done this a hundred times. Like we should've been doing this all along.

"You slept hard," she says.

"You wore me out," I tease, voice low.

Her eyes sparkle. "Are you complaining?"

"Not even a little."

I reach across, brushing a crumb from the corner of her mouth with my thumb. She catches my wrist, holds it there for a beat too long, like she doesn't want to let it go.

"I meant what I said last night," I tell her. "I will do everything to make you feel safe. I'm not leaving."

Her smile fades a little. "I just...I've waited a long time to feel safe again. Really safe. I don't want to keep bracing for the goodbye."

I nod, standing up. I walk around the table and kneel beside her chair. "No more goodbyes."

Her eyes shine, and she leans forward, pressing her lips to mine. It's slow and sweet, just like everything else this morning. She tastes like coffee and sunshine.

When we pull apart, she rests her forehead against mine.

"You hungry still?" she asks.

I grin. "Not for food."

She laughs, soft and breathless and kisses me again. The storm is gone. The world is quiet. And for the first time in a long time, I feel like maybe I don't have to fight so hard anymore.

* * *

It's Sunday, and the bookstore is closed. We're curled up on Willa's couch, under the old quilt with Cobweb asleep on our lap. The bookstore below us is quiet, full of dust motes dancing in the sun and stories.

She's in my arms, legs tucked under her, her cheek against my chest. And we're just...*here*. Still and settled. Breathing the same rhythm.

But I feel her hand resting on my chest, right over my heart. I feel the questions in her fingertips. The things neither of us has said yet. The heaviness we keep pretending isn't there. So I start. Not because it's easy. But it's *time*.

"I have to tell you something," I tell her softly.

She lifts her head slowly. "What?"

"Old Pete's sick."

"What do you mean?" she asks, looking stricken.

I nod, my throat feeling tight. "A few days ago, he came by the tree farm and told me."

"Oh, Tate..." Her fingers slide into mine.

I stare at the fire. "I'm not sure if he wants everyone to know. But I think after last night, you should know. But maybe he doesn't know how to tell everyone. Saying it out loud feels like it's real. And I don't want it to be real."

She squeezes my hand. "I hate this. But he doesn't have to do this alone. I want to be there for him."

I exhale, shaky and low. The kind that's been sitting in my lungs for years. "He told me I'd be the one to look after Wisteria Cove when he's gone."

Willa's eyes soften. "He trusts you. And he knows you have a heart even bigger than his."

"Yeah. Which is insane, right? I've done nothing to prove I'm worthy of that trust. I've let people down." I pause, blinking hard. "I thought we'd have more time with him."

She brushes her thumb across my cheek, and I see a tear streak down her cheek. "I know. I always thought that when I got married, he'd be the one to walk me down the aisle. He told me that he would after my dad died."

"I want to be present for every minute of this life that I can and be there for those I love," I say with conviction. No matter what happens, we are all in this together.

Her breath catches, but she doesn't speak.

I sit up a little, needing to look her in the eye for what comes next.

"There's something else," I say. "Something I've never told anyone."

She nods once. Silent. Ready.

"The day my dad died..." I stop, my jaw clenching. My hands curl into fists before I force them open. "My dad and I had plans. He wasn't supposed to go out that day. Stupid, right?"

She shakes her head, eyes already shimmering. "Not stupid."

"But then your dad..." I swallow hard. "He radioed in that he needed my dad."

She's silent. Completely still.

"And my dad went," I say, my voice flat now. "And I had a bad feeling. I had even asked to go out with them. But he had shrugged me off and said he didn't need me."

I see it hit her. Like a wave to the chest.

My voice cracks when I continue. "I know it wasn't your dad's fault. But part of me...part of me needed someone to blame."

"And you blamed my dad," she whispers.

"Yeah. I did. For a long time."

Tears slip from the corners of her eyes, but she doesn't look away. "I always wondered if you did."

"I know it was just an accident." I press my hand to her cheek. "I was angry and broken and drowning in it."

"We didn't know how to hold grief," she says, her voice cracking.

I nod. "And I held it wrong. I held it until it poisoned everything."

Her lip trembles. She leans into my palm like she's been waiting for this moment to happen between us so we can finally get past it, something that was keeping us from being fully together. It's gone now.

"I should've dealt with it sooner," I whisper. "I'm sorry."

She climbs into my lap and wraps her arms around my neck, burying her face in my shoulder.

I hold her. Tight. Like I'm making up for every second I didn't before. And she cries. She cries for her dad. For mine. For Old Pete. For us. And I let her. Because for the first time, it feels safe to fall apart.

We sit like that until her tears slow. Until all that's left is the warmth of our skin pressed together, the steady rise and fall of our breathing.

"I don't want to carry all this sadness anymore," I say.

"I know," she whispers.

She leans in and kisses me softly and slowly and a little shakily, like we're rewriting the past with our mouths.

Her hands cradle my face like she's afraid I'll disappear. I kiss her back like I never want to leave again. Because I don't. Because *this* pain—the love, the mess of it—is real. And it's ours.

We curl back up under the quilt, tangled and quiet, her head on my chest and my heart steady for the first time in years.

"I love you," I whisper into her hair.

She sighs against me, her body soft and warm in my arms. "I love you, too."

Chapter 27
Willa

You were the lighthouse the whole damn time,
weren't you?
Even when I was too blind to see it.
You kept shining.
And I'm finally ready to sail home for good.
-Tate

The smell of old books and cinnamon lingers in the air, but my eyes aren't on the stack of books beside me. They're on the dock, and more specifically, on him. Tate Holloway's wearing that navy flannel that makes my knees weak, sleeves rolled to the elbows, hair a little wind-tousled from the harbor breeze. He's laughing, a full-belly, eyes-crinkling, head-thrown-back kind of laugh, as Old Pete yells something at him from the bench near the bait shop. But I know there's a heaviness behind those eyes. It's a heaviness of what's coming, but I know he's soaking up every minute that he can right now.

Pete gestures wildly with his hand while Tate ties something off on a skiff like he's finally chosen this place and let himself take root. The knot in my chest loosens a little more. And my heart breaks a little, wondering how many more moments we'll have like this with Pete.

I tuck a blanket under my arm, grab two steaming to-go cups of hot coffee behind the counter, and head for the door. Cobweb meows from her window perch as I pass, flicking her tail like she approves.

The chill hits me the second I step outside, but I don't care. The path to the dock is layered in golden leaves and the harbor hums with life, seagulls crying, water slapping against boats, someone hammering in the distance. Wisteria Cove is calm and alive, a reminder that life goes on even after storms.

Pete sees me coming before I say anything. "Well, if it isn't the prettiest book witch in the harbor."

"You only say that when I bring you coffee," I tease, passing him a cup.

He sniffs dramatically. "Ah, perfection in a cup. What's the secret to your coffee, Willa?"

"A pinch of cinnamon in the grounds," I tell him, not even hesitating as I unfold the blanket and lay it across his lap. "And this is so your knees don't turn to brittle sea glass by lunch."

"Rude." He playfully rolls his eyes, but he tucks it around him anyway. "Now, I *know* something is up. Because you'd never tell anyone your coffee secrets unless they're dying."

I give him my best smile, even though I feel my eyes ping with a sting of tears and scoot in closer next to him. "Someone's gotta keep you safe."

"Thought you'd be glued to your shop, guarding your spell books and carrying that cat everywhere." He says, obviously not ready to talk about it yet.

"Cobweb can hold down the fort for a few minutes."

We both watch Tate for a moment, the soft creak of the dock settling beneath our weight. He's working and getting his boat cleaned up from last night; it looks like.

I glance at the old man beside me. His cheeks are ruddy from the wind. His hands shake a little as he lifts the mug. But his eyes...they're bright. Sharp. Holding more stories than the entire second floor of my shop.

Pete doesn't look at me. "You know, don't you?"

I rest my hand gently over his on the bench between us. "I know that you're sick."

He stiffens for half a second. Then sighs. "Big mouth. Knew he couldn't keep that to himself."

"He did. He didn't tell me right away. I could just...tell something was weighing him down." I squeeze his hand. "You've always been the anchor of this town, Pete. The cranky, salty, slightly terrifying anchor."

"I prefer charmingly cantankerous."

I smile. "Sure, that works, too. Seriously, though. We're not gonna let you carry this alone. Whatever you need, I'm here. We all are. No one in this town is going to let you go at this alone. You're not alone in this."

He swallows hard, and I see the flicker in his expression, like he's not sure whether to cuss me out or cry. "Damn it, Willa."

"I know." I lay my head on his shoulder, and we both stare out at the harbor.

He clears his throat, takes another sip of coffee. "I'm not used to this whole 'people giving a damn' thing."

"Well, too bad. You've spent your whole life taking care of this place. Now it's our turn to take care of you."

He turns to me slowly, blinking faster than usual. "You really mean that?"

"With every beat of my sappy little witchy heart."

He laughs, and then, just for a second, his fingers tighten around mine.

"You remind me of your mom," he says, voice suddenly rough.

That knocks the wind out of me. "Yeah?"

"She always been full of spitfire and heart. Never backed down. Always knew when someone needed a hand to hold, even if they didn't say it. Just like you."

"Well," I say, voice catching, "I had good people to raise me."

"Yes, you did," he says, taking a sip of his coffee and smiling as if he knows a secret no one else knows.

We sit there a while, just watching Tate fix something along the dock with that signature Holloway determination.

"He's just like you, you know," Pete murmurs. "That's why you're both so perfect to run Wisteria Cove and look after everyone."

I look at him.

"That boy's been looking for a place to land for years, but he found it. Unlike you, he didn't have an excellent mother to raise him."

My chest tightens. "Yeah, he got robbed there."

Pete grins. "Look at him. He's got his very own stubborn Maren girl and a town full of fools who love him. What else does a man need?"

"A cat in a hoodie pocket?"

Pete laughs and coughs again, wiping at his eye like it's just wind. "You're gonna make an old man cry."

"Better tears of laughter than sadness.'"

Pete snorts and nods.

Tate looks up and spots us. He smiles, with that impossibly handsome smile, and heads our way, wiping his hands on a rag.

"Hey, what's all this? Please say that's for me?" he eyes the coffee in my hand.

"Willa's on nurse duty," Pete says snidely. "And emotional support patrol. Real bossy about it, too, you big mouth."

"She's good at that," Tate says, his gaze settling on me with something soft. "Real good."

I hand him his coffee, and he smiles gratefully and takes it. "Thanks."

And just like that, the world feels a little less heavy. Because we're not alone. Not in grief or in love. And never in the messy life that we get to do together.

* * *

By the time Tate and I walk into Marco's for a big family dinner, it smells like garlic, melted cheese, and heaven. Seriously. If heaven had a scent, it would be the buttery crackle of garlic knots and the yeasty, almost-sweet scent of fresh dough rising under the wood fire. Add in the mouth-watering aroma of tomato sauce, the peppery sizzle of sausage, and the faint sweet smell of basil in the air, and it's enough to make your knees buckle. Yeah, this is heaven.

Marco himself waves from behind the counter, tossing a disk of dough high into the air like he's conducting a symphony. "Willa! You bring the entire coven tonight or just your favorite boy toy?"

Tate coughs behind me.

I glance back and smirk. "Don't be jealous. You're second only to pizza."

Tate leans down, mouth near my ear. "I'm fine being second. As long as I get dessert."

I flush all the way to my fingertips and nudge him with my hip.

Our group floods the front like a pack of joyful chaos. Junie darts straight toward the vintage Ms. Pac-Man machine with Ivy on her heels. "Let's do this!"

Finn, already in a backwards cap and hoodie, is hooting and slamming buttons on the pinball machine like a grown child. Remy groans, but smiles. He follows behind with a parental slouch that says, *this is my circus and yes, these are my monkeys.*

Rowan slides in beside me, shaking leaves from her curls. "Are we feasting or summoning spirits tonight?"

"Why not both?" I laugh.

Lilith and Donna are already making a beeline for Marco's favorite booth, the one by the big front window with the deep red leather seats and cozy candlelight.

Old Pete stayed home tonight, said something about his knees and Netflix. I think he just wanted to be horizontal by seven, and honestly, respect. He's been through a lot. He hasn't told anyone else yet, and we're waiting for him. I suspect Donna knows because Pete and Donna have been close friends for years. Donna, Pete, and my mom are like the caretakers of the town. They know everyone and look out for all. Not much gets by those three.

We all pile into seats and corner booths, coats flung onto hooks, scarves hung on chairs. Wisteria Cove is rapidly descending into the colder season, and the weather is brisk tonight. The table stretches out in mismatched chairs and elbows, and Marco himself slides over with the first round of garlic knots so hot they steam.

Tate grabs one, breaks it in half, and offers the bigger piece to me with a wink. I accept it like it's a diamond ring. Because honestly? In this town, a warm garlic knot is a love language. The garlic knots are perfection.

"Okay," Ivy says, bouncing in her seat as she plays Tic Tac

Toe with Junie on her paper menu. "We are ordering everything."

"Agreed," Finn says. "Appetizers are just a warm-up lap. I'm here for the buffalo chicken pizza and the meatball sliders."

"And the prosciutto fig flatbread," Rowan chimes in, eyes glittering. "We're feral tonight."

Tate raises his hand like we're in school. "And a full order of fried ravioli. It's not a real Marco's night without that."

"Can confirm," I add. "Also, we're going to need a takeout box before the food even arrives."

Junie tugs on Ivy's sleeve, looking up with big brown eyes. "Can I have more quarters?"

Ivy glances toward Remy.

But before he can even dig into his wallet, Tate pulls out a handful from his flannel pocket and hands them over like a vending machine prince.

"What?" he says as Junie squeals and runs off. "Everyone knows you can't come to Marco's and not play the games. It's like a childhood rite of passage. Just passing the baton here."

I lean closer to him, heart turning into a puddle. "You're such a softie."

He smirks and whispers in my ear. "Only for you. And pizza. Also, there's nothing soft about me when I think of you."

Town gossips are definitely watching us from the other tables. You can feel it, the curious glances, the subtle smiles, the phrase "finally" whispered between shared appetizers and sneaky glances in our direction.

Lilith sips her iced tea and chats with Donna and watches us with satisfaction as if they've been planning this for decades. Wisteria Cove friendships exist on a whole different time line, seasons and soup nights, and gossip is shared like sacred rituals.

I catch Remy watching Ivy as she and Junie huddle over the

claw machine by the window. There's something in his expression that's not just fondness. Interesting. Very interesting.

The appetizers land, and we're all ready to dig in. Piping hot fried ravioli, bubbly marinara, meatballs nestled in soft bread with a mountain of melted cheese, and arugula salad with shaved parmesan and lemon oil that smells so good it doesn't even count as healthy.

We pass plates and steal bites. There's laughter, overlapping stories, forks clinking, and enough warmth to melt the fall chill still clinging to my skin.

Marco drops off the pizzas himself. "One mushroom truffle. One buffalo. One margarita. And one special, which is Tate's favorite. Bacon, sausage, jalapeño, and a secret, very special ingredient."

Tate lifts a slice like it's holy.

We eat until we're full, and then we eat some more. Everyone wraps up leftovers to take home, except Finn, who's still picking at his like a hungry raccoon.

"I'm gonna need a nap and a full moon detox after this," Rowan groans, stretching.

Donna dabs her mouth delicately and says, "Well, you do need to stay in good health. I might write you into my next book."

The table goes silent.

Then Ivy gasps. "Wait. What?"

"You heard me." Donna's eyes sparkle. "You never know when I'll be inspired by someone I know. Especially when they act out a real-life love story right under my nose."

She doesn't even look at me, but I feel the heat crawl up my neck anyway.

"Oh my god," Rowan groans. "If she writes you in, it's happening. That's the Wisteria Cove spell!"

"I don't make the rules," Donna says with a sip of her iced tea. "But I do write them."

Ivy snorts and grins. "Does that mean if you write me in, I finally get a happy ending?"

Remy chokes on his soda.

Donna arches a brow. "I think you mean happily ever after, honey."

Ivy flaps her napkin dramatically. "No comment!"

Rowan wiggles her eyebrows and murmurs. "Someone needs to get laid."

"Rowan!"

"Oh please," she says, waving a breadstick. "We've all seen the way Derek is. You need a real man."

Tate leans into my ear again. "What the hell is happening?"

"Chaos," I whisper back. "Absolute, beautiful chaos."

The dinner winds down, plates scraped clean, dessert offered and declined only because no one can move. We bundle up and head into the night with takeout boxes and full hearts.

On the walk home, the town is quiet again. Leaves crunch under our boots, and the smell of wood smoke curls in from chimneys along the harbor.

It's just me, Tate, Ivy, and Rowan now. The four of us in a loose row, full of carbs and chaos.

Donna peels off toward her house, calling, "Good night, darlings! Don't do anything I would write about. Wait a minute, definitely do that!"

"Ivy," Rowan says slyly. "Do you need a ride home? Or are you gonna sneak onto the tree farm and climb some trees?"

We all know she's talking about Remy. The energy between those two has always had sparks. Ivy's still with Derek, but they're so on again, off again. We are all rooting for the off part. Derek doesn't treat her right and never has. You won't find him at these dinners because he doesn't like any of us, and he doesn't mind letting that be known. The last time he came to dinner he had so many digs about witches and how bad we all were. Ivy was so embarrassed, and he hasn't been back since.

"I hate you," Ivy mutters, but she's smiling.

Tate wraps an arm around my waist as we climb the steps to the bookstore. "This town," he says.

I smile. "I know."

He leans down and kisses the top of my head. "Remind me never to leave it."

"Deal."

And just like that, we disappear inside, back into the glow of the bookstore's light. Safe. Full. A little ridiculous. But entirely, wonderfully home.

Chapter 28
Tate

The next night we follow Remy and Junie out to the farm, and I head to the back of the property where the cabins are located.

"It's so quiet and peaceful out here. I can see why Remy loves it out here," Willa says softly as we wind down the side road to the cabins.

"It is. I wanted to show you something and see what you thought," I say as I pull in front of one cabin that's dark.

"Okay," she says hesitantly as she zips up her coat, and we get out.

"Remy says I can have this one, and I wanted to know if you wanted to make a home here with me," I turn and say quickly, "I know it's fast, but I want to make a home for us."

Willa's eyes go soft, and she says, "I love it."

"Really?" I say as I pull her into me, and she nods.

I tip my lips to hers and kiss her softly, holding her tightly. I pull back and stare at her, wondering how the hell I got so lucky with Willa. "Okay."

"It's pretty magical out here," she says as she runs her fingers over the front porch railing and looks over at the porch swing. The cabin overlooks a pond that the moon reflects off of.

I open the door and turn on the light as she follows me in. It's small, but the natural wood makes it feel like a nice home. The black Buck stove in the corner is ready to be lit and make the whole space cozy. Remy has already stacked a fresh pile of wood outside.

"Yeah," she says softly. "We could definitely make this work."

Relief fills me. "Okay, I'll let Remy know."

Her arms circle me, and she pulls me in and kisses me. "Imagine what it would look like in here with a Christmas tree and decorated so beautiful. And all the snow outside. I would never want to leave."

"We can do that," I promise. "And there're plenty of trees to choose from."

"Well, that's good, because I want this with you." She kisses my cheek and lays her head on my shoulder.

I kiss her again, deeper this time, my hands sliding over her back, and for a second, the whole cabin feels like it's already ours.

Chapter 29
Willa

The snow's melted into little puddles along the sidewalk, and it's quiet this morning, and I'm grateful for it. It's a perfect pause between festival chaos and Thanksgiving prep. Today is a big baking day, and we are getting ready for our friends' feast tomorrow, a tradition we do every year.

Ivy perches on the stool at the counter, nursing a mug of tea while Cobweb purrs on the windowsill, watching the leaves flutter in the breeze on the ground, tail flicking in rhythm with the soft music playing overhead.

"You're glowing," Ivy says with a grin, nudging her mug toward mine. "What's it like to be finally, disgustingly happy?"

I laugh and lean against the counter. "It's amazing. Like, actually amazing. I don't think I've ever felt this grounded in my entire life. Like...I know where I belong."

Ivy raises a brow and gives me that big-sister-you-chose look. "How do you feel about moving out to the cabin?"

"I'm really excited," I admit, my cheeks warming. "Tate and I—" I pause, heart fluttering a little just saying it out loud. "We're building something real. It's...a life. A future. I didn't think we'd have this."

I take a breath, trying not to get emotional. "We're decorating the cabin this week. I already found the perfect garland for the fireplace. And I ordered stockings. One for me, one for him, and one for Cobweb."

Ivy gasps dramatically. "Family stockings. You're officially a family."

"I'm really happy," I say with a grin. "I want all of this. The traditions. Christmas pancakes and morning cuddles and coffee on the porch. I want to wake up with him and fall asleep knowing that we're together and have our own home."

"You said all of that with the dreamiest look on your face," Ivy murmurs. "I never thought you'd actually settle down. You said yourself over the years that you were going to be a cat lady above the bookstore. Hey...nothing wrong with that, but you really have done a one-eighty. It was amazing to watch."

"Because it feels like the chapter I've been waiting to write or read." I sip my tea and glance out the window, where the harbor glints just beyond the rooftops. "Rowan's going to move into the loft while she gets the shop ready to open, and I'll still run the bookstore, obviously. But now there's a rhythm to everything. There's balance."

Ivy stares into her mug for a moment. "I'm so happy for you.

Really, I am. I mean… it's like watching someone step right into the life they were meant for."

There's something wistful in her tone, a flicker of longing that tugs at me. She hasn't talked about what happened with Derek. The latest is that they got in a big fight, and I didn't get all of the details, but I gathered it was bad. I'm pretty sure Rowan is ready to hex him big time.

"I want that, too," she says softly, not meeting my eyes. "Not your exact life. I mean, I'd totally steal your man if I thought I had a chance—"

"Ha," I snort and see her laughing.

"I'm totally kidding. I love Tate like a brother. But I'm not blind. He's hot."

I snort and sip my tea and tease. "Okay, so you're into brothers. Got it."

She rolls her eyes. "I want something that's mine. A plan and a dream. To finally have a place to land. I'm tired of hopping jobs and not having a place to belong."

"You're not floating, Ivy. You're going to find your happily ever after."

She laughs. "Thanks. I don't know about that. I'm pretty sure things are over with Derek. I just want to matter to someone, you know? I want someone to love me and show up for me like I show up for them."

I reach across the counter and wrap my fingers around hers. "You matter more than you'll ever know. This town would fall apart without you. And something good's coming. I can feel it."

"I hope so," she says, her voice thickening a little. "I'm trying so hard to believe that."

"You're magic, Ivy. And you deserve to feel it, too."

Just then, the bell over the door jingles. Tate steps inside, cheeks pink from the wind, a garland of pine boughs looped over one arm and a box of lights in the other. He catches my eye and grins with that easy, heart-wrecking grin that undoes me every time straight to my core.

"Sorry I'm late," he says, setting the box down. "Had to wrestle with Old Pete and Donna about which bulbs were too 'damn tacky' to go on the harbor poles."

"He's particular about his harbor poles," I say.

"Don't I know it." Tate glances between Ivy and me. "Should I come back later?"

"No," Ivy says, hopping down from the stool. "You're the muscle we need. You can help us string those up before we get distracted again."

He salutes, all warm flannel and muscular forearms, then starts unspooling the lights. I catch Ivy watching him for a second before she whispers, "Yeah. I see the appeal."

"Brother fucker," I whisper-tease back.

"Yeah, that one's all yours. I might just become the cat lady who ends up living above the bookstore," she says with a wink, then heads toward the back to check on the new shipment of books that just arrived.

I step over to Tate and wrap my arms around his waist from behind. He stills for a second, then turns and pulls me into him like he's been waiting all day.

"Hey," he murmurs into my hair. "You excited to decorate at the cabin later?"

"Only if you promise to do it shirtless while drinking cocoa."

"Maybe," he smirks as he pulls back and brushes his knuckles over my cheek. "You okay?"

"I'm perfect. How are you doing?"

"I'm great now," he says as he pulls me tighter, planting a kiss on my head.

And for the first time in my life, I mean that with no hesitation, any fear. I feel like I'm exactly where I'm supposed to be.

Cobweb jumps from the windowsill onto Tate's shoulder, her tail flicking dramatically.

"I guess she's perfect, too," I add. "She wants in your hoodie again."

"Of course she does," Tate says, as he gets her adjusted in her custom pocket. I had to order him more hoodies with the pockets because she expects to be carried around and worn now.

As he strings lights across the front window, I watch him, without doubt or fear, but with a heart full of peace. This isn't the part where I brace for the storm. This is the part where I decorate the life we're building, knowing the foundation is solid, the love is real, and the lights will shine, even on the darkest nights.

* * *

The last-minute shoppers have dwindled down, and we're getting everything ready for our big Small Business Saturday shopping event. Ivy and Rowan have been busy helping me get all the desserts baked for our enormous family dinner at Mom's. Every year she outdoes herself, and this year she has invited most of the town.

The bookstore smells like pumpkin pie and apple crisp, and the chili pot on the stove is working overtime against the chill that crept into Wisteria Cove overnight. Ivy's curled on the window bench with her legs tucked up beneath her, sipping one of my cinnamon honey lattes and absentmindedly tossing a stuffed mouse for Cobweb.

"We were at Donna's last night," I tell her. "Remy's in his busy season, and Donna's on deadline, so he's scrambling to find help with Junie. There was some mention of him needing help."

Ivy raises her brows. "What kind of help?"

I grin at her. "A nanny. He's hoping to find someone to stick around through Christmas, ideally a live-in arrangement. Just while things are crazy with the tree farm and the nursery."

Ivy blinks. "Interesting."

"What do you think?" I ask, trying not to sound too excited. "You're amazing with her. She adores you. Remy trusts you. You've known each other forever. And you need a place and some stability right now."

Ivy looks like she's trying to argue, but the words won't come. I can see her wheels turning behind those sea green eyes. Ivy has always struggled as the younger sister who looks nothing like Rowan and me. Rowan and I both have dark hair and are tall. Ivy is short and curvy, with red hair that is always wild, and sea-green eyes. She's bright, vibrant, and outgoing, while Rowan and I are more subdued. When we were little and rotten, we used to tease her, saying someone must have adopted her. But little did we know our dad had the same red hair that had already turned gray. She favors him, and we favor our mom.

Tate joins us and leans his hip against the counter, arms folded. "She's not wrong," he says casually, though he's smirking like he saw this coming a mile away. "Remy's in over his head. He's burning the candle at both ends. Not sure how long he can keep going, and Junie is bored at the shop every day after school until bedtime. She needs someone who can take care of her and let her enjoy the holiday season, instead of just sitting in the barn every day."

"I do really love Junie," Ivy says, "But I'm not even sure that Remy likes me. He barely says a word to me."

"Oh, he likes you just fine," I snort with a wave. "He gives you the same looks I've caught you giving him. Silently checking each other out."

Ivy laughs and shakes her head, looking nervous. "I don't know about *that*. And living with him? Isn't that a little weird?"

"It doesn't have to be permanent," I offer gently. "Just the season. Through New Year's. He's got the space. You'd have a warm bed, a place to cook in, and a job you're good at. That's not weird. That's practical."

"And you two are definitely scheming," Ivy asks, side-eyeing both of us.

"Maybe just a smidge," I say sweetly.

"Not me," Tate adds, holding up his hands and grinning.

Ivy gives us both a look and pets Cobweb, stroking her soft fur and sighing.

"I'm serious," I say, voice softening. "You've spent so much time taking care of everyone else, Ivy. Maybe it's time you did something for you. Even if it's in the form of a nanny job for a cute five-year-old who wants you to decorate cookies and build blanket forts."

Her face looks quiet and thoughtful.

"You really think he'd want me?" she asks after a beat. "I mean, to do that?"

Oh, he definitely wants her, I think to myself as my eyes widen with a grin. Tate gives me a look.

"I know he would. And Junie already thinks you hung the moon. Just give it a shot. Worst case, it's a few weeks of magic and mess." I say matter of factly. "If it doesn't work out, you can just come work with Rowan and me."

She lifts a brow, and mutters, "I mean it does sound like fun..."

"Of course, you could also fall in love and end up wearing matching Christmas pajamas," I say with a smirk.

"Don't tempt me. You know I love a romantic love story. Only just not with Remy. I don't think he likes me...or really anyone. I can tell. He looks at me as if I'm annoying." Ivy bites her lip, staring into her mug.

"He looks at everyone like that," I tell her. "He's looked like that since his ex, Sloane, left."

"I'll think about it," she says finally. "It does sound kind of...right."

"Right is the word for it. You both need this. End of story."

Tate chuckles from the counter. "Now who is meddling."

"Shut up. You know I'm right," I tell him with a look.

He gives Ivy a two-finger salute and disappears into the back, humming some ridiculous tune under his breath.

I look at Ivy, and there's a spark in her eyes that wasn't there before. It looks like hope. Something I haven't seen since Derek got ahold of her.

Chapter 30
Tate

The scent of roasting turkey hits me the second I open the door to Lilith's house. Warm and buttery with that cozy undertone of herbs and something savory, maybe spiced pears or those glazed carrots Willa keeps dreaming about. Honestly, it's probably all of the above. I missed out on these dinners while I was away, and now that I'm back, I'm looking forward to them.

"Our friendship feast is a sacred event," Lilith declares, her hair pinned up with glittering gold sticks, a cranberry-colored apron tied over a flowy black dress. "And I need a strong back and capable hands. Tate, you're with me."

"Yes, ma'am." I set the pies Willa brought down on the table, already covered in mismatched dishes and desserts.

She hands me an oven mitt and gestures toward the turkey like it's a sacred artifact. "We're basting. Gently. Like you're coaxing secrets from a dragon."

"I don't even know what that means," I mutter.

She smirks. "And yet you're doing it beautifully."

I grin and bend down to check the oven, the heat hitting my

face in a blast. The turkey looks perfectly golden brown, glistening, surrounded by orange slices and herbs.

Lilith leans close as I close the oven door. "You know, I'm thankful for you this year," she says softly. "You've brought something back to this house. To my daughter and to this town."

My throat tightens. "Lilith..."

She pats my shoulder. "Don't get weepy on me, Holloway. There's still cranberry sauce to stir."

By the time the guests start pouring in, the house smells like heaven. Candles flicker in the windows, the fireplace is roaring, and the backyard has been strung with fairy lights like she's hosting a wedding instead of a potluck.

Old Pete sits in the kitchen, fixing the leg of a creaky wooden chair Lilith rescued from the shed.

I pause for a second, watching him. His hands are steady, his face focused. Willa walks up behind him, pressing a jacket around his shoulders. They whisper. I can't hear what they say, but I see her kiss his cheek, and I swear I see him wipe his eyes.

This town and these people...they wrap themselves around you when you're not looking and claim you.

Ivy shows up late. She's wearing a rust-colored dress and boots, but her eyes are red like she's been crying. Willa catches her first, drawing her into a hug while Rowan hurries over with a glass of wine and a concerned look.

"What happened?" I murmur to Willa as she passes by.

"Boyfriend trouble," she whispers. "She said he tried to keep her from coming today. Said he hid her car keys."

I frown. "That guy's a walking red flag."

Before dinner's ready, the house is full, with Finn and Rowan bickering about deviled eggs, Donna and Lilith laughing together, and Pete sitting near the fire, watching everyone with contentment. Ivy is playing dominoes with Junie while Remy sneaks glances at her from the kitchen doorway. And me?

I belong here. Somehow, in all the mess of the past, I landed in the middle of this noisy, heartfelt, ridiculous chosen family.

And when Willa threads her fingers through mine on her way to the table, everything settles.

The lights dim slightly. Everyone gathers around the main table, with so many chairs and mismatched dishes.

Lilith stands at the head, lifting her glass. Her hair is wild, and her lipstick smudged from sipping her wine glass. She's radiant.

"I want to say something," she begins, and the room hushes. "This year has been a year of shifts. Of heartbreak. Of healing. And yet, we're still here."

Her eyes sweep across the table. "We've had losses, and our hearts have been cracked wide open. But what I've learned, and what this town has taught me, is that the heart always finds a way to keep beating. And real love sneaks in through the cracks to settle where it belongs."

I feel Willa's hand tighten in mine.

Lilith's voice softens. "I'm thankful for each of you. For the old friendships and the new. For messy beginnings and unexpected second chances. And for chaos, magic, and the people who show up when it matters most, because we never know when a moment may be our last."

She lifts her glass higher. "To the ones we love. And the ones who love us back."

Then the sniffles start. Ivy wipes her eyes. Finn pretends he has allergies. Even Donna swipes a forefinger under her eye.

We raise our glasses, and we drink and feast.

Later, after too many helpings of everything, when the candles have melted halfway down, and Junie is asleep on Donna's lap, I lean over and kiss Willa's temple.

"You okay?" I whisper.

She nods, eyes shining. "More than okay."

Outside, snow begins to fall again, and it's a soft, quiet, like the town is sighing with contentment.

Willa reaches for my hand under the table and squeezes, and I squeeze back.

I don't need to say it. It's all right here in the way Lilith puts me to work and treats me like I've always been her son.

It's all right here in the firelight flickering on Donna's glasses as she types something into her phone, probably already dreaming up the next novel. And in the way Rowan pulls a soft blanket around Pete's shoulders when he falls asleep snoring on the couch.

And in Willa's hand, warm and sure in mine. Yeah.

This is what home feels like.

* * *

The harbor's quiet after Thanksgiving. The water's dark and slick, so dark that it makes you think too much if you stare at it too long.

I walk the dock alone, hands in my jacket pockets, boots scuffing along the damp planks. The scent of salt and cedar hangs in the air, and off in the distance, a gull cries like it's mourning something it can't name.

The old boat's still there.

She's still weathered now, with her paint chipped, ropes fraying at the edges as she leans into the dock like she's tired. Like she's waiting for permission to rest for good. There's so much I wanted to do to bring her back to life and make my dad proud. But I think family is most important, and my dad would be proud to see me happy with the people who I love and who love me. I look around at this life that I'm building, and I can feel him. He would fit right in if he was still here.

I press a hand flat to the side of the hull. "Thanks for everything you taught me Dad," I whisper.

The breeze kicks up, and I swear the boat groans in response, like she remembers everything, too.

I stand slowly, swallowing hard. "Goodbye, old girl."

I'm about to turn away when I hear boots on the dock behind me.

"Figured I might find you down here," Donna says, out of breath.

I blink and look over my shoulder. She's in her usual long coat, scarf tucked in tight, hair swept back in a tight bun.

"What are you doing here?" I ask.

She walks up beside me, slowly and carefully, like she knows this moment is heavier than it looks. "Well," she said, "I came to give you something."

She hands me a manila envelope.

"What is it?"

"Open it."

I tear it open, half-expecting a manuscript or one of her handwritten recipes for mulled wine. But it's a deed.

The deed to the boat. In my name.

I freeze. "What...what is this?"

Donna gives me a small smile. "She belongs to you."

"Donna..." My voice breaks. "Why?"

"Because you weren't ready to let her go. And this town looks after each other," she says, stepping closer. "And so do you now. You didn't realize it, but you're one of us; you always have been. You've been holding pieces of this town together since you got back. Whether it's helping Remy, or fixing things for Lilith, or just showing up for Willa. You are a big part of our town's heartbeat, Tate."

I shake my head. "I can't—"

"You can," she says, firm. "You've got this wild, stubborn loyalty that your father never had the courage to live into. You love hard, Tate. And this boat? It doesn't have to be a ghost anymore."

I look down at the deed again. It feels heavier than paper has a right to be.

"It's yours now," she says. "You decide what it becomes. Scrap it. Sell it. Restore it. Make it a charter boat, a shop, a floating bookstore, hell, build a crab shack on it. I don't care."

She smiles, soft and a little sad. "It's a blank page. A fresh start. Just be happy, son. You deserve that."

The wind shifts again, colder this time, and I let the words settle. "You're really giving this to me?"

"I'm not giving it to you, the whole town is," she says gently. "It's time to start building your own legacy now. The town pulled together and bought this back for you."

I don't realize I'm crying until I feel the tears on my cheeks. I swipe them away with the back of my hand and laugh under my breath. "I don't even know where I'd start."

"You'll figure it out," she says. "Start with what this town needs. And what you need. You'll find the middle."

We stand in silence for a minute, both of us looking at the boat.

Then I ask quietly, "What do you think he'd say? My dad."

Donna hums. "I think he'd be proud. And a little pissed that you're gonna do it better than he ever did."

I huff a laugh.

"But you're not him, Tate," she adds, voice firmer now. "You never were. You have to be you. You can't live his life. You have to live yours."

I nod slowly and look up at her. "Thank you. For this. For everything."

Donna steps forward and hugs me, tight and warm. "I love you, sweetheart. Just take care of her. And yourself."

She starts back toward town, coat flapping, leaving me with the boat and the silence and the possibilities.

I climb aboard for what feels like the first time. She's really mine.

The deck creaks under my weight, and the cold air bites at my cheeks, but something stirs deep in my chest, something I haven't felt since I was a kid standing at the bow, pretending I was headed toward some brave new life. I feel hope.

I walk to the stern, lean against the rail, and stare out at the open water. The future used to terrify me. Now I think maybe I'm ready to chart my own course. With Willa, naturally.

And whatever that looks like, this boat's coming with us.

Chapter 31
Willa

Willa,

You once told me you hated unfinished stories.

So here's mine:

It's still you.

It's always been you.

I just need you to help me write the ending.

—Tate

There's something sacred about the quiet here. The hush of snow falling outside, the slow crackle from the fireplace, the warmth of Tate beside me beneath the quilt. My cheek presses to his chest, and his fingers trail lazily up and down my arm, suggesting he is in no hurry to start the day, and for once, I am not either.

Cobweb perches on the dresser, tail flicking with judgmental rhythm, as if we're her favorite soap opera, and the season finale isn't delivering fast enough.

"She's watching us again," I murmur into Tate's chest.

"Probably wants breakfast," he mutters, voice gravelly with sleep. "Or a front-row seat to our scandalous display of cuddling."

I snort and nudge him with my knee under the covers. "Scandalous? We haven't even gotten to round two yet."

Tate laughs, then stretches, pulling me tighter to him. His body is all warm muscle and sleepy comfort. If I could bottle this moment and keep it forever, I would.

Eventually, we untangle ourselves and make our way to the kitchen. The windows are rimmed in frost, and the snow outside sparkles like someone dusted the entire world in sugar.

He makes our coffee, and I make the toast, slathered with butter and honey, and we sit on the little bench by the window, knees touching, watching the world slowly wake.

I look over at him, at this man who came back into my life like a shipwreck survivor who still remembered how to swim, and I think: *This is what home feels like. With him. He is my home. It's with him. Wherever he is, that is my home.*

Later, we bundle up and head to town. The bookstore is closed today, a rare gift I gave myself, but we still stop by to check things. As we make our way down Main Street to the shop, hand in hand, people call out to us with smiles and laughter.

"Morning, Willa and Tate!"

"Looking cozy, you two!"

"Did Tate finally propose or what?"

We laugh and wave. The snow crunches beneath our boots. The wreaths on the lampposts sway in the breeze. Everything smells like cinnamon, pine, and possibility.

We haven't talked much about marriage, but we both know this is it. This is what we want, and we have it. Whatever else comes, has time to get here.

Inside the bookstore, the air is warmer, richer. The smell of the cinnamon broom near the door mingles with the evergreen garland I wrapped around the ladder. Warm lamps light up the space, and I swear even the books feel cozier.

I run my fingers across the spines as we pass the romance section. Tate does his usual routine, checks the back for deliveries and fixes anything that needs fixing.

My mom arrives midmorning, wrapped in a plaid shawl, cheeks pink from the cold.

"There's my favorite bookstore witch," she says, pulling me into a hug that smells like sandalwood and peppermint. "And my favorite brooding fisherman who finally stopped brooding."

Tate grins. "I still brood occasionally. In moderation now."

She hands me a wrapped package. It's heavy and warm, like it holds secrets.

"What is this?" I ask.

"Open it."

I peel back the brown paper to reveal a thick, worn recipe book. The cover is soft with age, the pages full of notes in the margins and smudges of flour.

"The Maren Family Spellbook," she says with a wink. "It's not just food. It's memories and magic and a family treasure my mother passed down to me when I was ready. Now I'm giving it to you. I have one for your sisters that I made when they're ready, too."

Tears prick my eyes. "Thanks, Mom."

"For when you make your own magic," she adds, giving Tate a meaningful look, "now that you have your own home."

Later, we leave Cobweb at the bookstore. We check in with

Rowan and Finn, who are deep in discussions about floor samples for Salt & Root.

Tate and I take a walk along the harbor. The bench where Old Pete likes to sit is dusted with snow, but we brush it off and sit close, sipping our coffees that I brought from the bookstore.

The water is calm today, the fishing boats bob gently, and the gulls are quiet. The world feels paused, like it's giving us a moment.

Tate slides his arm around me. "I was thinking about the boat," he says.

"Yeah?"

"Donna told me I could do whatever I wanted with it. I was thinking about doing tours. Maybe even one of those harbor cruises with cider and stories. Something fun that makes people fall in love with this place the way we did."

I rest my head on his shoulder. "You'd be great at that."

He presses a kiss to my hair. "Maybe I could call it The Second Chance."

I laugh, squeezing his hand. "You're getting soft, Holloway."

"Just trying to keep up with my hopeless romantic of a girlfriend."

"Girlfriend, huh?" I tease and nudge him.

His hand slides into mine, and he holds it tight. "Yeah, my girlfriend. What do you want me to call you?"

"Girlfriend is fine." I smile and lean my head on his shoulder.

We sit in silence for a moment, watching the world shimmer with frost and fading light.

"This isn't a dream, right?" I whisper.

Tate turns to me, eyes warm and sure. "No. It's real."

* * *

Tate's hand is warm in mine, gloved fingers curled around my mittened ones, and even though the wind bites our cheeks, I feel flushed with something warmer than the December air.

"This one?" I ask, stopping in front of a tall, slightly crooked pine.

Tate squints. "It's a little lopsided."

"Exactly," I say. "It's got personality."

He chuckles and gives the trunk a tap. "All right. You're the boss, bookstore girl."

"I'll remind you of that next time you try to argue about where the garland goes."

He leans in and kisses my forehead, then hoists the tree over his shoulder like some kind of lumberjack Santa Claus. "Deal."

Back at the cabin, we crank up the Christmas playlist on the old record player with Bing Crosby crackling under the needle and Cobweb weaves between our feet like a tiny, judgmental supervisor.

The cabin smells like pine and cinnamon and warm cider. The fire crackles, and the snow outside thickens until it blurs the world beyond our frosted windows.

We decorate barefoot. Tate strings the lights while I unwrap more ornaments we've collected. A ceramic book. A little felt fish. A glittery ornament that says *First Christmas in the Cabin*. We hang them slowly, laughing, kissing between each one.

"Careful," I say as he reaches high for the top branch. "If you fall and break something, I'm not helping. I'll just say 'told you so' while the paramedics take you away."

"Spoken like a woman truly full of holiday spirit," he deadpans.

"You're lucky you're cute," I reply.

He grins down at me. "Luckiest man alive."

Once the tree is glowing in the corner, lights twinkling against the dark wood walls, I head to the little table by the window where I've stashed a folder. Tate flops onto the couch, legs stretched out, one hand lazily stroking Cobweb's fur.

I pull out a few sheets of paper, half-doodles, half-plans and hold them up.

"Okay," I say, heart skipping a little. "Don't laugh."

Tate sits up, interested. "What is that?"

I hand him the sketches. "I couldn't sleep last night, so I started thinking... what if your boat tours weren't just tours? What if they were stories?"

He flips through the pages. My sketches are rough but full of heart, little flyers with waves and anchor illustrations, bookmarks with quotes and history snippets. One has a mockup of a flyer with the tagline: *Wisteria Harbor Second Chance Tours: Where Every Journey Has a Story.*

"You wrote all this?" he asks, voice quieter.

I nod. "I figured...you'd captain the boat, tell stories. Local legends, history, ghost tales. Maybe even a sunset poetry cruise if you're feeling brave."

He snorts. "You want me to read poems to tourists?"

"No," I grin. "But I might sell them to them."

He flips the page again, then looks up at me. "This is... incredible."

My throat tightens. "I just thought, if we're building a life, maybe we start building the dream part, too."

He pulls me into his lap and kisses me like I handed him the keys to something sacred. Like I opened the door to a home he didn't know he was allowed to want.

But he just shakes his head and reaches into his flannel pocket. "No. It's perfect."

He pulls out a small, clear glass bottle. Tucked inside, rolled up with a bit of twine, is a tiny note.

I blink at him. "Tate..."

He shrugs, a little sheepish. "I've had this one ready for a while. Just waiting for the right moment."

I uncork the bottle carefully and slide the note out with trembling fingers.

It reads:

"This time, I'm not drifting. I'm anchoring to you."

Tears well instantly. I press the note to my heart, chest aching in the best way.

"You're going to destroy me with these, Holloway," I whisper.

"Good," he murmurs, brushing a kiss to my temple. "Because you ruined me first."

I kiss him back, slow and sure and deep, and when we finally pull apart, the fire's dimmed to glowing embers, and the tree sparkles beside us like something out of a snow globe.

We stay up late talking about the tour business, too excited to sleep about who we might hire in the spring to help, whether Marco would cater boat picnics, and if Old Pete could be talked into sharing his legendary sea stories.

Tate lays back on the couch, one arm around me, the other gesturing at the ceiling like he's already dreaming it into reality.

"I could take people around the harbor," he says. "Tell them about the old lighthouse keeper who fell in love with the baker's daughter. Or the sea captain who left a bottle in the waves for his wife every full moon."

"And I'll sell bookmarks in the shop," I say. "And maybe write up some little booklets to go with the tours."

Tate grins, eyes sparkling in the firelight. "Willa Maren Holloway, storyteller of the sea."

"Willa Maren Holloway?" I tease.

He shrugs. "Just seeing how it feels to say." He laughs and pulls me in again.

And when we finally head to bed, the tree glowing in the corner, Cobweb curled at our feet, and dreams of a new kind of future dancing behind our eyelids, I know this isn't just another chapter.

It's the prologue of a brand-new book. And we're writing it together.

Epilogue

Tate

Let me tell you something.

This boat? This was once my father's pride and joy. Back then, it smelled like diesel and regret, creaked like it hated its own existence, and had more rust and fatigue than anything.

Now? It's a damn *floating storybook.*

There're twinkle lights strung from bow to stern, warm cider in thermoses with crocheted cozies, a little portable heater tucked under the console, and custom wood benches Willa insisted needed "a cozy slouch factor." She painted them herself in shades called things like *Sea Mist* and *Oyster Pearl,* which I'm ninety percent sure are just fancy ways of saying blue and white.

I pilot the boat. She tells the stories. And somehow, it works.

"—and that's the spot right there," Willa says into her mic, her voice soft and singsong as we round the bend near Lovers' Rock. "Where the lighthouse keeper fell in love with the baker's daughter. He lit the lantern every night for her, even after she moved away. Every single night for twelve years. And if you want to read more, you can buy the book at Wisteria Books & Brews."

The group on board gives the appropriate "aww," a few of them sipping cider, one kid sneaking a second cookie from the basket. Willa winks and hands him a few in a napkin.

I glance at Willa. She's hired more help at the bookstore and joins me on the tours we schedule. She's standing near the bow, hair twisted into a messy braid, cheeks flushed from the cold, her scarf trailing in the wind like she's the main character in a Hallmark movie.

She catches me watching and winks.

Lord help me.

"Fun fact," she continues. "The baker's daughter eventually came back and opened a bookstore. Right here in Wisteria Cove."

A few passengers murmur with recognition.

"Wait," a woman whispers. "That's her."

"Right?" her friend says, clutching her coffee cup. "That's the couple from the flyers. They're really married."

I cough to hide my laugh. We're not married. Yet.

But I'm not about to correct them. Not when Willa's glowing with happiness like that. Not when I know, in every bone of my body, that she's my forever.

We pass the dock, and Old Pete's there, bundled in his coat and dozing on his bench like some magical sea wizard who's watching over everything. I swear he still knows more about what's happening in this town than anyone. He's hanging in there and he's getting the best care from everyone.

Remy strolls down the dock with Junie beside him with her

own thermos and a balloon sword. She shouts, "GO FASTER!" and nearly drops the thermos.

Remy catches it, unbothered as Junie yells, "YOU GOT THIS, CAPTAIN TATE!"

I raise a hand in salute. "Aye aye!"

Willa rolls her eyes but laughs, the sound curling around my ribs and settling there like it's home.

I slow the boat as we pass beneath the lighthouse. It's glowing gold in the late afternoon, casting its beam across the water like something out of a postcard. Willa turns toward me, her hand slipping into mine, her fingers squeezing gently.

"Ready for the next chapter?" she asks.

I grin. "Aye aye, captain."

Our passengers clap. I think someone wipes a tear.

Honestly? This is the life.

After the tour, we dock the boat and thank our little group of dreamy-eyed tourists, who swear they're coming back for the Valentine's cruise we just made up and started planning last week.

Willa hops down to the dock and immediately slips on some water.

"Careful," I say, catching her before she face plants.

She mutters something, but I kiss her anyway. Right there on the dock in front of everyone.

Old Pete whistles from his bench. "Get a cabin, ya horny sea biscuits!"

Donna, who somehow appeared behind him with a notebook in one hand and a chocolate croissant in another, says. "Oh, I *am* using that line."

Willa pulls back, panting. "She's writing us into her next book, isn't she?"

"Definitely a strong possibility," I say. "Should I be worried she called me a horny sea biscuit?"

"Probably."

That night, back in the cabin, I find her curled up by the fire, cat on her lap, sketching ideas for a new tour, the "Winter Solstice Love Stories" ride. She looks up when I walk in and asks, "Think we can get Remy to dress up like a sea ghost?"

"No," I say. "But we could probably get Finn to."

Willa lights up. "Oh my god. Yes. He *would*."

I sit beside her and hand her a tiny bottle.

She tilts her head. "Another one?"

I nod.

She opens it. Unrolls the paper. Reads it slowly, her lips moving.

"Will you marry me?"

She says nothing for a second. Just looks at me like I *am* her whole damn world. I love it when she looks at me like that.

And then she kisses me like we've still got a thousand more chapters to write.

Which, for the record, we do. Because I'm not going anywhere. I'm not drifting anymore. I'm anchored. To her and this town. And I wouldn't change a thing.

Bonus Content

Want more Willa and Tate? Check out this bonus scene for The Pumpkin Spice Spell when you sign up for Erin's newsletter! Scan the QR code to get your bonus scene:

Mistletoe & Magic

Chapter One
Ivy

The breakup wasn't even the worst part. The worst part was that he kept my dog.

My Lola.

"I miss her," I rant as my sister Willa turns her old tan Jeep Wrangler with the heater that barely works half the time onto the winding road that leads into Wisteria Cove.

She had picked me up at my townhouse in Boston when my boyfriend Derek and I'd had a fight and he'd told me to leave.

The asshole had even been nice enough to pack a bag for me and set it by the door before I woke up. He wanted me gone so his new girlfriend could move right in. Ultimate betrayal.

"I was the one who took care of Lola and did everything for her. She was supposed to be a gift from him. And Derek just— what? Gets to keep her like *I'm* the one who cheated? Why are Lola and I being punished because Derek can't keep it in his pants?"

"It's not right," Willa replies, shaking her head angrily on my behalf. "He's an actual reindeer turd in human form. But can I point out something hilarious? You're sadder about losing the dog than losing him."

Damn. She's right. I love my dog. But I definitely fell out of love with Derek.

I fall back against the passenger seat headrest with a dramatic groan, the fluff from my hood poofing up around me like I'm drowning in a marshmallow. "I knew it was over for a while, and I just didn't want to add it to my list of failures. What am I going to do now? I've had so many jobs in the last five years. No one takes me seriously in Wisteria Cove anymore. My ex is a sleazy, emotionally constipated, controlling criminal defense attorney who is threatening me with legal action if I try to take Lola. And my best friend—now his new girlfriend— wasted no time moving in with him before I was barely even out the door."

I'd wanted to lose it when I opened the door with my bags, thinking Willa was here to get me and realizing instead it was Kristin, my best friend who had been screwing Derek the whole time we were together.

The way she wouldn't meet my eyes and had turned with her bags and said, "I'll come back later."

"Go fuck yourself, Kristin!" I'd yelled at her as she scurried down the street like a rat. Girl code doesn't mean a thing to her. Just take whatever you want, I guess. I should have known when she stopped coming to girl's night out that something was up, but I realize now that was when she was with Derek.

Derek's betrayal didn't hurt as much as Kristin's did. I felt humiliated because I would confide in her about Derek and she would listen. All along she was screwing him, and I trusted her. I told her everything, and she pretended to support me and encouraged me to break up with him. Now I know why.

"Ex-best friend," Willa corrects. "Also, she's a massive turd, too. I think we should hex her."

"Yeah, she is. She can have Derek. I honestly should have left him sooner. I'm an idiot for not figuring this out and leaving when you guys tried to warn me."

I pull out the thermos and take a long sip of peppermint cocoa that Willa brought for me because she's literally the best and has her own cafe in her very own bookstore.

I know what Willa is probably thinking. She and my other sister Rowan repeatedly tried to tell me to leave Derek and that he was bad news. I never listened. And the truth is, I thought maybe I could help Derek. Sometimes I'd see glimmers of the person he could be. But then he'd flip back to the asshole that he always was. He would make me feel so badly about myself and subtly suggest that he was the only person who would ever tolerate me. And if I broke up with him, he would just be another failure, like all of the jobs I've had.

Sometimes I can still hear Derek's voice in my head, telling me nobody would want me or put up with my shit.

So, I stuck it out, hoping that it would get better. It only got worse.

"Kristin didn't take your man; she took your problem, and I actually can't think of a better consequence for either of them than each other," she says disdainfully as she makes her way back to Wisteria Cove.

I nod, because that's all I have in me. I am so tired of fighting with Derek and how he treated me. But it also feels like I'm going back home to Wisteria Cove with my tail between my legs.

"It's all going to work out. And now you get to be a nanny to Junie. It's a great job for you until you can figure out what *you* want to do. This is actually great. You are amazing at so many things," Willa says as she holds her hand out for the thermos to take a sip.

"I don't know... Are you really sure Remy is okay with all this? I mean, don't get me wrong—being a nanny for Junie sounds absolutely amazing. And not to mention living at the tree farm at Christmas. It sounds magical and all that. But Remy is just...I don't know. I need to think about something long term. I guess I could do that while I'm there..."

And honestly working with Remy would be...a dream. He's so freaking mysterious and devastatingly handsome. He's got the whole grumpy single dad thing down. And I would love to work with Junie. This truly would be a dream job for me.

"Remy's mom was at the bookstore with me when you called me and said that this is perfect timing for everyone. She said that he really needs your help," Willa says as she hands me back the thermos.

Donna is Remy and Finn's mom. She's also an incredibly famous author, like Nora Roberts-famous, and has written over a hundred bestsellers in the past few decades. If towns had grandma's, she'd be Wisteria Coves. Our very own royalty. We all love her so much. I guess if Donna says it's okay, it must be okay.

But I'm still not completely convinced. "It's just that every time we've been at things together, Remy barely talks to me or acknowledges me. It's like he doesn't even *like* me," I say as I glance out my window at the neighborhood, where every house looks dressed for a storybook holiday. Porches are wrapped in garlands and big red velvet bows. Wreaths hang on every door. Windows glow with paper snowflakes taped on some of them, and I can see trees inside, twinkling and ready for presents.

Snow dusts the sidewalks. A pack of kids waddle in puffed coats, bundled like marshmallows, dragging bright red sleds. Their laughter skips across the street and lands in my chest.

Someone's chimney sends up a ribbon of smoke that smells like cedar and comfort. The air slips in through the crack in my rolled-down window and brings pine, a hint of sugar, and something buttery that has to be coming from the corner bakery. It wraps around me like a memory of mittened hands and a mother's scarf tied snug under my chin.

Across the way, a neighbor lifts a strand of lights and the bulbs blink one by one, soft gold. The whole world feels softer, whispering that I am exactly where I am supposed to be. Coming home to Wisteria Cove feels right.

Willa breaks through my thoughts and smirks. "Donna may have mentioned that he's been extra grumpy with the holiday season approaching at the tree farm, so he definitely needs your help. Besides, Junie is a great kid. You always have fun with her. Plus, Remy is not bad to look at. Maybe you two of you can work out your issues together over the holidays. If you know what I mean," she wiggles her eyebrows.

"I'm not emotionally ready to handle a hot, grumpy single dad, Willa." I say dryly.

"Oh, so you admit he's hot," she smirks.

All right, I've *always* had a crush on Remy. Age gap is one of my favorite romance tropes, and Remy definitely gives off the vibes. He's thirty-five and heart stopping handsome. He's only nine years older than me, so my fantasies of Remy have always been chef's-kiss perfection. Of course, I am not telling Willa any of this. Or that I named my favorite vibrator Remy.

Nope, she doesn't need to know any of that. And this might be exactly why I'm having second thoughts about working with him. Because it's not just second thoughts, it's some seriously dirty thoughts. Working for someone I've had a crush on for so long is likely to bring on complicated emotions. And I'm feeling complicated enough these days.

Willa lives in a cabin out on Remy's tree farm with her

boyfriend Tate, who works as a manager for Remy. She and my other sister, Rowan, would tease me mercilessly if they knew I had a thing for Remy, and I *most definitely* have a thing for Remy. I think any hot-blooded woman with a beating heart would have a thing for him.

First of all, he's tall—at least six foot two. Derek was maybe five foot six. I'm not crying over a man who isn't even six feet tall. Remy's got that dark hair, brooding storm-gray eyes, sexy jawline. And he's built with buff arms like a bodybuilder, only I know for a fact he got that body naturally working his tree farm.

Yeah, I'm a goner for Remy Bennett. Even though he's always been that unattainable book boyfriend that you dream about and never a reality. Until today. Today he's a reality. And a great distraction from Derek and his bullshit.

"I think you two would be good for each other," she smirks. "And you know Donna is right. This is a good opportunity for you both. Remy needs help, and you need a job with a place to stay. Win-win."

"I'm not like you and Rowan. I don't have my shit together like you two. I'm a mess," I say quietly. "What if I let him down?"

"I don't know why you think that," she says, glancing over with a look of concern. "You are totally smart, cool, and a knock-out. So what if you haven't found your passion yet? Maybe it's Remy." She cackles at the last part.

My sister Willa has always had a gift for spot-on intuition. My other sister, Rowan, is an apothecary and yoga instructor, who I fill in for occasionally. Both are really beautiful and successful. I don't have the same gifts they do; in fact, I don't have any gifts. People widely know and respect our mother, Lilith, as the town sea witch. Do they ride on brooms? No, but they all definitely have gifts.

I'm just Ivy. The girl who has had dozens of part-time jobs

and can't seem to get her shit together and find herself. And today, getting kicked out of the town home that Derek and I shared and moving back to my hometown is just another failure I guess I can add to the list. Poor Ivy can't keep a job or a man.

I sit up higher in my seat as we pull into the drive for Bennett Tree Farm. It's like something out of a snow globe. big, beautiful red barn dusted with fresh powder comes into sight, surrounded by towering evergreens wrapped in string lights. A hand-painted sign reads "Cut Your Own Joy." I don't know who painted it, but I want to hug them. I glance back and realize maybe Junie did that. It's adorable.

"This is like...if Hallmark had a baby with a Pinterest board," I breathe. "Wow. Remy has done a lot to the place in the past few years since he took it over."

"Welcome to your new life," Willa says. "You're going to have so much fun here. I love living out here, too."

"I don't even know how to nanny. What if Junie decides she doesn't like me?" I say suddenly, feeling nervous.

"Last year, you made a giant gingerbread replica of Hogwarts for fun." She glances over and laughs.

"What?" I say with a shrug. I guess I am a big kid at heart.

"It's hilarious that out of all the jobs you've had, being a nanny is the one job you haven't had yet," she teases. "I feel like I'm dropping you off for your first day of school."

"All right, not fair." But it is ironic, I guess. I am notorious for having had a ton of part-time jobs everywhere. I've done it all. From dog walking, pet sitting, serving, bartending, cleaning houses...I've mostly done it all. Some would say I'm a jack of all trades, but I just haven't found what makes me happy. Willa is successful with her bookstore and coffee shop, Wisteria Books & Brews. And Rowan is opening up her own apothecary shop, Salt & Root, next to the bookstore, where she'll have a yoga studio on the top floor and her apothecary on the bottom. We've all been working and saving to go in on it together. It's going to be amazing when she finally gets it up and going.

We pull up to the one-bedroom cabin that Willa and Tate live in on the Bennett tree farm property, and head in and get Cobweb, her cat, to bring with her back to the bookstore.

"Can you grab her carrier?" she calls as she heads to the back of the tiny space.

"Yeah," I say as I look around and find Cobweb curled up on their bed on a blanket in their cozy, rustic home.

Outside, the cabin glows like a lantern through the trees. A wreath hangs on the red front door, woven with cedar, eucalyptus, and a few sprigs of wisteria, that our mom likely gave her, tied with a bright red ribbon. A stack of split logs is tucked beneath the overhang, dusted with snow.

Inside, stockings hang from boat hooks Tate mounted into the beam, knit in cream and red. The Christmas lights throw a soft glow of gold across the room, catching on the framed black-and-white photos of Wisteria Cove and the little watercolor of the harbor that Willa loves.

The tree stands near the big window, tall and full, dressed in a mix that is pure Willa and Tate. Hand-cut paper snowflakes from the bookstore craft night. Cinnamon salt dough stars. Glass baubles in shades of sea foam and smoke. A driftwood star crowns the top, sanded smooth by years in the water. Bright red ribbon winds through the branches, and tucked between needles are small bookish ornaments: tiny open novels, a miniature typewriter, a copper bookmark charm.

On the dining table sits a long runner of linen, scattered with pinecones, taper candles in mismatched brass holders, and a bowl of oranges studded with cloves. The kitchen is strung with a simple strand of lights over the open shelves, reflecting off polished copper pots. A kettle rests on the stove. Mugs wait with candy canes hooked over the rims. Every corner has a touch of them. A stack of well-loved Christmas records near the record player. A basket of knit throws by the couch. A jar of wish papers on the coffee table for guests to write a hope and toss into the fire.

The whole cabin feels like a held breath and a warm hug, the kind of place where you can hear the snow hush outside and the quiet promise of the season settle in your bones.

"Come here, Cobweb," I whisper as I stroke her fur and pull her up to my chin and kiss her soft head. "You're a good baby, aren't you?"

She meows softly and snuggles into me. "Time to go to the bookstore, Cobweb."

The front door opens, and Tate comes in. "Hey," he calls to me as he pulls the door closed behind him and glances around.

"Hi," I call back, waving with Cobweb's paw.

In an instant, Cobweb is off of me and over in Tate's arms. He strokes her fur and murmurs to her. "Where's Willa?"

"Right here," she calls as she comes out of the bathroom and goes to him, wrapping him in a hug and kissing him. Those two are endgame and goals.

I grin at them; they're so cute. Crazy cute. I knew Derek wasn't for me when I saw how good it was for Tate and Willa. And I want what they have someday.

Someday.

"What are you guys doing here?" he asks me, still holding Willa.

"Today's Ivy's first day as Junie's nanny," Willa says as she grabs the cat carrier and loads up Cobweb. "I've got to get to the bookstore. Mom's watching things for me, and she's probably rearranging everything as we speak. Can you take Ivy up to the house with you on the side by side?"

"He hired a nanny?" he asks, giving me a confused look.

"Ummm...well, yeah. What do you mean?" I ask nervously, feeling my emotions roll over me.

Tate shrugs, "I didn't realize he hired someone. Actually, you know what, this is great. He's been having to miss a lot of work, and he's been really stressed out lately. This will be a big help to him."

I shrug. "Donna said it was okay, and I assumed—."

It's about that time that I realize that Donna probably set us up. I should've known. Great.

Heat crawls up my neck. My smile feels pasted-on, and I picture Remy walking in and finding me here, uninvited, like a stray cat who wandered into his kitchen. The old worry flares fast.

You do too much.

You're in the way.

You read the room wrong.

I think of my suitcase by the door, how easy it would be to zip it, mumble an apology, and disappear before anyone has to say it out loud. I can already hear the story I will tell myself in the car. *No harm done. You tried. It was a misunderstanding.* Only it wouldn't feel like a misunderstanding. It would feel like proof.

I try to breathe. The house feels warm and safe, and for a second, I let myself want it. I want to belong here. Then doubt slides in again, quiet and sharp. If he didn't say *yes*, if he didn't say he wanted me here, then I'm trespassing on the softest parts of his life.

I glance toward the doorway, half expecting Remy to appear with that guarded look he wears. My chest tightens. I could make a joke. I could spin this into something breezy and charming. That is the old reflex. Smile. Minimize. Make yourself smaller so no one can hurt you when their jabs land.

I straighten instead. If I'm going to be here, it has to be

because he wants me here. Not because his mother nudged the chess pieces around and called it fate. The thought steadies me. I can ask him. I can risk the answer. My heart knocks against my ribs like it's trying to get out, but I lift my chin anyway.

Please let him want me here. And if he doesn't, let me be brave enough to hear it.

Want more of Wisteria Cove?
Scan the QR code to read Remy and Ivy's:

Mistletoe & Magic

Want more of Wisteria Cove?
Scan the QR code to read Remy and Ivy's:

About the Author

Erin Branscom is a creator of happily-ever-after's, crafting spicy, Hallmark-like romances that make readers fall head over heels for charming small towns. When she's not writing heartwarming stories, Erin can be found anywhere there are dogs, with a cup of coffee in hand, or lost in a good book. As a passionate Scorpio, she brings intensity and heart to everything she does. Dive into her world and discover love, warmth, and a touch of spice in every story.

Acknowledgments

To my family. I love you all and you are my reason for working hard every day. I'm so thankful for all of you and your support. To all my readers, thank you for always showing up for me and being excited!

Freedom Valley Series
Falling Inn Love
Baked Inn Love
All Inn Thyme
Love Inn Books
Forever Inn Love
Snowed Inn

Bridger Falls
Forever To Me
Wild As Her
Always You

Non-Fiction
Writers Inspiring Writers with Jennifer Probst

Wisteria Cove
The Pumpkin Spice Spell
Mistletoe & Magic
Hexes & Honeysuckle

Cozy Creek Collection
Fall Too Well

You can find all of Erin's books on her website:
Erinbranscom.com

Hexes & Honeysuckle

Want more of Wisteria Cove?
Scan the QR code to read Finn and Rowan's story:

* 9 7 9 8 8 8 6 6 2 0 2 6 9 *